ONE SUN TWO CONTINENTS

Leta Wilson Parker

Author's Tranquility Press
ATLANTA, GEORGIA

Leta Wilson Parker/Author's Tranquility Press
3900 N Commerce Dr. Suite 300 #1255
Atlanta, GA 30344
www.authorstranquilitypress.com

Ordering Information:
Quantity sales. Special discounts are available on quantity purchases by corporations, associations, and others. For details, contact the "Special Sales Department" at the address above.

One Sun Two Continents/Leta Wilson Parker
Hardback: 978-1-964037-86-8
Paperback: 978-1-964037-17-2
eBook: 978-1-964037-18-

Dedication

This book is dedicated to Jane Wilkinson, my partner in doing what we have never done before, together. Sometimes stars across resulting in an explosion of beauty, fun, excitement, adventure, and friendship. So thankful that you were the star that crossed mine!

And this book is dedicated to my Egyptian family Saber, Amel, Asan, and all the guys at Ride Egypt. You are my family by choice and love. I hope this book relates my love of Egypt and my love for you!

And lastly, the lady that changed mine and Jane's life, Emma Levin of Ride Egypt. A late-night invitation and a promise of fun, excitement and adventure which has been unmatched in a lifetime! You are my friend forever in my heart and I am forever grateful.

The word Egypt conjures images in the mind of ancient pyramids, the mysterious Sphinx, the beauty and allure of the Nile River, and the never-ending sands that go nowhere and everywhere. But along with the ancient sites and history that Egypt boasts, it is the love stories that have come from Egypt since the earliest of times that have captured and held the imagination of mankind. The stories of devotion, lust and desire have been passed down through the centuries for man to ponder and interpret and retell to future generations. Egypt is a land of dreams and magic and mystery, but most of all, Egypt is the land of love, passion and sadly, loss

Isis and Osiris

A story of love of life and soul that predates civilization passed through the sands of time from one tongue to another. Tum was the Great He/She of all universes. The whole, the complete, the perfect, but was lonely and so within itself created and bore the gods that begat two children heaven and earth. From the love between heaven and earth the gods Ra (the sun) and Thoth (the moon) came to be along with thousands of souls that had rested within Atum (the stars). With the creation of Ra (the sun) and Thoth (the moon) time began. Their love was legendary and one envious of their love tore them apart and allowed them to only touch from afar at dawn and dusk.

Eons passed and more gods were born of Nut the mother god. The siblings were Osiris, brother, son, father, husband watcher in the dark. Then Isis, woman, wife, widow, dancer, goddess of desire, mother of a god. Horus, whom the mortals call Hero, the divine son of a divine couple, twice-born, once in Heaven and once on Earth. There was Nephthys, lady of the house, mistress of the shadows. Finally, Seth, warrior, and rebel. All gods in the womb of Nut waiting for their destiny.

All the gods were players in the realm of creation with Isis and Osiris marrying. It is said their passion was so boundless and intense that they lay with each other for eight thousand years and Isis lay in the crook of his arm for eternities in adoration and devotion. Their lovemaking was epic with rapture in their hands and hearts, deep rivers of passion and sensation, soaring like birds in the sky among the stars with the constellations as their entities to count and name. Few know that it is the Egyptian gods Isis and Osiris that first experienced and passed on to mankind the joy of love and physical affection.

All families encounter strife and conflict and so it occurs among the gods. Ra, the sun, became absorbed in his own beauty and power and began to scorch the earth destroying life and drying oceans and rivers. His siblings, particularly Seth, rose up against him but the sun only shone brighter. So bright that half the day it blocked out Thoth, the moon.

Ages continued and the gods found their purpose and went about with their affixed duties. All but Seth. Seth harbored hate and resentment and brooded constantly. One day when opportunity presented itself Seth took his anger out on his brother Osiris. At a celebration he tricked Osiris, who thought Seth was of changed character, into lying in a jeweled coffin that was shut, sealed, and thrown into the Nile.

It was Anubis (the god of embalmment) that told Isis of Osiris fate. Isis took on all levels of mourning walking for years across Egypt asking all if they have seen her husband in his jeweled coffin. She received her answer when in exhaustion she lay on the riverbank with even crocodiles shying from her grief and despair. In her dream she was given the vision that Osiris and his jeweled coffin were swept to sea and landed on shore instantly becoming a tamarisk tree.

Isis went on the search for the tree for centuries looking for her beloved Osiris. Upon finding the tree in which her cherished was enshrined she begged for her husband and brother to come out to no avail. At that time a king and his army came by. Eyeing the tree, the King had his soldiers cut down the tree for him to use in the building of his home. With Isis crying in terror and hysteria the pieces of the tree and Isis were put on a sledge and hauled away.

Time passed and Isis hid her identity to work in the king's house where the pillars made of wood contained Osiris. She was a nanny to the owner's male child and before long, her fondness for the child led her to begin to impart godly attributes and powers to him. One night the mistress of the house discovered her baby in front of the hearth in flames with a swallow circling him.

At the last moment before all was lost, the swallow swooped down, turned back into the form of Isis and saved the child.

The mistress of the house was so grateful she had the pillars taken down that held the roof and replaced. She gave the pillars of Osiris to Isis who cut into them and removed the coffin of Osiris. With great anguish the coffin was once more placed in the Nile. But Seth's revenge did not stop. He retrieved the coffin and cut it into pieces and spread them wide and far. And once more Isis walked and searched the lands of Egypt for centuries to find the pieces of her lost love.

Once found she created an altar in his honor for all to remember him. But a miracle occurred as she continued to express her grief and woe. She conceived a child from her deep longing. The child was named Horus. Named after Isis's brother Horus, with whom Isis shared the womb of Atum long ago before time existed, and so, began a new generation and era of Egyptian gods.

But the love and passion of Isis and Osiris were the model of human love for all mankind. Devotion, loyalty, and commitment were born of Isis and Osiris as well as physical expression of love.

Foreword

Spencer left the party to seek a few minutes of peace and quiet. He hurried to his office knowing that Mal would make excuses for him. She knew he had his limits on celebratory affairs. His disappearance would not draw attention from anyone.

Not that the day Mal had planned had not been delightful. There was a private family lunch before the party to celebrate his 65th birthday. He sat at the head of the table and as he perused the occupants, he drifted to how different the faces were to those that once sat at this table. Cav would be sitting at the head with Genevieve at the other end. The middle would include Mallory and him and other guests. On many occasions, Gil, Mallory's uncle, and his parents would fill the empty spaces. But the years had passed fast and furiously. He now sat at the head of the table looking at his son, his daughter, Yousuf and their families. The table was full of much of his life and happiness.

Mallory and he had created a blessed and fulfilling life. The kids were the joy in both their lives. Ginny was a doctor, married to a doctor and currently raising three boys. She had little interest in riding, only seeing broken bones and cracked heads connected to horses. His son also was not particularly interested in the barn or horses. But actually, carried on the legacy of family veterinarians. It was a proud day when he hung his shield, Spencer Ewing Jr., DVM, beside his grandfather. Spencer's father was beyond proud to have him join him in practice. It was Yousuf that became Mallory's prodigy, friend and partner in all things pertaining to horses. Yousuf had his place at the table due to his loyalty to the family and to the family business. They were a strange bunch no doubt. But they had lived as a loving, supportive family for many years. And for that Spencer was thankful.

It was at the party that the guest list expanded considerably. Mal loved throwing big and lavish celebrations for any and all occasions. So, for a while he grinned and greeted and mixed and visited. But it was after his visit with Yousuf that he almost sprinted from the party to his office in the barn. Spencer approached Yousuf.

"Yousuf, how did your visit to your homeland go?" Spencer asked bracing himself to hear of Egypt. He had avoided the question at lunch. Even now decades later the thought of the beautiful, magical mystery of Egypt brought wanting through his body.

"Well, Spencer. The show was a total success," Yousuf replied.

"I hear you and Zulfagar stole the show," Cav further commented.

"Yes, Zulfagar was outstanding as expected. There was surprise that a Texas bred Arabian would carry bloodline traits found in Tawfik lineage, the legend icon of the Zabr bloodline. The Zabr family took notice of how exquisite Zulfagar is. They are very impressed with our Texas based breeding program. We were, if you will excuse the expression, heads and tails above other horses and riders. The competition for red and white though was intense," Yousuf replied but not boastfully.

"And your family?" Spencer inquired. He had met Yousuf's family many years ago. Spencer had been a good friend with Yousuf's grandfather who had passed some years before.

"Family is well. We enjoyed our visit," Yousuf said as he took Spencer's arm and guided him into a private area.

Spencer knew before they had taken two steps what was coming. He found himself holding his breath as he realized after over thirty years finally something from her. The excitement that he felt at just being told she sent her best or hello from an old friend … was plain foolish. But nonetheless his expectation was creating havoc with his psyche.

"I spent time with Sekhmet Zabr at her request," Yousuf quietly stated.

Spencer thought he was going to faint at hearing her name. He was an old man, a grandfather for goodness' sake, happily married for decades reeling like a teenager.

"She gave me this for your hands only," Yousuf said as he handed Spencer a scroll of papyrus.

Spencer could feel her in the paper. He could feel she had touched it, held it. In all these years, he had questioned himself many times if their connection was what he remembered or the way he wanted to remember. But when he held this scroll, he knew. Their connection had been real, unique, and once in a lifetime.

Spencer arrived at his office and almost locked the door feeling like he needed to be secretive, but realized he was being silly. No one was going to come looking for him. The band had started, people were dancing and partying. Mallory would be flitting about making sure everyone had food and drink. He was in his safe place.

He set the scroll on the desk. There it was in her perfect handwriting his name, not Spence, but Spencer. He closed his eyes and began to go where he rarely allowed himself to go. Even after all this time, he could remember those few months like it was yesterday. He was an old man, but he never forgot. He never really ever let it go, and so he indulged himself and began to recall …

Chapter 1

Spencer sat in his office at the barn half attentive to the speaker phone as Mallory, his fiancé, regurgitated mundane details about the upcoming engagement party. She recited a never-ending list of his guests, her guests, tables, sitting charts, food, beverages, entertainment, decorations, and then of course her dress and hair and make-up, and new concerns with the venue. He leaned back in his chair with his booted feet on the desk, crossed his arms stared at the ceiling watching the fan making redundant circles and feeling a kinship with the mechanical fixture.

She chattered, he made appropriate hum-ums and virtual nods as expected. Why when he loved Mallory as he did, was all this pomp and splendor simply boring to him. He felt more like a trophy for a round robin golf tournament than a man making the decision of his life.

He found no reason for all the hullabaloo. After all he and Mallory had been together since high school and through college years and were currently living together. He would have preferred a quick trip to a tropical paradise, a wedding on the beach with just a few invited and then return to continue with their life. He just did not get this pretending as though their relationship was brand new and shiny. He loved Mallory but he felt like he had been married to her all his life.

"Have you ordered your tux?" Mallory inquired.

"Yes," Spencer responded.

"Ok, because you know that a western tux cut correctly is hard to locate," Mallory fretted.

Spencer sat up in his chair and began to search on his phone for tux sales in the area.

"My dress is sky blue. I haven't definitely chosen colors for the wedding, but I am thinking of honoring Sky by using sky blue as a color. What do you think?" Mallory probed.

Spencer was snapping a picture of a tux retailer and thought to himself at the same time, "of course honor your horse in our wedding. Wouldn't expect less of you Mal."

"Sky blue, mauve peach, with a splash of yellow. You could wear a baby blue or peach or yellow sash and bow tie," Mallory lost in her dream sent Spencer over the edge in the conversation.

"Mal, I will not be wearing any baby blue or yellow or a peachy mauvy sash at my wedding."

"Spence!" Mallory protested.

"Mal, end of discussion. We are getting married in June. We have plenty of time to dress me in white and black. I will have a tux for the party but need to run right now. See you at home tonight."

"Okay! To be continued," Mallory consented.

Spencer disconnected the call and looked at the calendar bemoaning to himself the next few months between now and the wedding. He reminded himself he would have to be patient with Mal. This was her day. Her wedding day. Her dream "come true" day. But as he initiated the call to the tux shop, he wondered to himself, "when does my dream come true?" And then he immediately admonished himself. He was living the dream. He should be grateful and rid himself of this feeling that life was passing him by.

Mallory on the other hand ended the call thinking life was perfect! After years of waiting for Spence to make up his mind as to his best options for his future, he had finally succumbed to her father as the best opportunity. It came with a newly built home on the ranch with her parents down the road and Spencer second in command of a thriving horse barn. He actually ran the ranch and barn while her dad entertained his hobby horses and served as a figurehead.

Cavanaugh King or Cav as his friends called him, Mallory's father, was renowned in the equestrian world. The King Ranch had been untouched for generations in the breeding, training, and sales of elite performance horses in several disciplines. Mallory's family owned and operated a 5,000-acre ranch and a prominent barn that housed valuable equines involved in both English and Western disciplines. The actual facilities included a forty-stall, modern updated barn with two covered arenas and two outside arenas for training and exhibitions and numerous round pens, paddocks, and expansive, green fields for long term turn-out of horses.

The ranch had been renamed King Equestrian Center in the late seventies when the original King Ranch was split between Cavanaugh and his brother Gillespie. The two brothers shared a history of rivalry, jealousy, conflict and sometimes it seemed pure hatred of each other. When the senior Kings died, they could not operate the one ranch in accord, so they split the ranch down the middle using the creek as the boundary. Each brother took 5,000 acres and flipped for who would take the acreage with the homestead and facilities in place and who would build. As it turned out, Cavanaugh won the flip for the homestead and Gillespie held this against Cavanaugh all their lives. Grudges and transgressions had been long standing between the brothers.

The division of the ranch should have resolved any differences between the two Kings. But the competition between the brothers heightened as both tried to outdo each other in breeding and training. Both sought the best horses, the best trainers, the best groomers, and caretakers. The years did not resolve the problems or mellow the brothers. However today Mallory was totally untouched by her heritage. She was floating in the euphoria of being the bell of the ball at her engagement party. She would insist on looking her absolute best and having her good-looking cowboy fiancé on her arm would hopefully make for a stunning couple.

She had been hurt by the gossip for years as to why the handsome, single, totally desirable Spencer Ewing would be exclusive with Mallory King. She was not nearly as pretty as he was handsome. She knew that her riding since she was a child resulted in a boyish look to her. She kept her dishwater blond hair short. She was thin with little curves. She rarely wore make-up and usually was either going to or coming from the barn.

But their mutual love of horses had bonded them as teenagers, and she had somehow managed to hang on to Spencer. Four years of high school, four years of college, two years of living apart and two years of cohabitation. And finally, last month at the Baxter-Smith National Dressage Competition held in New York, he proposed.

Her life was perfect. She lived on her childhood home spending her days with beautiful, talented, majestic, award-winning steeds and coming home to the man she loved. The infinite patience she had developed over the years in training horses paid off. He finally chose her. She was having the engagement party of her dreams and then moving on to plan the wedding of her dreams with the man of her dreams to live her dream life. Mallory King was ecstatic about her future.

Chapter 2

Spencer grabbed his phone and left his office proceeding to the nearest tuxedo shop. He used his walkie talkie to notify Matthew his foreman that he was leaving the property. He drove down the long leader road passing the wooden rail fencing where a small herd of horses grazed ignoring his truck, while others looked up with interest, and a pair galloped beside the fence racing him to the gate. He had been around horses all his life, but he still marveled at their beauty, grace, and strength.

He had grown up on a farm himself, although on a much smaller scale then the King Equestrian Center. His father was a veterinarian, as was his father before him. The Ewing Animal Care had been open for over seventy years until he broke the chain. But Cav King had successfully lured him to take over his operation. He could spend another two to four years in school or go to work for Cav and make more money than he ever could as a third-generation vet. Although he was shy of the prestige and visibility the position offered, Spencer knew that being part of the King family and married to Mallory would be a life well lived.

Mallory wanted to return home after they graduated from the university, and she also wanted Spencer to come with her. Spencer over time had become accustomed to pleasing Mallory, who had been an only child with a silver spoon and did not take disappointment well. So, they returned, and Mallory moved in with her parents while he moved into an apartment.

The first year at home went well for Mallory and Spencer. He relished having his own place and space. It gave him a refuge to get away from the circumstances that went along with working for Cav King and being seriously involved with Mallory King. He worked for Cav as his right hand and enjoyed becoming more familiar and knowledgeable of large ranch operations. He also enjoyed being up close and personal to legendary horses and in the inner circle of international breeders and trainers. Mallory set about her equestrian activities and building the house they currently lived in. She approached both with her normal obsessiveness and was fixated over every detail. A mode that over the years Spencer had learned to cope with but found annoying, nonetheless.

The second year had been full of Mallory pushing marriage and Spence taking over the ranch agenda. Spence was not necessarily opposed to either circumstance. He just wanted to make the choice, the decision, himself. But Mallory had called the shots since he could remember and he knew that when they took the trip to New York, he was expected to get down on one knee.

He wished he could say it was because he and Mallory were madly in love and could not live without each other. But the truth be known, if he had not proposed and Mallory had not placed in the competition, he would have been responsible. He felt sure her performance was tied to his proposing.

He could not face going home with Mallory blaming him for losing. He was not sure exactly when or how or even why, but he had become responsible for making Mallory happy. So, he proposed consenting to life and family with Mallory and managing and eventually inheriting the celebrated and lucrative enterprise, King Equestrian Center.

His phone rang and broke his reverie on his way to purchase a tuxedo for his engagement party. He had a couple of tuxes in his closet that he had been requested to wear at different King functions, but Mallory wanted him in new duds for this party. It was particularly important to Mallory, and he mentally set his mind to make it special for her.

"Hello," Spence answered.

"Spence," Cav King greeted Spencer.

Spencer knew that Cav was in a stir about something by the sound of his voice.

"Spence, where are you at? Matthew said you had left the property."

"I'm on an engagement party errand. What's up, Cav?"

"Well, too much to discuss over the phone. I am not at the ranch. Misses and I are in Dallas and staying the night in town," Cav explained.

"Oh, okay. So, when do you want to talk?" Spence ask tiring of the suspense.

"Well, we probably won't have a chance until the party tomorrow night. I'll just wait till then," Cav offered.

"All right. We'll see you and Genevieve tomorrow evening then. Mal is super excited. I'm surprised she and Genevieve are not plotting and planning tonight," Spencer ended the conversation.

But he could not help but notice the strange sound in Cav's voice. And he couldn't be sure if he was hearing what he thought he was hearing or was just strung out over the party himself. And now Cav was throwing out a pending, important mystery conversation. Spencer consoled himself that maybe after this party, the stress and anxiety surrounding his impending marriage would lessen.

Chapter 3

Spencer completed his errand, ran by the barn, and then headed home. The home that Mallory built. It was a country home with a wraparound porch, all white with an abundance of windows and skylights. The house was open and cheerful and perfect just like Mallory. Fresh flowers sat on the table in the dining area and a basket of fruit on the kitchen island. Decorated simply but amply and mainly pictures of Mallory and her horses. She also included family pictures and a wall of her with Spencer over the years.

The photo library began when they were young up to the current date with a space left for a wedding photo. Mallory made that perfectly clear to Spencer when she created the gallery. Spencer was not sure if he liked the wall or not. It was a reminder of the years that had passed. He and Mallory were so young when their friendship began. And that young friendship had turned romantic and into a lifetime commitment. Neither had dated others nor stepped out of the confines of what their life was designed to be.

Their love came slowly and over much time. It was built on friendship, common interests, common goals, and values. All the elements that a lifetime commitment should be built upon. But deep down in the recesses of Spencer's mind and spirit, something was absent. They had it all and Spencer knew he should be grateful. He was living a life that so many others only wished for. He rationalized that being at your pinnacle at age twenty-nine could leave someone feeling a bit lost and unfulfilled.

Spencer entered the house and went directly to the bedroom to get out of his jeans, having left his boots in the mud room. Mallory was in the kitchen cooking dinner, and they acknowledged each other with a casual greeting when he came through Spencer was bracing himself for the upcoming inexhaustible conversation about the engagement party that he knew was forthcoming. He soothed himself, musing it would be over in a matter of hours.

"How was your day?" Mallory immediately asked when he entered the kitchen area and sat down at the bar picking up a carrot from salad makings and crunching down.

"Busy as usual. And yours?" Spencer asked.

"Well, the florist is not able to get into the venue to decorate the tables before six and they are saying not enough time. The venue is being unreasonable saying they have an afternoon affair and need the time to clean up and set up before vendors come in. I tried to reach mom, but she didn't answer. So, I just told the florist to hire an extra people to get it done before 7:30 when guests start arriving."

Spencer tried to look attentive and interested, but he knew that Mallory would leave no stone unturned to make things perfect. It was the world she lived in. A bubble where everything was precise and detailed. Sometimes he wanted to track hay into the house, or spill wine on the white carpet. He wondered if the horses that Mallory so diligently trained in the subtleness of dressage felt the same desire to just kick out or buck occasionally just to shake Mallory's perfect existence.

"My dress is not fitting right. I cannot wear a deep V and bigger than life the seamstress left a deep V so I may end up wearing a little black dress to my own engagement party. Again, I could not get in touch with mom to sort that out," Mallory was close to whining.

"Your parents are in Dallas overnight at the Fairmont," Spencer informed her.

"What?" Mallory looked up.

"Your dad called me earlier," Spencer further enlightened her.

"Mom did not say anything," Mallory pondered.

"Sounds like it was impromptu. They will be back in plenty of time for the party tomorrow," Spencer casually clarified.

"Well, I hope so. Not like mom to just leave me with all the details and not tell me," Mallory pouted.

The remaining hours of the evening were spent on routine activities. Dinner, cleaning up and afterwards both Mallory and Spencer spent time on the computer and watched the evening news. Then it was off to bed where both did some bedtime reading and a kiss goodnight, lights off and both drifting off to sleep thinking of tomorrow.

Mallory with images of her party tomorrow night as her guests fawned over her plans for the wedding and honeymoon. Spencer having self-dialogue that this was his past, present and his future. He would become grey haired living this choreographed existence in which he was ingratiated.

Chapter 4

Spencer awakened on Saturday knowing he would be slammed. It was the weekend so the barn would be hectic and demanding and of course, the party that evening meant additional chores to meet Mallory expectations. She was already reviewing lists and problem shooting knowing that everything was a disaster waiting to happen. He was grateful to get dressed, grab a cup of coffee and head to the barn.

"Bye ... I will be back to help after I make sure all is well at the barn," Spencer offered going out the door. Mallory was on hold, so she nodded her goodbye and smiled while rolling her eyes at the phone.

Spencer scooted out the door to his truck and drove down the lead road to the barn. The property consisted of the big house that Cav and Genevieve occupied. It had been built in the thirties and boasted huge rooms with high ceilings, huge closets, and a large kitchen with a family room connected. The house had been remodeled several times over the years. So, although an older home, the updates kept it comfortable and vintage beautiful. Mallory had built her house down the road from the big house. Her house, although considerably smaller, provided adequate space and comfort for him and Mallory. It was unsaid that at some point he and Mallory would occupy the big house.

The barn was in full swing when Spencer arrived. Riders, trainers, and horses filled the barn aisles. Arenas were full as were the round pens. The stable crew were working in stalls and tending to horses. As Spencer walked the barn everything appeared to be in order. That was till he neared the back entrance of the barn.

"Damn it Gil, you do not have any interest in the Fadjur bloodline. Why all of sudden are you undercutting me with Royce on that filly I'm looking at?" Cav was talking to his brother and obviously irritated.

"Hey, you don't have any exclusive on his horses. I have as much right as you to approach him," Gil defended his obvious stealth methods to buy a horse underneath his brother's nose.

"Gil, you look for opportunities to stab me in the back. I don't know what is up that here we are seventy years later still fighting the same battle," Cav responded exasperated.

"Cav, you need to get over yourself. You don't hold any restrictions on what and who I buy from. If I want to make an offer, that is my business."

Spencer was destined for the barn office and did not like walking in on this conversation between the King brothers. Their dislike of each other was legendary. Spencer did not want to navigate those waters any more often than he had to. And most everyone in the county felt the same way.

"Spence!" Gil exclaimed glad to have a distraction to Cav's anger over the Royce filly.

"Hi, Gil. Hi Cav," Spencer greeted.

"Well, popped the question and you and little Mallory are finally tying the knot! Early congratulations! You two are quite the couple!" Gil proclaimed.

Gil was sincere in his sentiments for Spencer and Mallory. He watched them grow up and fall in love and he admired their relationship.

"Thank you, Gil," Spencer responded but was looking for an out and an end to this conversation.

He knew it could get awkward if the brothers continued to argue. But to his surprise, Gil seemed done with the conversation and made his exit saying, "Bye now, Spencer. Although I am a scoundrel, I am family and I welcome you to this fold. Such as it is. I will enjoy celebrating with everyone tonight at the party in your honor," Gil parted with his comments to Spencer ignoring Cav.

Cav said nothing. Spencer smiled and bid Gil goodbye.

Spencer turned to Cav, "I didn't think I would see you until tonight."

"I couldn't keep Genevieve away. She wanted to come home early so she could help with loose ends. She and Mallory were on the phone early this morning," Cav responded.

"So, what did you have on your mind yesterday when you called?" Spencer inquired.

"Well, several things we need to discuss but I don't have the time right now to get into it. We'll make time tonight or in the morning," Cav was putting Spencer off, and Spencer knew it.

But Spencer quit a long time ago trying to second guess this multi-millionaire who could finance any cock-eyed scheme he could dream up. Spencer was guessing by Cav's behavior that a scheme was on the horizon. Cav was avoiding talking until he had his ducks in order and Spencer also noticed that Cav did not seem particularly upset that Gil was going after the filly Cav wanted. The gentlemen said goodbye and Cav was off to his interests and Spencer turned his attention to matters in the barn.

"Mom, why didn't you tell me you and dad were going to Dallas yesterday?" Mallory finally inquired. Mallory had postponed asking why her mom had been secretive about her plans in Dallas.

They had spoken early that morning but were in panic mode taking care of last-minute issues with the party. But now most everything had been ironed out and Mallory was curious why her mom had not shared their plans to stay overnight in Dallas.

"It was last minute, Mallory. We had a dinner invitation from the Brinkmans and decided to accept. It was a late dinner, so we stayed with them," Genevieve replied.

Mallory instantly realized her mom and Spencer's story did not match. But at the same instant decided Spencer must have misunderstood.

The afternoon passed quickly, and later Spencer was sitting at the island in the kitchen when Mallory walked out dressed for the party. He was taken aback by how beautiful she was. Her hair was shining. She had pulled it to one side with a gardenia tucked behind her ear. She rarely wore make-up, but tonight was the exception. Her blue eyes were popping with color and excitement matching her dress of blue. The dress was modest in cut and style, but she wore it well. Spencer was proud of his beautiful bride to be. She was talented, intelligent, pure class and she loved him to a fault. At that moment as he watched Mallory spin to show off her attire, he was very much in love and incredibly happy with the life that was unfolding for him.

The engagement party was held at the Long Branch convention center. An opulent, western venue used for large gatherings of all kinds. Walking into the Long Branch was always an experience the first time.

The hall boasted western furnishings and décor to include velvet, overstuffed round sofas and plush, leather accent chairs. The hall was luxury carpeted with massive velvet curtains hanging over the eight-foot stained-glass windows. The focal point of the hall was the ten-foot solid oak bar with gold foot rails, a surface with mirror reflection, and highly skilled craftsman carving on the ten-foot edge. Behind the bar a massive mirror hung with an etched border reflecting a large portion of the room and all the beautiful people. Along with the lavish surroundings the service and food were legendary. The waitstaff circulated making sure everyone had a fresh beverage and a plate of gourmet hors d'oeuvres.

Spencer and Mallory arrived at the party to be greeted by almost a hundred guests. They stood in the receiving line for well over an hour greeting dignitaries from all walks of life both local and statewide. The King brothers were well known and respected not only in the equestrian world but rubbed shoulders with the elite of Texas. Spencer noted that Mallory basked in the attention and limelight as one person after another hugged and fawned over the bride to be. He shook more hands than he had shaken in his life and heard repeatedly what a lucky chap he was.

The line finally evaporated, and dinner ensued. The head table consisted of him and Mallory and their parents and the best man and maid of honor. He had chosen his father as his best man. When he thought of his college friends, he realized he was not close enough to any of them to ask them to be his best man. His life had been dedicated to Mallory, even in college. So, calling on his dad, his best friend for life, was an obvious choice.

He noted that his mother and father made a handsome couple. His dad had remained in shape for a sixty plus year old and he sported a head of striking white hair. His mother also had remained thin and trim and was a lovely lady. She had Italian roots and still maintained her natural dark hair that he had inherited. Her complexion was clear and with fewer wrinkles than most. She had aged like fine wine and had been an impeccable homemaker, mother, and wife to his father. Lelia Ewing harbored a love of animals and was the ideal partner for a second-generation veterinarian. Spencer loved his parents and appreciated the life they had given him, albeit not as affluent as Mallory's birthright.

He glanced down at the table and noted that Cav and Genevieve were also looking quite dapper. Cav was conversing with Spencer's dad and Genevieve was visiting with Mallory's maid of honor. Cav looked somewhat stuffed into his tux and did not appear totally comfortable with his stomach straining against the sash. Cav was not a particularly handsome gentleman. He was stocky, overweight, and balding. But Cav had a presence. He had the assurance and confidence of knowing that he was important, and people listened when he spoke.

Genevieve was smiling and visiting, but Spencer noticed she seemed to drift off during the conversation. She would look into the crowd and go he did not know where. Genevieve, although a very pleasing and delightful person, was not a particularly pretty woman. She was thin to a fault and had recently become thinner. Her features were angular and hard. She wore glasses that hid any beauty found in her eyes. She had her hair cropped short and never wore make-up.

Genevieve did not have to depend on looks to demand respect and admiration. She had trained and exhibited dressage legends. One of the leading equestrian touring companies in the country depended on Genevieve to start and initially train their horses. Cav had been the wealthier of the two when they married, but Genevieve had increased their wealth and stature in the equestrian world tenfold. Because she was without a doubt a worldwide renowned equestrian.

Spencer's reverie of the family at the head table was broken by Cav banging his glass with his fork to get everyone's attention. "I want to thank all of you for coming and helping us celebrate these two young people as they begin their life together. I think I speak for Delzel and Lelia that we are thrilled our families will be bonded, and we will be proud grandparents someday," Cav paused as the audience laughed. He continued, "We invite you to finish your dinner and then we will have music and dancing for the balance of the evening. Please come by and visit Genevieve, Lelia, Delzel and me. By all means mingle and have a wonderful evening," Cav graciously invited.

The crowd evolved from dinner to the dance floor. The music was provided by a famous DJ that kept the group on their feet. Mallory danced with almost every gentleman in attendance and

Spencer also made the rounds out of politeness. It was his dance with his future mother-in-law that left him somewhat bewildered.

"You are lovely tonight, Genevieve," Spencer started the conversation as they began to dance.

"Thank you, Spencer. It is a lovely night to be lovely!" she replied and continued, "Mallory is certainly in her element! Spencer, I am so happy for the two of you. This is a mother's dream. To know that your daughter will be loved, cared for, and taken care of when you are not around to …" Genevieve stopped suddenly and looked at Spencer. Her look indicated she was about to let a cat out of the bag. He had no idea why her statement was so sobering or why she became instantly secretive. He was processing this surprising conversation when he heard loud voices from the direction of the bar. Genevieve also heard the commotion.

"Good grief. That is Cav and Gil at it again. Get over there, Spencer. Stop it before it gets out of hand. How embarrassing!" Genevieve exclaimed. Spencer practically bounded across the room to where Cav and Gil were standing facing each other like two bull buffalos.

"What the hell are you talking about, Gil? You bought that filly today! You bought the horse I had a deposit on! How the hell did you do that Gil? How?" Cav was bellowing and observably exasperated. Gil was looking smug on the other hand.

"Cav, you are making a spectacle at your daughter's engagement party. We can discuss the details of my purchase another time," Gil complacently offered.

"Do you have the damn horse at your place or not?" Cav questioned.

"Guys, please. This is not the time or place!" Spencer interjected.

"Yes! Cav! Gil! I cannot believe you two! Mallory will be mortified!" Genevieve walked up behind Spencer looking as angry as the brothers.

Both brothers looked at her, glared at each other and then Cav walked away and disappeared into the crowd on the dance floor.

"I am deeply sorry and truly regret ..." Gil began to apologize.

Genevieve did not let Gil finish his apology. "Gil, you came here tonight not to celebrate Mallory and Spencer, but to play the one-up game with Cav. I would appreciate you staying clear of Cav for the evening and flying under the radar, so my daughter and friends can enjoy this occasion," Genevieve admonished.

"Certainly, Genevieve. Again, my sincere regrets."

Gil walked off with that and joined a group at the other end of the bar. Spencer noticed that Genevieve had put her hands to her forehead in frustration. But on second thought, he believed she looked physically ill.

"Genevieve, are you okay?" Spencer inquired.

"Yes of course. I just have a sudden headache. Those two could cause anyone's head to hurt," Genevieve explained. She continued, "Go find your fiancé and dance with her! Have a good time! Forget all this nonsense!"

Spencer gave her lean torso a hug and did as she asked. But he noticed later she apparently had slipped out of the party. He concluded she must have been more upset than he thought. But he did as she suggested, and he found Mallory and led her to the dance floor for a cuddle-up slow song.

"So, what was all the ruckus about?" Mallory asked Spencer.

"Your dad and Gil. The usual. Hope it did not upset you," Spencer empathized.

"Good grief no! They have acted like that at every social function both have attended all my life! I would be surprised were they not to clash in public! You know, keep the feud alive for all to enjoy and speculate about!" Mallory was totally unconcerned about the incident, so Spencer let it go.

The interactions with Genevieve were like apparitions in his mind that things were off, and he was sure she was not herself. But his thoughts became loss as her daughter was in his arms looking up at him with love and hope and dreams of the future and he was looking at her returning the love and hope for the future that shown brightly.

It was later that evening when all, but a few had left and the staff began to clear tables and clean up, that Spencer had a chance to speak with Cav. He found Cav having a private drink in an alcove off the main room that featured a rolled and pleated leather booth behind curtains.

"May I join you?" Spencer asked.

"Sure! Have your parents left? I failed to bid them good night," Cav lamented.

"Yes, they left a while ago. But they knew you were inundated with guests to attend to."

"No problem," Spencer assured Cav.

"I would say the party was a total success!" Cav remarked.

"Yes! Mallory was pleased with how it all turned out," Spencer replied.

"She wasn't upset with Gil's and my tiff?" Cav asked.

"No, she knows what happens when oil meets water," Spencer joked and went on. "Sorry that Gil made the deal behind your back. Can't imagine Royce taking a deposit and then selling the filly to Gil," Spencer remarked. Spencer was truly pondering the circumstance.

"Well, because he didn't," Cav stated, and Spencer looked confused.

"What do you mean? Didn't you put a deposit down on the filly?" Spencer looked quizzically.

"Yes. Yes, I did. But I also took it back," Cav now looked smug while Spencer looked perplexed.

"I thought … I thought you wanted that filly," Spencer was obviously confused.

"Well, Spence, that is what everyone thought. But I never honestly put a deposit down on the horse."

"What?"

Spencer looked at Cav inquiringly. He did not understand.

"I made a deal with Royce you bet. But it wasn't to buy the horse. It was to make Gil think I was interested, no, obsessed, with the horse, so Gil would pay Royce top dollar probably twice what the horse is worth," Cav continued.

Spencer was not sure if he was shocked by Cav's deceit or impressed with the ingenuity of outsmarting his brother or disgusted at the lengths the King brothers would go to undermine each other.

"Now don't think too badly of me, Spence. I didn't want him to pay that much for the horse. That was his fault and stupidity. What I wanted was to distract him," Cav explained.

"Distract?" Spencer asked.

"Yes. I need Gil looking the other way and thinking he has the upper hand. While I make the deal of a lifetime. The deal that will end all future conflicts because I will have the ultimate horse, the ultimate bloodline. Gil will never be able to compete," Cav imparted his motivation behind his actions.

But Spencer was completely in the dark as to what Cav could be talking about. His first thought was this was just another one of Cav's extravagant expenditures to pay for his latest pastime.

"Okay. Would you like to elaborate?" Spencer was tired of being in the dark.

"Well, I do want to give you all the details. Because you have to be my decoy. But not tonight. I am suddenly extremely tired and want to go home to Genevieve. I'll answer all your questions tomorrow," Cav stated.

"As you say, Cav. I'll be interested to hear how all this unfolds. I am grabbing your daughter and calling it a night too."

"Good night, Spence. Oh! And Spence. How do you feel about Egypt?"

"Egypt? Like Africa Egypt?" Again, Spencer was aghast as to what Cav could possibly be plotting or scheming to top Gil.

"Yep!" Cav answered.

"Have no interest or desire to visit or do business in Egypt," Spencer said frowning.

"Well good night, Spence," Cav dismissed him.

"Good night, Cav," Spence slid out of the booth and went to look for Mallory.

"Ahhhhhhh, but you will son. You will be my eyes, ears and legs and help me pull off the coup of the decades. There will be no doubt which King brother has the best of the best. You will, my son, soon journey to Egypt," Cav said to no one but himself as he toasted thin air.

Chapter 5

Spencer took his time the next morning getting to the barn. Mallory rose on schedule to be at the barn at 5:30 AM. She maintained a routine that she had adhered to for years. Early morning rides to train horses, lunch and then lessons in the afternoon and evening. Mallory's organization and living on a schedule had been a habit since she was young. She treated time like it was a valuable commodity that she had to protect and distribute with extreme care.

Rarely did Mallory just relax with nothing to do and nowhere to go. She was obsessed with everything in her life and her personal curse that it had to be perfect. She kept things clean, slick, and simple so she could maintain her unrealistic expectations. Spencer occasionally entertained the passing thought that even he was scheduled, convenient, and simple to choose as a boyfriend, fiancé, and husband.

Mallory would not beat the bushes to find a mate. Spencer was sure of that. She found him when they were young and determined he checked off all the boxes, so she just planned their lives accordingly. He was somewhat flattered that Mallory found him worthy of being included in her self-made utopia. But he sometimes wondered how Mallory would handle disappointment …. real disappointment.

As it turned out, he did not see Cav for several days. Cav did not come to the barn on Sundays. Spencer only made appearances to make sure all was running as it should. He and Mallory usually attended church service after Mallory's early rides and spent the afternoons either riding leisurely together or separate activities. Sunday dinner was normally at Cav and Genevieve's home. But Genevieve begged off the night before at the party saying she would be too tired to socialize. So, it turned into several days before Cav and Spencer actually had an opportunity to visit.

Cav did surface at the barn later that week. He chatted with a couple of patrons and then found Spencer.

"Spence, I want you to come to Gil's with me," Cav invited.

"Why are you going to Gil's?" Spencer was instantly less than enthusiastic at the prospect of a meeting between Cav and Gil. He could be walking into a ring with two angry bulls that pace, paw, grunt and then explode. He had refereed this behavior more times than he wanted.

"To appropriately admire the Royce colt, what else?" Cav picked up on the reluctance of Spencer to come with him. Cav also knew why. "Don't concern yourself, Spence. I will keep things low-key. But we need some time to talk, and this will give us that time." With that Spencer grabbed his hat and Cav followed Spencer to his truck to head to Gil King's ranch.

Unlike Cav, Gil never renamed his ranch. If one were to guess, probably just because Cav did. Gil built his home on the far side of the creek as far away from Cav as he could be. Although there were better homesites around the creek, Gil did not want to live one inch closer to his brother than he had to. So, it was a twenty-minute drive from the Equestrian Center to Gil's.

The King land holdings as a whole was as picturesque as it was functional and successful. The land was acres of green pastures separated by wooden rail fencing with ponds and tanks scattered across the terrain. The two ranches were separated by a creek that ran through the entirety of the ranch which offered beautiful tree lines with lush natural grapevines in the trees filtering down to the creek. The creek itself was always running with water except during severe drought and had served as a playground for fishing and wading for several generations of Kings.

Spencer knew most of what he knew of the King brother's feud from his father. When he started dating Mallory in high school, his father related the details as best he could. The story was the brothers hated each other from birth. They were only eighteen months apart, so they could be mistaken as twins. The ranch was owned by Porter and Grace King at that time, and it was said that the boys drove both of them to madness from the beginning. As babies they hit, bit and threw toys at each other. What was considered as baby boys being baby boys became more serious when they became toddlers. There were constant fits from one or the other because their brother took something away or ate the last cookie or climbed in mama's lap first. It didn't matter. One or the other was unhappy or mad at the other unless they were both sound asleep. Grace was a nervous, anxious wreck dealing with the dueling babies.

Porter often soothed Grace with promises that when they were a little older, past the unreasonable toddler years into their youth, they would mellow. They would become more civil, less jealous, less combustible. Porter would tell her to have patience. But he was wrong. The toddlers as young boys were more spiteful than ever, attacking each other with weapons, destroying the other's property, and constantly dissing and disrespecting each other.

Cav had once described it to someone. Think about sharing everything, your home, your parents, your friends, your horses, your baseball bat, anything, and everything with someone you hate, you detest, you wish was not in your life. But you wake up every day and deal with hatefulness, maliciousness, and just him period.

By the time the boys became teenagers, Porter was more involved with their relationship. He was a mild manner man that did not seek out conflict. The battling of his sons totally dismayed him. He was called upon more than once to intervene to stop the boys from seriously hurting or killing each other. It was then that Grace would tell him to be patient. They will mature and become men and leave all this foolishness behind them.

She was wrong. Well into their manhood they continued to be adversaries. If one drove a Chevy, the other drove a Ford. If one rode a black horse, the other rode a white. If one thought the fence should run north and south, the other thought the fence should run east and west. They went to rival universities and to the current day still have robust conflict over sports. There was also a rumor that the brothers had courted the same woman which resulted in unforgiveable and unforgettable bitterness between them.

Porter was in anguish dealing with his two sons and trying to mediate every disagreement. It was said that he worried constantly about the future of the ranch when he no longer could actively run it either due to illness or death. He could not imagine Grace having to arbitrate her way through the anger and clashes. As it turned out, Grace went peacefully before Porter. When Porter followed a couple of years later, the brothers agreed for the first time in their life. They concurred they would split the ranch. With the death of their parents, the brothers were no longer required to interact as peaceful loving brothers except on occasion which was a relief and a release from a life sentence.

After the split the brothers seemed to have called a moratorium. Spencer's father commented that it was a shame that after Porter and Grace were gone, they decided to leave each other in peace. Cav was busy remodeling the house for his wife and making improvements to the ranch. He worked twenty hours a day networking, hiring, and rebuilding his part of the ranch.

Gil was equally busy building his home and barn and amenities on his property. He built a lavish five-bedroom ranch villa and an equally extravagant barn facility. It appeared for several years the brothers had buried the axe and were content to run their individual barn and business irrespective of each other. But it was tribal knowledge that the peace was not lasting, and they clashed at almost every opportunity over the years.

"Spence, we have trouble on the horizon," Cav began to talk in the truck on the way to Gil's.

"Why do you say that Cav?" Spencer's heart sank as he realized that Cav really was upset over that Royce filly.

"Well, I know that you and Mallory think that everything is sugar and spice right now. But I think you need to know it is not. I need a co-conspirator to appease Genevieve," Cav shared.

Spencer was shocked at Cav bringing Genevieve into the conversation. This was obviously not going where he thought it was going. An awkward silence ensued as Spencer tried to figure out exactly what to ask Cav, "Cav, I don't understand. You need to explain a little further," he finally broke the silence.

"Well, I don't have all the information. We are waiting for the results from the tests last week. But it appears Genevieve …" Cav's voice broke. Spencer was in shock and slowed the truck down to delay arrival at Gil's. Cav cleared his throat, "It is possible that Genevieve has brain cancer, aggressive brain cancer." Spencer pulled the truck over to the side of the road and stopped. It was a country road so even though he was blocking the lane, he wasn't concerned.

"Cav, what are you telling me?" The shock was apparent in Spencer's voice.

"Spence, we may lose her. We may damn well lose her."

"How long?" again shock and disbelief in Spencer's voice.

"Well until the doctors have their test results and make some decisions, we don't know anything for certain. But Dr. Mahoney is going out on a limb and saying if they find what he thinks they are going to find, six months to a year," again Cav's voice broke a little.

"Cav, what do we do? What can we do?" Spencer was devastated.

He had over the years developed a real affection for Genevieve. And needless to be said, being that close to a living equestrian legend had been priceless. To process the fact that she had brain cancer was unfeasible. In the same thought he thought of Mallory. She was incredibly close to her mom. Mallory will be inconsolable. He did not realize that he had said that out loud until Cav responded.

"Yes, she will be. That is why Genevieve does not want her to know until there is no other choice. She does not want this year ruined for Mallory. She doesn't want Mallory to postpone her wedding or competition plans. She believes she may have the opportunity to be there. She is insistent we keep this from Mallory for the time being. We are enlisting your help to assist us in keeping this a secret. Cover for us when we are at the hospital, whatever. Just be there and lie through your teeth until Genevieve is ready to tell Mallory."

"What? You want me to lie to Mallory? We have never lied to each other, Cav. I want to respect Genevieve's and your wishes but lying to Mallory!" Spencer exclaimed.

"I realize what we are asking and if it comes down, I will assure Mallory you had no choice but to honor her mother's wishes. She will be upset with both of us, but she will get over it. There will be much more to concern her if this all comes to pass," Cav replied.

"So, Genevieve could be on her death bed when we walk down the aisle?" Spencer almost choked on the words.

"Well, I would hope that is not the case. I don't have a crystal ball, Spence. I don't have the answers. I know that Genevieve is determined to see Mallory married. I must support her in that goal no matter whether I believe she can make it or not. I am asking for your help also."

"Of course, Cav. I don't know that I agree with you and Genevieve on this path. Mallory will be really hurt and feel very betrayed," Spencer stated uncertainly.

"No, Spence. She will be sad and heartbroken. And for the first time in her life, we may not be able to stop the inevitable. Come on! Let's get this meeting over with! See the filly! Brag on her! Let

Gil gloat! And then get out of here. You and I have other business to talk about."

Chapter 6

The visit with Gil went better than expected. Spencer was still reeling from the news that Cav had delivered on the way over, he could not imagine how this was going to affect Mallory. He did not feel right keeping this secret and he didn't see how Genevieve could fight brain cancer and keep it from her daughter.

Gil took them to a stall in his barn to view the Royce filly. He and Cav made small talk walking out to the barn. But tension was in the air. Gil went in the stall, haltered the filly, and brought her out. If you did not know her background, you would still know you were looking at a horse of impeccable breeding and lineage.

The horse's color was unusual for an Arabian. She was golden in areas that deepened into shades of browns that ended in deep dark brown. Her legs were dark brown with no stockings. Her abundant mane and tail were coal black. Even as a young horse her step was high and regal. Her eyes in the Arabian tradition were large and expressive. Her neck was arched, muscular, and elegant and set on strong shoulders with a chest destined to be broad and solid. Her movement was the epitome of Arabian movement, free flowing, floating, and effortlessly gliding across the ground. In Spencer's estimation, the filly was destined to become one of the most lucrative purse winners in the nation.

Cav was suitably respectful and complimentary of the filly. He commented on her striking color and of course her flawless movement. He was correctly polite, but yet seemed to exhibit a bit of envy. Gil was like the cat that ate the canary. He knew that he had overpaid for this filly, but to see the look on Cav's face made it well worthwhile.

"I'll be interested to see the future of this baby," Cav offered.

"What? You don't think I can give this horse the future it deserves?" Gil was instantly offended.

"No Gil, I did not mean that at all. Actually, right the opposite. I believe she has a phenomenal future, and I will be following her and your success."

"Humph!" Gil muttered.

"Gil, may I bring Mallory over to see her?" Spencer quickly intervened. They were close to leaving on a good note and he was going to make that happen if at all possible.

"Why, sure Spence! I always enjoy seeing Miss Mallory." Gil amicably agreed.

Mallory was the only child of that generation. Gil never married and did not have children. It was often thought Gil coveted Cav for his equestrian celebrity wife and charming and equally talented daughter. But Gil sincerely had a soft place in his heart for Mallory. She affectionately called him uncle, and he loved her for overlooking his relationship with her father.

Finally, Cav and Spencer said their goodbyes. Both congratulated Gil on the filly and climbed into Spencer's truck. At first there was an awkward silence. Spencer was at a loss as to what to say. He could not believe that Genevieve had brain cancer and could die. She was an icon in the horse world. She rose to fame as a young rider competing in the Olympics and winning gold three times. Genevieve's fame was international, and she was wealthy in her own right for her endorsements and appearances. She trained many of the finest dressage horses in the world. It was a badge of honor to ride Genevieve's horse. Her picture was flashed across equestrian magazines and websites continually. She always looked regal, in control, confident and unshakeable. Spencer admired her and was in awe of her. This news left him anxious, realizing that this time next year, she could be gone. He could not wrap his mind around that.

"So, Spence, what do you think of that horse?" Cav broke the silence.

"No doubt she is one fine Arabian. I'm with you. Interested in seeing what becomes of her. Gil should hire the best to train her," Spencer responded.

"Yes. When Mallory sees that horse, you know, and I know that she is going to want to get her hands on her. If he approaches Mallory with that proposition, you might want to discourage her."

"Okay," Spence responded with a statement, but it came across as more of a question.

"No, not because I'm jealous and don't want her to help Gil with the horse. It's because if things go right, I will have a horse that will make that one look like a Clydesdale," Cav explained.

Spence was shocked. "What was Cav up to now?"

"Would you care to explain, Cav?"

"Well, not at the moment. I have a few loose ends to tie up before we have the conversation. Just keep Mallory occupied and give Genevieve the space she has requested to deal with whatever this is that could destroy her," Cav stated.

Afterwards, Spencer took time at the barn to absorb the information Cav had shared with him. Again, he could not believe this dynamic lady was at risk. He could not imagine what she must be going through. Looking at everyone and everything and knowing it is almost over. She would never see grandchildren or Mallory in the Olympics and so much else.

Spencer went home a different man that night. He was softer and more attentive to Mallory as she rattled on about different horses and patrons at the barn. His heart broke when he thought how different she would look, and she would talk if she knew of her mom's condition. He had such sympathy and empathy for her, and he couldn't even tell her. All he could do was hold her and silently extend his compassion.

Chapter 7

The next couple of weeks went by without any more major revelations. September is an active time at the barn as riders and horses prepare for fall exhibitions and competitions. What drew comments even from Mallory, was Genevieve's absence from the barn. But Mallory learned that her mom was writing a new book and was trying to meet an ambitious deadline. That appeared to satisfy Mallory for the time being.

It was late in September that Genevieve did visit the barn for the first time in weeks. Spencer was shocked that she looked much like her normal self. She was not showing any signs of illness, other than maybe a loss of weight. But Genevieve was thin anyway, so the loss was subtle. She looked in on several horses and greeted patrons. She seated herself in the bleachers around the outside arena and watched Mallory ride and train a Friesian stallion destined for a touring company. The King family and their handpicked trainers had trained horses for the company for decades.

Spencer approached Genevieve not sure what he was going to say.

"Hi, Spence. Watching our girl ride. She is such an accomplished rider," Genevieve said with genuine pride and admiration. Having Mallory follow in her footsteps was her true life's ambition. She had Mallory riding before she could walk. Cav often chastised Genevieve for putting that baby on a horse. Genevieve often teased him over the years as Mallory's star rose that Mallory was that baby that she put on a horse.

"That she is," Spencer agreed.

She gestured for Spencer to take a seat beside her.

"Spence, I want you to know that I appreciate your support of Cav and me during this difficult time. I do not want my circumstance to destroy one second of Mallory's happiness as she plans her wedding."

"Genevieve, I understand your intent is to protect Mallory. But I don't understand how you think you are going to keep this away from Mallory."

"Well, at this time, I am taking things a day at a time. Depending on how things progress will determine decisions in the future. But we must live in the present and right now everything is as good as it gets."

Spencer just shook his head in agreement, but inside was pondering if he really agreed with her. Was she the bravest person he had ever known or was she in denial? He did not know. She stood to leave.

"Spencer, we are expecting you and Mallory over Sunday for dinner. Cav is grilling. Okay?"

"Sure, Genevieve. I'll let Mallory know."

Genevieve waved at Mallory, blew her a kiss, and left the barn.

Sunday proved to be a beautiful day and perfect for the dinner at Cav and Genevieve's. Mallory and he arrived bringing dessert and wine. Mallory and Genevieve busied themselves in the kitchen with sides. He opened the wine and took a glass to Cav who was outside grilling.

"Here ya go, Cav." Spencer handed Cav his wine and sat down in a patio chair to visit while Cav cooked. Cav eventually shut the grill and took a seat also, "Thank you, Spence. I'm glad you came out. I want to run something by you."

Spencer became all ears. Finally, Cav was going to share the scheme that Spencer had been suspicious of for some time.

"Spence, I might as well just lay it on the table. I have the opportunity to introduce the Zabr Arabian bloodline into our horses. We will be the only breeder in the US to have the bloodline and will have without question the elite of domestic Arabians in the US."

Cav paused to let this sink in. He had purposefully used a couple of key words. Zabr Arabians were legendary all over the world. The bloodline had been protected by the Zabr family for centuries. Only the family becoming more progressive with younger generations taking over the family business could foster such an opportunity.

Cav continued to explain that when he and Genevieve attended an event in England last year, he met one of the Zabr cousins that was high ranking in the Zabr equestrian business. Cav had cultivated the relationship and recently he had been invited to Egypt to explore bringing the bloodline back to America.

Spencer could see the pride and pure joy in Cav's demeanor as he dreamed of having a Zabr Arabian horse in his barn. Both knew that Gil could go to the ends of the earth, but he would never top a Zabr horse. Zabr Arabians were the pinnacle. They were so protected that most equestrians had only seen pictures of them. The Zabr's alone had preserved the best of the earliest ancient horse pure bloodline. Cav's highest aspiration was to bring them to the ranch.

"Go to Egypt. You are going to Egypt?" Spencer inquired.

"I can't go, Spence. I can't make the trip health wise myself. And more importantly I can't leave Genevieve. I want you to go, Spence. I need you to go to Egypt and close the deal. Bring back my golden specimen. Help me make this barn renowned for you and Mallory as you carry on. Your future will be dealing with multimillion dollar horses. I need you to go to Egypt for me, Spence. There is no one else."

Spencer sat silently taking in what Cav had shared with him. No doubt that Zabr Arabian horses in their barn would put them in another stratosphere in the equestrian world. What those horses would be capable of in the American sports and equestrian competitions would be unmatched in stamina and heart.

But doing business in Egypt would not be easy. They were talking about an exchange of millions. He felt sure the Egyptian government would be involved in such a transaction between an American and Egyptian. He also was not sure he could trust what he brought home was what he bargained for. How would he know if he did not witness the process of semen retrieval, and would the Egyptians allow that? Many questions were running through his mind as he grasped what Cav was asking him.

"Take Mallory with you. Make it a vacation for the two of you. See the sites. She will love being involved," Cav volunteered.

"Cav let me talk to Mallory. When are you thinking of us going?"

"October, Spence."

"October, next month … actually, practically this month!" Spence exclaimed.

"I know. But I want to strike while the iron is hot. Things could change and we might not be able to make the deal later. I need you to book your flights and go as soon as possible," Cav instructed.

Spencer sighed, "I will talk to Mallory tonight when we get home. Does Genevieve know about this?" Spencer asked.

"Spence, there is nothing I do or have done in forty years that Genevieve does not know about. She is my partner and best friend. I can only hope that you and Mallory will have such a relationship. We have always had each other's back. She is supportive of this and excited to see it happen. So, another reason to make haste."

"Then let's not dally," Spencer replied standing.

The evening provided the perfect ambiance, so Mallory and her mom set the dinner table on the patio. Cav dished up the grilled main course and they sat down to dinner with a toast from Cav.

"To the family and a future, we can all look forward to," as glasses clinked. He reached over and kissed Genevieve on the cheek.

Spencer was touched. In the years he had been associated with this family he had never seen affection between Cav and Genevieve. He wondered if Mallory was picking up on the red flags everywhere that things were not the same.

The four dined talking barn, horses, trainers, and competitions. All four were knowledgeable and had an opinion to share. Although Genevieve was the true horse whisperer among them, she always listened respectfully to their feedback. It was halfway through the meal that Cav broached the subject of Arabians and Egypt. He could not wait to get everyone on board so he could move forward.

"Mallory, we need to have a family discussion that stays at this table," Cav began.

Mallory looked at Spencer rolling her eyes, "That means we are not to tell Uncle Gil."

"Well, yes or anyone else for that matter. This is confidential. We all need to agree that it will remain so," Cav instructed.

Spencer picked up his wine glass, everyone followed suit and a toast was made to the unspoken pact of what Cav was to reveal. Mallory sat looking quizzical as she toasted. Cav began.

"I have cultivated a relationship with a gentleman that I met in England last year. We met at one of the socials and seem to seek each other out at remaining events. Your mom met him, and he was impressed to know and hang with the husband of Genevieve King." Cav laughed at his own witticism and others followed suit. It was known among all of them that Genevieve was the star in the family. However, never had Cav been resentful of Genevieve's success. He continued.

"As it turns out the gentleman was there for the exhibition piece, and it was his first time to participate in a western show. Western meaning Europe of course. His handlers were exhibiting several Egyptian Arabians. Because he was new to the crowd and the event,

I showed him the ropes and we developed, as I said, a friendship. A friendship that has continued up to this time."

"So, when is he shipping us a horse?" Mallory sardonically asked, thinking she knew the end of this story. Spencer was surprised that she was not more excited about the chance to train an Egyptian import.

"Well, it's not that simple, Mallory. The man's name is Saad. Saad Zabr," Cav let that sink in for a minute.

"Zabr Arabians! Are you kidding?" Mallory was not believing her ears as Cav silently acquiesced … yes. She looked at her mom who in turn also indicated concurrence. She looked at Spencer and he raised his eyebrows. "You have purchased a Zabr Arabian? You are kidding me!" she asked again.

Mallory was confused because everyone knew that the Zabr stable was off limits and had been forever. The horses were protected and considered more valuable than the Mona Lisa. The Zabr Arabians were direct linage descendants of the original Arabians that dated back to 1100 BC. Only the Zabr family and ancestors had ownership of the horses.

In the 1920's after the war, the current Zabr patriarch in a gesture of friendship gifted a horse to the English royal family. This stallion was bred numerous times, and his offspring were considered a more refined Arabian and sought after. But the actual ancient lineage had been bred out of the breed currently recognized as Arabian in most of the world.

"No, they will not sell a horse. But I may have a donor deal," Cav revealed.

"May?" Mallory was questioning the possibility of this being real.

"They are not your usual do business on FaceTime and boom it's done. They want a visit. They want to meet face to face the person that will be responsible for the insemination, care of the mare and ultimate care and training of the horse. At this point they want a share of the horse. I plan to negotiate them out of that ownership," Cav stated.

"So, you are going to Egypt?" Mallory was instantly dismayed.

Her father, although feisty, was not really in shape to travel across the world. And although she had not said anything, she was worried about her mother. She wasn't herself. She was hiding behind writing her book, and she wasn't riding or training. Before Cav could answer.

"No, Cav is not going, Mallory. We are," Spencer spoke up.

"We!" Mallory exclaimed.

"Yes, your dad has asked me to represent his interests in Egypt. He has suggested that you come with me, and we make it a holiday. See the Sphinx, the pyramids, float down the Nile," Spencer said.

"Is it safe?" Mallory inquired.

Cav spoke up, "You will be with a Zabr envoy at all times. They will take care and keep you safe."

"Wow! Egypt!" Mallory again exclaimed.

Spencer could see that Mallory was getting on board. And maybe getting Mallory away from the barn and the horses and in a totally different environment would be good for them. They were both so tied to the barn that they were victims of routine. They were not married yet, but Spencer felt like they were old and looking back instead of looking forward.

"All right. When can we go? It would have to be after Japan in April," Mallory asked.

Cav looked at her with eyebrows furrowed. "Next spring is entirely too long to postpone this trip. You need to go immediately. By the middle of next month at the latest."

"Dad, I can't do that! I am in intense training with Sky for Japan. Not to mention a wedding I'm planning. I am in the middle of training, and I have horses making breakthroughs. I am committed here until after Japan," Mallory argued.

"Mallory, this is not my timetable. I am negotiating with a family that number one does not have to negotiate about anything, and who will think nothing of cutting the dialogue off at a moment's notice. This is very shaky ground. We must move on with this. You will have to turn your horses over to someone else for a couple of weeks," Cav said sternly.

Later when Spencer and Mallory were at home.

"I can't do it Spence. I can't just drop what I'm doing and go chasing my dad's idiotic ruse. You don't believe they are really going to give up an ancient held treasure to a Texas horse ranch. I am so close to getting Sky where he needs to be to go to Japan next year. But we have to win the shows in between and a week off might as well be a month. We can't afford that kind of downtime. Not now."

Chapter 8

The conversation continued at breakfast the next morning. "I was hoping that sleeping on it would change your mind," Spencer half stated – half asked.

"Spence, don't you think if I could see my way to go with you I would! But to jump up and run across the world to God knows where to God knows what chasing after one of my father's covert plots to undermine my uncle? Go! You go! Humor him! But I cannot. I simply cannot." Spencer bowed his head in defeat.

Later that day, Cav came by the barn. He was looking worn and old sitting at his desk in the barn office where Spencer found him.

"Hello, Cav," Spencer greeted.

Seeing Cav looking quite grave. Spencer shut the door behind him.

"Hello, Spence." Cav responded.

"Are you ok, Cav?"

"The news is not good, Spence. Not good at all. They gave her six months, less than a year. They are suggesting treatments that are invasive and with terrible side effects. She has refused treatment."

Spencer sat for a moment letting Cav's words sink in. He silently reasoned if Genevieve refused treatment, she would most likely be on the short end of the timeline. "Cav, I don't know what to say. This is a nightmare," Spencer was at a loss. "How did Genevieve take the results?"

"She is stoic as to be expected. Nothing shakes her... not even her impending ..." Cav's voice trailed off.

"What can I do to help you ... help Genevieve?" Spencer asked.

"Just continue to keep this from Mal until Genevieve is ready to tell her. That is number one. Genevieve and I had the discussion coming back from Dallas. She wants everything at the barn to run as usual. She is removing herself from day to day. She knows at some point her behavior will tip Mal off, but she wants to spare her as long as possible."

"Sure. I suppose I should postpone Egypt to stay here with Mal," Spence uttered.

"No!" Cav said sharply. Spencer looked at him shocked. He was thinking with all this going on that pursuing this pipedream in Egypt would take a backseat.

"No. I want to make this deal before Genevieve is …" Cav hesitated, "I want her to know that we have the Zabr bloodline in our barn. It will be my last and best gift to her besides Mal. If anything, I am depending on you to get to Egypt and make that deal as soon as possible."

Spencer softened and explained his objection. Spencer was feeling a lot like Mallory as far as going to God knows where to do God knows what.

"Cav, Mal has refused to go to Egypt with me. If I go, I won't be here to help you navigate the waters here."

"That is exactly right, Spence. I need you to go and get back with no delay. I have no idea how much time we have to make this happen. We are in a race with God."

"Okay then. If going to Egypt is how I can best help you, then I will make travel arrangements as soon as you tell me the details of the trip," Spencer acquiesced.

"I will visit with Saad and get back to you," with that statement, Cav dismissed Spencer.

Spencer stood to leave but turned before he opened the door. "Cav, I will be remembering Genevieve and you in my prayers. My heart is broken," Spencer sincerely tendered.

"Thank you, Spence. I take great comfort in knowing you are a part of this family and will be here to manage the barn and take care of Mal. I'm afraid that I may not be able to manage either for a while."

Spence nodded and left, leaving Cav to sort through his feelings.

Chapter 9

Spence spent the next few days looking at itineraries to Egypt. Mallory continued to insist that she could not go. So, after several discussions he relented that he would be traveling alone. He put his flight itinerary together and he waited.

It was several days before Cav approached him. However, Spence was preoccupied with an early winter storm in the forecast. It was forecasted to be the worst in decades for Texas with two different fronts bringing record snowfall.

"Hi Spence, got time for a cup of coffee?" Cav asked Spence nodding to Spence's office for a private conversation.

"Sure, Cav."

Spence and Cav entered the office with Spence shutting the door behind them. Cav took a seat in front of the desk and Spence retreated to his place behind the desk.

"Coffee?" Spence offered and turned to the credenza behind him and began pouring from the already brewed beverage. Cav shook his head yes to the question.

"I have lined things up for your Egypt trip," Cav started the conversation and Spencer became instantly dismayed. He had hoped that the deal would fall through.

"You need to leave next week," Cav sipped his coffee and shared his timeline.

"Next week!" Spencer exclaimed his surprise at the impending timeline. He had hoped maybe the end of October first of November and be back for Thanksgiving. In his mind he was not sure he could plan a trip across the world in a week.

"Is your passport current?" Cav asked.

"Yes, but I haven't cleared my calendar, we have a big storm looming, I don't think Mallory is ready for me to waltz out the door in a week," Spencer objected.

"Spence, I do not call all the shots on this. You are the guest of the Zabr family, and they have invited you next week. Pack a bag, get a ticket, and go. They will meet you at the airport and take care of everything else."

"Okay, Cav. I will do as you request. But you do realize with me gone, Genevieve absent most of the time, the barn will fall on you and Mal?"

"I know, Spence. We'll get through. You will be gone what four or five days? We can delay most issues until you return."

What could not be delayed was the premature fall snowstorm that became an unprecedented blizzard that moved in that week. Temperatures were below freezing for over a week and snow carpeted the ground and every nook and cranny. Tree limbs, telephone wires, roofs, fencing, even the backs of livestock, all surfaces were covered with inches of cold, wet snow. All structures were subject to coming down due to weight from the snow. Communications on mobile phones and the internet were interrupted as well as major power issues and freezing water pipes.

The barn and homes were built well, but days of below freezing were unusual and an unparalleled event. The outbuildings roofs were in jeopardy and outside pipes and hoses in the paddock had to be protected to prevent freezing. Constant water had to be available along with hay for the paddock horses to fight the cold. Some horses had to be blanketed and kept in stalls with hay for the night. It was a taxing undertaking to take freeze preventive measures for the barn, the paddocks and all the dwellings on the property including the homes.

Electricity or lack of became an issue so generators were pulled out to keep the barn activities going. If a horse and rider could rise above the overall freezing temperature to tack up and prepare for a ride, then the indoor arena gave some relief from the cold and training could continue. But the weather conditions prevented most from coming to the barn. The roads were dangerous and being on the side of the road should a vehicle fail could be fatal in a short period of time.

Mallory and Spencer were working hard trying to cover all the bases. They were short staffed due to the weather and unpassable roads. Horses had to be fed and monitored for their reaction to the cold. Most horses, unless aged or ill can handle cold temperatures. But this storm was not just a dip into freezing. It was the prolonged exposure to below freezing into the single digits that put everything at risk, man, beast, and systems.

Mallory was sitting in the arena in front of one of the exterior heaters trying to stay warm when Carson Redden joined her smiling a greeting. Carson was a long-time friend of the family and had worked for the family since before Mallory could remember. He was foreman for many years but with age had become Spencer's right-hand man and continued to handle many of the functions at the barn. Carson had supervised many of Mallory's first rides as a little girl and cheered her on as she developed her skill level to rival her mother. Carson was well thought of at the barn and Mallory could not imagine a day without him.

"How ya do'n there Miss Mallory?" Carson inquired.

"Just great! My touché is freezing, my feet are freezing, my nose is not even there anymore, my hands are numb," Mallory groaned.

"Might want to consider going home and taking a hot shower and hunkering down in front of the fire," Carson suggested.

"Well, unfortunately Spence is in the field troubleshooting, so I have to stay here until closing," Mallory grumbled.

"Nahhhhh, I'll close her down. You look beat Mal, go home get warm and get some rest. We have another three days of this according to the forecast."

"And what are you, Carson? The invincible snowman?"

"No, but I have had the easy duty. I have been in the truck with a heater most the day," Carson grinned wickedly.

"You Judas! Where are your wet hands and feet and cold ass?" Mallory looked at him accusatory.

"I save those for cold shower days. Now get your wet hands and feet and cold ass home. I will let Spence know where you are at."

"Thanks, Carson! Dad is going to call and threaten to come down but don't let him. Assure him all is fine, and horses are not dying of exposure and the barn has not burned down or fallen down from the snow, or any other imagined catastrophe he can come up with. He doesn't walk well enough to be skating on ice and snow and we do not need a broken hip."

"I will see to that, Miss Mal," Carson assured her.

"Mother is behind closed doors working on her book as usual these days so she most likely will not be down. I can remember when she thought the barn would not survive a crisis without her input and hands-on management. Now it's like, eh, you and Spence take care of it."

"Well, I admit that is a change and unlike your mother," Carson agreed.

"I was counting the other day, and I don't think she has been to the barn but about five or six days this past month. She has pretty much turned her students over to me or other trainers. Her horses are sitting idle. All she seems interested in is this book and meeting her editor's deadlines," Mallory bemoaned.

"Well, all books end so keep your criticisms to yourself, Miss Mallory. That would be my advice. Sometimes what we see is not the whole picture or the real picture. We look through a lens that distorts reality into what we think or want or believe. Keep an open mind and let your mom be your mom. She loves this barn, and she loves her horses. She'll be back with a vengeance, and you'll be wishing she were writing another book."

Both laughed as Mallory stood to go home. Carson began to escort her to the door.

"So, are you ready for Spence's trip and taking over this barn?" Mallory inquired.

"Well, it will just be a few days. Once we get through this storm shouldn't be a big deal. Of course, there is going to be some major clean up and repair on the other side of this," Carson advised.

Carson opened the outside door and a Christmas postcard unfolded in front of them. Eyes were blinded by the white blanket that covered the world. Trees and fences were etched into the icy porcelain background. The glistening and glare almost hurt the eyes as one peered through the falling snow trying to focus on something not white. The stock tank usually visible from the door was nonexistent having fallen victim to the coverlet of white powder. Where there was usually chaotic busy activity in the arena yard with riders and horses preparing to ride, today there was only silence. The grey sky that loomed above the trees and snow was claustrophobic, feeling low and menacing. The cold was silent, intrusive, and bitter, and Mallory wanted to go home to warmth and dryness.

"Well, his flight was to leave Saturday. DFW is shut down, I think. Or at least it was. Who knows now? It's been so long since I have seen the news," Mallory stated.

"Well, we'll see what the boss man says. You get home. I'll talk to him when he gets here to see what his plans are," Carson winked and grinned as Mallory headed for her truck to take her where she longed to be. Which was out of this ice age, deep freeze and warm and cozy at home.

That evening Spencer arrived, warmed up, and they were drinking a glass of wine waiting for the phone to ring. When it did, Spencer gave Mallory a knowing look and answered his phone.

"Hello, Cav," he greeted and put Cav on speaker phone. He was expecting the call after he had left Cav an earlier message.

"Spence, you cannot postpone this trip. You cannot! You must not!" Cav bellowed.

Cav was obviously beside himself. Spence shook his head as Mallory shrugged her shoulders giving a body language message of "what did you expect?"

"Cav, there is not a choice here. I cannot leave in the middle of a winter storm for many reasons. You would not leave the barn at a time like this," Spencer reasoned.

"I would if it meant millions on the balance sheet. I would if I could not change the plans in place. I would if I didn't have any other choice and you have no other choice. You must go to Egypt this Saturday!" Cav was practically roaring.

Mallory pointed at herself as if to say, "do you want me to talk to him?" Spencer shook his head no. He didn't see any reason for her dad to get upset with her. She and he had talked earlier and decided to postpone the trip.

"Cav, talk to the Zabr's and tell them the situation here. Tell them we have a storm that is putting unbelievable strain on our systems, our animals, our clientele, and our staff."

"Spence, do you think for one minute that an Egyptian sultan who lives in the Sahara Desert is going to understand or give a fuck about a snowstorm in Texas?"

Nefertari

Nefertari was born in 1370 BC and given a name synonymous with beauty and intrigue. Her name means "beautiful companion." And she became just that to one of the most notable, powerful pharaohs of all time. Her birthright is speculation, but at the age of fifteen she came to Ramses II and became his first wife. An honor beyond all honors given to a woman at that time.

She was known for her fashion and makeup. Her beauty certainly was the draw for her pharaoh, but she also educated herself and became a military expert. She could read and write hieroglyphics, which was a rare skill at the time. She was an asset as a queen to Ramses II and a success as a ruler herself for twenty-four years. She was known for her exquisite loveliness, remarkable intellect, and becoming noteworthy in politics and military matters.

Ramses II, known as Ramses the Great ruled Egypt for sixty-seven years in the 19th Dynasty, the second longest rein in the history of Egypt. He was known as a strong, ruthless ruler that waged successful military campaigns on behalf of Egypt. Most famous being that against the Hittites. The campaign lasted sixteen years and was notable because it ended with a peace treaty being signed by Egypt and the Hittites. The first peace treaty recorded in history.

Ramses was innovative in his leadership and led Egypt to prosperity unlike any known before. He was a revered and admired pharaoh that gained reputation for his building of Egypt temples and monuments. He was legendary as an explorer, monarch, and warrior. A man among men that was madly in love with Nefertari, his first wife. Ramses is said to have had two hundred wives, ninety-six sons and sixty daughters, but it was Nefertari and her four children that he held in the highest regard and esteem.

Their love was legendary and celebrated by Ramses by his construction of temples and colossal statues not only in his honor and image but Nefertari as well. His enduring love for her is demonstrated by the massive temples and statues he erected in her honor with poems of love written by him for her adorning the walls. Her tomb in the Valley of the Kings is one of the most beautiful even today. He further displayed his devotion and admiration by building her statue at Abu Simbel, the same height as his and adding a second temple dedicated to her. She died of unknown causes, and he remarried. But his love for Nefertari a woman unlike any other at the time, remained a legend and renowned.

Chapter 10

Saturday evening found Spence boarding a non-stop overnight flight from New York to Cairo. The snow and unreasonable temperatures did subside, but in its place the melting left a muddy mess with fencing down, pipes busted, trees fallen, flooding in outside facilities, and the list went on. He had some comfort that Carson was more than capable of handling things, but he felt guilty leaving him to do it. But Cav gave him and Mal no option or he would not be here.

He settled himself comfortably in first class ordering a drink and thinking to himself, "What am I doing? I will get off this plane in Cairo, Egypt."

Spencer had done some traveling in his time. He and Mallory had visited several island destinations over the years for beach trips. They had visited England and France several years back right after college. But he never considered a journey to Egypt. No, he could honestly say that Egypt was low on his list of countries to visit. He turned on his private tv, put on headphones, finished his drink, and settled down for his twelve-hour flight.

****

With Spencer's abrupt departure for Egypt, Mallory found herself at home that evening feeling a bit lonely. He left early that morning for the airport as she was heading to the barn. A hug and a casual kiss and she sent her fiancé off to the other side of the world. She could not help but wonder why the insane urgency of this trip. Her dad's insistence that Spence leave with everything in a ruckus at the barn was unforgiveable.

She was supposed to be planning a wedding. But she was here dealing with plumbers and repairmen, her mom was incognito again, and her fiancé was on his way to another continent. She knew her dad and she knew that not even an Egyptian sheik could pressure him into anything that her dad didn't see fit to do. Cavanaugh King did not respond to bullying unless he was doing the bullying. Mallory clasped her hands underneath her chin and contemplated her spinach salad and hot tea.

"Red flag. Definite red flag there," she uttered to herself.

But as she began to slowly have dinner by herself, she could not figure out why or what the red flag was all about. Just a feeling she had that there was more to the story. But then how much more could there be. Her father had basically sent her fiancé off to some god forsaken sandbox to deal with extraordinary people that might just cut his head off and he had to go immediately.

"Definite red flag," she again muttered.

It was a bit later as she relaxed in her tub she began to think about the day. She had actually been able to work Sky and he was coming along splendidly. She knew that he would take the purse in Japan with all the blue if she could just keep them both on track with no injuries. Next stop would be the Olympics! She hoped that her mom would be at the barn today to give her a few pointers and a critique. But her mom had hardly shown her face at the barn in several weeks. Even the bad weather had not enticed her to come down and check on the horses. When Mallory inquired a couple of times about her uncharacteristic absence, her mom claimed to be writing her book. But writing a book would not keep her mom from the barn and the horses.

"Red flag. Another red flag." Mallory again lamented.

There seemed to be red flags everywhere. She knew she was prone to anxiety and panic attacks, so she needed to shut this red flag dialogue down. But it was later in bed she had her final thoughts.

She initially was engrossed in thinking about her wedding as she fluffed her pillow and tried to accustom herself to being in bed alone. She was picturing an outside garden wedding with greenery and beautiful flowers. Her dress was soft and romantically billowing in the breeze. And then she thought of a church wedding. A long aisle to walk in classic satin with buttons down the back all the way to the train. She would have to make an appointment for her and her mom to look at dresses and discuss the venue. Which brought her back to her mom's absence from the barn. She also had been complacent about the wedding planning.

"Red flag. Add one more red flag."

Mallory could not imagine why her mom would be missing in action when it came to wedding planning because of a book. It was as though the things that were most important to her mom, her horses, the barn, wedding, carried no importance. Not like her mother at all. But how would Spence going to Egypt connect with her mother's strange behavior? And if they were connected, did Spence know something about her family and the barn that she was not privy to? Mallory had a restless and sleepless night as red flags and questions played havoc with her slumber.

Chapter 11

Spencer awakened from his night aboard the flight feeling jet lag and lack of true rest. The stewardess bought him coffee and a menu for breakfast before landing in Cairo. He used a wet cloth to wake himself up, looked out the window at a world that he could only remember from eighth grade geography. He was not planning on sightseeing, but since he was in Cairo, he might take a few hours and see the Sphinx and pyramids. He would have to see how his time went. He wanted to conduct business and leave this desert as soon as possible.

A short time later the plane landed, and Spencer began the routine of deplaning, getting through customs, and fetching luggage. He walked out of the cool, drab airport into the warmth and brightness of the Egyptian sun. Having left Texas in the aftermath of an unprecedented snowstorm with freezing temperatures for days, the heat from the Egyptian sun was welcomed by him. He felt as though a cozy electric blanket encased him with promise and assurance.

He did not feel he was stepping into a foreign, strange country that made him feel awkward and fearful. He felt strangely at home and peaceful. Spencer put on his sunglasses and began to peruse the drivers holding up signs. He spotted the driver holding a sign saying, "Welcome Spencer Ewing." He waved at the driver and in a few minutes his luggage was loaded into a private vehicle, as was he, and they were off to the Zabr home and stables in Cairo.

Spencer's first impression of Cairo was that of chaos and time worn. He felt like he had stepped back into another time. One multi-story building after another with what appeared to be twelve or more floors stacked against each other. Most were all the same sandy brown color with balconies and windows used as clotheslines for drying laundry. The street was jammed pack with vehicles of all sizes and types with little organization as they vied for space.

It was when they came to a bridge connecting Giza and Cairo that Spencer asked the driver to stop. The driver obliged pulling over. Spencer got out of the limo and stood looking at the Nile River. He was in awe. The Nile ... the longest river in the world ... the river Baby Moses was placed in ... the river that Cleopatra, Marc Antony, and Caesar traveled upon ... the river that has given life to this part of the world since early beginnings. Spencer felt like he should kneel and pay homage to this historical body of water. He was amazed at the impact that a few minutes in Egypt had upon him. He felt absorbed, engaged, seduced and he could not explain why. But as he stood on the bridge over the river Nile absorbing Cairo, Spencer began his love affair with Egypt.

Chapter 12

The drive through Cairo was a myriad of sights and sounds. The multi-story, brownstone buildings were residences with businesses on the bottom floor. The driver explained that businesses were often family owned. When members of the family marry and create new generations, they cannot buy or afford to buy land. They just continue to build on top of each other. From almost every balcony laundry was strung out to dry and children peered through the openings at the street below.

The streets were crowded and in turmoil with activity. As traffic tried to move down the street, the frenzied activity of people, horses, camels, donkeys, carts, bicycles, vendors and more crowded into the narrow passageway slowly making their way to their destination. Spencer was enthralled. He had seen such scenes in movies but to actually experience this street in Cairo, to hear it as well as see it, was incredible. Spencer began to relax. He actually was excited and thrilled to be here. He knew that he was going to enjoy Egypt after all.

They finally drove down a dusty, narrow street and stopped. Spencer exited the car and walked down brick steps into a set of double doors. His driver followed him with his luggage. A gentleman met the driver, paid him, and then turned to Spencer.

"Mr. King?"

"No, my name is Ewing. Spencer Ewing. I'm here on behalf of Mr. King who could not make the trip for health reasons." Spencer immediately became nervous. He was told that everything was arranged. There would be no issues. They knew he was coming. But the look on this gentleman's face told him a different story.

"I see. Please sit and I will return shortly," the gentleman gestured with his hand to one of the velvet sofas that adorned the small room. Spencer sat down watching the man leave and was instantly upset.

Here he was in a strange country, he knew no one, and obviously they didn't know him. It concerned him that he didn't know the language or the currency. He assumed he would be able to find his way home again, but it was an ominous notion at this point.

"Mr. Ewing, I welcome you!" a man entered the small room coming down the steps from another door. Spencer stood up to shake hands.

"I am Mohammed Zawahiri and I am pleased to meet you. I will be with you in your Egyptian travels most times. Let me welcome you."

Spencer immediately felt relief, as well as suddenly very tired. His jet lag had caught up with him, "Thank you. I am pleased to be here."

"Are you hungry, thirsty, what do you need after such a long journey? Do you want to go to your accommodations?" the gentleman inquired.

"Yes, I could use a bathroom and maybe clean up. A snack would be great," Spencer began to feel better that his own room, a shower, and maybe a few minutes to rest was in his future.

"Of course, your luggage has been delivered to your suite. I will order cheese and fruit. Tonight, you will have dinner at a very good eatery and can view the pyramid show. I will be joining you. But you have time to rest and relax before dinner tonight," Mohammed reassured Spencer.

They walked up the stairs that Mohammed had come down earlier into a luscious courtyard. A pool was in the center with a hot tub and Egyptian fountain on the opposite end. Small tables with chairs were on the pool deck and an overstuffed couch and chairs with a coffee table sat under a gazebo. He could see part of the building on the other side of the pool, so he surmised that it was built New Orleans style with the house around the courtyard. The house appeared to be two stories with third story parapets on the corners. Mohammed led him up a center staircase to the second story to his room or suite as it turned out to be and bid goodbye until dinner.

The room, while not luxurious, was more than adequate with a sofa, several tables, and a desk. The second room was the bedroom with a large bed and wardrobe and a bathroom off the bedroom. The bath had a shower only. Which was not much more than a slanted floor to the middle of the bathroom with a circular shower curtain. After one shower Spencer relented that it was mop the bathroom floor after every shower. However, it did have a vanity with a sink and the toilet was American. He had been warned that it was possible for the toilet to be a hole in the floor, so he knew he was in what might be considered luxury in Egypt. He showered, he mopped, he snacked, he slept.

He awoke what he thought in Egyptian time was about four in the afternoon. He knew there was about a six-hour difference in the time zones, so he decided to call Mallory. She would still be awake, he was certain. He sat down at his window which overlooked what appeared to be a dirty and gravel courtyard but with a street or path leading to it. He had a beautiful balcony and view from another entry, but the activity going on below in the dirt courtyard caught his attention as he was waiting to hear Mallory's voice in Texas.

"Hello," Mallory answered.

"Mallory, Mallory can you hear me?"

"Yes, loud and clear! Are you there? Are you in Egypt?" Mallory asked. Both were looking at static images of each other on the phone.

"I sure am. I have seen camels, the Nile, an unbelievable place, Mallory. I so wish you were here with me!"

"Well, if you knew what was going on here, I promise you I would rather be where you are."

"Lots of crap?" Spencer lamented.

"Just one mess, one catastrophe, one more upset boarder, rider, trainer after another. Did they save it all up for when you leave town?" Mallory sarcastically but jokingly suggested, "So, you look distracted what are you doing?"

"Oh, sorry. Looking out my window watching some riders come in," Spencer half muttered.

"Well, anyway. I am very worried about my parents, Spencer. Mother rarely comes to the barn. She has been here one time, saw the mess and left. Spencer, do you think they are getting a divorce? Spencer? Spencer, are you there?" The image became a picture of the ceiling that Spencer quickly adjusted.

While they had visited, Spencer was watching from his window as riders came in. There were four men on beautiful Arabians. Spencer noticed immediately the horses were stunningly adorned with headstalls that had colorful bangles hanging from them, breast collars that had matching bangles, beautiful blankets under the ornamental Egyptian saddles. The horses were magnificent in their Egyptian tack.

The riders rode in, dismounting when he noticed a late rider coming in fast and furious on a black Arabian with mane and tail flaring. The horse was stunningly adorned in silver and black tack. The rider was female, she was laughing as she full galloped into the circle, her head thrown back, her dark hair flailing in the breeze. Her horse half reared coming to a stop and she stay glued to him as though they were one! She slung her right leg over his neck and jumped off and never had Spencer had anything or anyone so impact him. She was breathtaking. She was beyond gorgeous in both face and figure and Spencer was truly dumbstruck.

"Spencer!"

"Ah, yes, Mallory! Sorry! I just saw the most beautiful thing I have ever seen," Spencer let the words come out of his mouth before he remembered he was talking to his fiancé. Mallory could see the strange look on Spence's face even through the phones. "Horses that much better over there are they?" Mallory asked, assuming only one thing could make Spence sound like that.

"Yeah, beautiful horses, absolutely beautiful horses," Spencer mumbled as he watched the exquisite beauty walk through a gate and disappear.

"Well, I'm happy you made it ok. You sound tired. Get some rest. Don't worry about things here. I'm sure it will all be here when you get back. Say hello to the Sphinx for me!" Mallory forced the cheerfulness.

"If I even see it. Good night, Mal! I love you and miss you."

"I miss you too, Spence. Come home soon!" Click, and both phones went black. Spence laid back across the bed and thought to himself, "and she never even said I love you back."

Chapter 13

Spencer dressed for dinner and went down to the courtyard. The waitstaff brought him a drink and he relaxed on the sofa taking in the local flora and color. The temperature was perfect, not hot with a gentle breeze. Spence inhaled the peace, the tranquility, and the beauty of the moment. He felt so far away from his life at home and the problems as they cleaned up and repaired after the storm. He felt untouchable, off the grid, under the radar.

Mohammed approached with a warm smile and indicated they should go. They left with the driver to navigate again the Cairo streets which were full of bedlam and confusion. The only source of light was headlights and neon storefront lights making the ride seem even more uncanny. Arriving at the restaurant, Spencer was taken aback. They entered a small sunken room that appeared to be someone's living room. He took in the scene admiring the authentic Egyptian furniture and décor. His passing thought was velvet, brass, and beautiful rugs everywhere. They ascended a small staircase to step out onto a circle terrace set with tables and chairs as found in any restaurant. He realized the restaurant had three such tiers at different levels with a rock ledge surrounding each terrace. It was dark and across the way he could see the pyramids. They were lit in different colors, blue, red, and gold. The sight was remarkable. He could not believe he was looking at some of the oldest structures on earth. And directly in front of the vibrant lit pyramids sat the Sphinx, one of the wonders of the world. Spencer was mesmerized.

Mohammed ordered for them which turned into the best chicken dinner with vegetables that melted in your mouth. Spencer watched the lights of the pyramid show and listened to the booming voice that described events and people of long ago. History was not of great interest to Spencer, but he felt himself being drawn into this ancient land and people. He found himself wanting to know more about where he was and what he was looking at.

In dinner conversation Spencer discovered Mohammed was a pleasant gentleman. He was great company for Spencer and seemed to enjoy his job. He told Spencer he was married but had lost his daughter years earlier. He was raising a grandchild that was orphaned at the time. He traveled Egypt doing whatever the Zabr family required of him. He was a third-generation employee of the family and was trusted and treated well. Spencer trusted him instantly, also feeling comfort that he was with someone that knew the country, the region and the people well.

"Mohammed, my intent was to come to Egypt, do business and return. But now that I am here, I would like to add a couple of days of sightseeing to my trip. I would be amiss to let this opportunity go. Can we change my agenda to accommodate a little sightseeing?"

Mohammed replied that he felt sure arrangements could be made for an extended stay. He also volunteered to accompany Spencer to ensure his safety and easy travel. He suggested a few sites in Cairo including the GEM, a new, elaborate, massive museum of Egyptian art, history, and treasures. Mohammed assured Spencer he would have an agenda for him in the morning. He suggested that Spencer might start the day with a ride in the desert.

Spencer was secretly pleased Mohammed mentioned riding, "Yes, I would very much like to ride in the Sahara Desert just to say that I have done it if for no other reason. But I saw some riders come in yesterday evening and could not help but note the horses were magnificent that they were riding. Were they Zabr Arabians?"

"Well, yes and no. They have Zabr in their lineage but are not true bloodline Zabr horses. You will see the difference when you visit the Zabr stable," Mohammed replied.

"Wow! I can hardly wait for that tour! The riders I saw, who were they?" Spencer continued to query.

"Well, I can only guess as I didn't see them. But a team is kept here to train, buy, trade horses that are used all over Egypt for different purposes. Keeping horses trained and cared for requires a lot of manhour and manpower," Mohammed enlightened.

"But I thought I saw a woman rider," Spencer probed.

"Hmmmmmm…that was probably Sekhmet," Mohammed guessed.

"Sekhmet?" Spencer repeated with interest.

"Yes Sekhmet Zabr. She is the most favored daughter of Leader Mohammed Zabr. She rides here often when she is in Cairo."

"She rides well from what I saw," Spencer offered his opinion.

"One of the best we have in Egypt. She is well known for participating in games and winning. One of the few women to be allowed and to actually ride and win contests," Mohammed further commented.

Spencer was totally intrigued by this female Egyptian equestrian. Not only was she drop dead beautiful, but she was also an accomplished equestrian from one of the oldest, richest families in Egypt. He was intrigued indeed.

Later that evening he climbed the stone stairs to the parapet on the corner near his room. He was high above the other buildings and could have seen for quite a stretch had it been daylight. But at present he realized he was looking at the same moon and stars he stared at in Texas just hours earlier. Although there was pandemonium in Cairo, here at the compound the evening was still with only the fountain below protesting the quietness. Again, he felt that distance from Texas. He felt a liberation that he had not felt before in his life. His dreams were full of pyramids, Sphinx's and an exotic Egyptian woman that rivaled Nefertari in beauty.

The next day as Mohammed promised, he spent a day seeing sites and treasures he thought he would never see but only read about. He felt touched by ancient history and knew that he would spend the rest of his life studying the ancient Egyptians. He found himself transported into hieroglyphics, papyrus, tablets, mummies, tombs, kings, queens, gods and goddesses. He was fascinated and his imagination ran wild with what once was.

He enjoyed all of it! The history, the people, and the food. Mohammed enjoyed watching this long, tall Texan with a hat like Mohammed had only seen in John Wayne movies becoming Egyptianized. After a long day they visited Old Cairo for dinner. They dined at a small diner that served an array of meats, vegetables, and a white cheese that Spencer had become very fond of. He spread it on pita bread, and it was a meal in itself.

Spencer was enjoying discussing the sites seen with Mohammed. Mohammed adding facts and stories that only locals would know made it all the better. Noting Spencer's undying curiosity of Egypt and its mysteries, Mohammed asked, "Spencer, there is more to see in Egypt than Cairo. You will visit Luxor when you visit the family, but may I suggest a swing by Aswan before you return home. There is much of interest in both Aswan and Luxor."

"Do I have time?"

"We can make time if you can make time. Will add another day or two to your trip. I can make the arrangements," Mohammed declared.

Spencer, intoxicated by what he had already experienced in Egypt with Mohammed as his guide, jumped at the opportunity to spend additional time and experience more of this amazing country. "Then do it! I will call home tonight and let them know my trip is extended," and he and Mohammed toasted to the new arrangement.

As they were parting Mohammed informed Spencer that the plan for tomorrow was an early morning ride in the desert and then they would fly from Cairo to Luxor where he would dine with family members at the compound that evening.

Later that same evening …

"Wow! Spence! You sound like you are on drugs … the drug of Egypt! I am totally surprised you have acclimated so quickly and so resolutely. Are you coming home this weekend riding a camel?" Mallory was a bit sarcastic after listening to Spence carry on about how wonderful everything was in Egypt.

He had been there less than forty-eight hours and seemed to have converted to a hundred percent fan of the place. She was pleased his trip was going well, but did he have to be so damn happy when she was across the world from him?

"I guess I do sound a bit nutty, but Mal you have to come back with me. You have to see this and be a part of it. It is life changing," Spencer could feel they were not connecting.

"Well speaking of life changing, we have a wedding to plan, and I am running into all kinds of crap! The venue does not like the seating chart I prepared. Something about the honorary table being in the wrong place and needing an exact number because we are close to the threshold. I have been dressing shopping and have not found anything that suits me. I want to go to New York, but Mom is resisting going and I can't figure out why except for that damn book that is all consuming! Dad is losing his mind waiting for your deal to go through. He is up all hours of the night. Carson found him wandering the barn the night you left crying and talking to himself. Again, I don't know what is up with him."

Mallory continued her rant, "Carson is doing a marvelous job of putting the barn and land in order, but it has been a chore with major hardships. They say that the storm was the worst ever recorded in modern weather recordkeeping. I did go down and check on Uncle Gil yesterday. He was sitting by the fire reading a book, drinking brandy and perfectly chilled. Why can't Dad be that way! We ventured out to the barn and took a look at his new project. She is a beauty! You are going to have to come home with one hell of a horse in a bottle to top her! I hated lying to him about your whereabouts. But the civil war continues."

Spencer listened as Mallory went on about the barn, the people, the good, the bad and the ugly. But Spencer did not relate to what Mallory was telling him. It all seemed so far off and beyond his control or influence. What can he do in Egypt about anything in Texas? Nothing! Absolutely nothing! And Spencer was astonished that it felt so good to be removed.

The conversation ended on a strange note once Spencer told Mallory that he was not returning this next weekend. He explained that his meeting had been delayed but he was flying to Luxor the next day and hoped to conduct business once he arrived. He was not certain of his return date or flight but when booked he would let her know. He could tell she was disappointed. He rarely disappointed Mallory or upset her perfect world. But as he stared at the starry, starry night of Egypt from the corner rampart, he knew that he wanted to stay and know more about this magical land and what it held for him.

Chapter 14

He awakened the next morning disappointed that this would be his last meal at the Cairo house. He had become fond of the outside dining room where he was served as a king at a long table with seating on both sides. The cuisine was always scrumptious with chicken and different types of vegetable dishes. The salad was the best he had ever put in his mouth. The fruit and veggies were so fresh tasting he had become addicted. He craved salad at every meal along with the Egyptian cheese that he spread on pita. He could easily make a meal with salad and bread alone. They did not serve iced tea or ice water so at breakfast he drank a soda, and he had wine with lunch or dinner.

He was dressed for riding and just as he finished with his breakfast, Mohammed appeared to escort him to the stable. Spencer was hoping to have time to look around the stable, but horses and riders were waiting on him in the back courtyard that he had seen from his window. His horse was presented to him in full Egyptian tack. The stallion was a burnt copper color unusual to even a cowboy from Texas. He sported a flaxen mane and tail. He was fitted with gold elaborate tack and an Egyptian saddle. He seemed calm and ready to do his job.

"I have been told to apologize that we do not have a western saddle in Cairo. If you ride in Luxor, they will have one there," the groomsman informed him.

Spencer climbed on the exceptional steed with dazzling garb fit for royalty. The saddle felt English with dangling stirrups, but it had a high cantle and pommel, so his seat was between the two. It would take some getting used to, but he was okay with it.

He was introduced and discovered he was riding with a member of the Zabr family who really did not seem to know who Spencer was. But the Zabr family member was also entertaining out of town guests which to Spencer's surprise were visiting from Russia. There was limited English among them so most communication was that of equestrian hand signals that are universal. Spencer concluded from the group that the Zabr family was large with tentacles all over Egypt and what one family order was doing did not necessarily affect another family order. He found that interesting that they would be connected but disconnected.

To reach the desert, they rode through the dirt roads of residential Cairo. The dwellings were meager at most without windows or even roofs. Barnyards were full of goats, donkeys, camels out the backdoor with dung pits not very far away. Along the road a canal floated trash and most likely sewage. Rusted water cans were on poles in front of the houses with tin cups tied to strings to drink from. Water buffalo were grazing in the front yards and acknowledged the riders. Children played in the front yards and yelled hello in English to the riders. The poverty was striking. But when he looked at the faces of the children, he realized that poverty was an adult term. These children did not know they were poor.

At times they were on busy streets with all kinds of chaos again filling the gaps. Cars, buses, horses, donkeys, camels, donkeys pulling carts, people walking, vendors hyping, all combined into a fabric of mayhem and noise. But Spencer noted that his horse walked through it all as though it had blinders on. Nothing seemed to faze his steed. He walked resolutely and unaffected.

They reached a 20 ft wall with two gates of equal height that were actual huge sections of the wall. The Zabr escort spoke with the gatekeeper and then two men swung the gates open. And Spencer was looking at the Sahara Desert. He followed the other riders but caught his breath as he realized where he was. His horse had muscled up under him expecting the ride to be fast and furious. But the riders all kept the pace at a slow trot as they began their trek across the desert.

The first thing Spencer noted was that his horse that had been so calm and relaxed in the streets was now geared up and ready to go but still under the command of his rider. The second thing he noted was that the desert was not hot and miserable as often described. Quite the opposite. It was the perfect temperature.

If being in the desert was not ethereal enough, the prayers boomed across this sandpile that stretched forever. The Muslim prayers are broadcast five times a day. They occur at the light of dawn, at noon, mid-afternoon, sunset and later at night. Spencer had not heard them in the noise of Cairo but here in the desert they echoed across the terrain. Spencer had to pinch himself. He was riding a fully Egyptian tacked fantastic Arabian stallion in the Sahara Desert listening to Muslim prayers. Home seemed extremely far away.

The morning was spent riding and racing the horses across the desert. The horses were forward moving and loved galloping full out across the sands. They rode to the Giza pyramids and the Sphinx and viewed them from horseback. Pictures were taken and lifelong memories were made for all of them. And Spencer became even more captive by Egypt and its offerings!

Chapter 15

Later that evening he and Mohammed arrived by flight in Luxor, and he was driven to what he would call a bed and breakfast inn. He had expected to be a guest at the compound, but Mohammed made Spencer aware that guests were rare at the compound. It was tradition from ancient times because guests in times past there were spies that could eavesdrop or overhear information that would be valuable to enemies. They would possess knowledge of the layout of the compound if someone planned to intrude or invade. The compound was for family only. But the family owned a large home not far from the compound that operated much like a hotel for guests of the family. The second home always had luxurious accommodations with a kitchen available and other amenities. There were outdoor areas for relaxation in the gardens and around the pool and staff at your beck and call for refreshment and food requests.

The home itself was massive and laid out in wings. Spencer's room was four large rooms. The sitting room was large with massive Egyptian furniture including sofa, tables, desk and other chests and armoires decorated in Egyptian colors and images. At one end of the sitting room was a large alcove draped with semi-circle sofas and skylights above. The bedroom was through a doorway and a step down. The massive bed sat on a platform with linen draping around the bed. A large picture window absorbed one wall which overlooked gardens. A skylight above the bed allowed natural light or a glimpse of the stars depending on the time of day. The third room was small compared to the others but was a dressing room with a stand-alone wardrobe and dressing table with toilet facilities. It was connected to the bath which was astonishing. The room was totally tiled from floor to ceiling. The ceiling was a Mosque dome with small squares of colored skylights placed throughout. The sun shining through the skylights resulted in colors dancing around the room which were captivating. A large sunken tub sat in the middle of the room. Spencer wondered "where was Mallory?"

****

Mallory was sitting in the arena watching the barn hand drag it methodically and precisely as it should be. In Mallory's world that was how everything should be managed, methodical and precise. Currently Mallory could not make sense of anything that was going on around her. She couldn't figure out if the world was going nuts or if she was.

She had a fiancé halfway across the world that had turned a three-day business trip into a week or more excursion because he apparently has been swept away by the wiles of Egypt. In the meantime, back at the ranch, she was half running things, trying to maintain her classes, attempting to keep Sky in training for Japan and plan the wedding of the century.

Doing it all while she was trying not to see what was becoming real before her eyes. She suspected that her mom was ill. Mallory could not for the life of her understand her mother's lack of interest in the barn activities or her horses. She claimed she was writing her epic book of training and horse knowledge, but Mallory was catching on.

She visited the big house yesterday evening and picked up the mail as she went in. She normally did not snoop. The family had always been an open book. But it was a stack of mail which made her suspect. She noted that the first envelope was from a doctor's office, then another envelope from a lab. Mallory did not mention the discovery to her dad or mom during her visit. Again, she did not want them to think she was snooping. But her radar was now on. Something was awry.

The barn hand finished up and waved a goodbye to Mallory as he motored out of the arena. She sat there alone in silence and tried to make sense of this feeling she had. She felt impending doom, a feeling she had never felt before. Mallory was always optimistic, moving forward, removing obstacles, taking risks, resilient, strong, always meticulous, and precise. She did not mope. She did not look at the worst of things. She was thankful and blessed and happy. She put her head in her hands. So why was she worried, tense, scared, and full of anxiety?

"Are things that bad?" Mallory jumped when she heard her mother's voice. She thought she was alone in the arena.

"Mom...you scared me! I didn't realize someone could sneak up on me like that!"

Genevieve sat down by her daughter. Mallory regarded her closely and could not help but notice she looked paper thin, she had dark circles under her eyes, and she did not move with the fluidity and grace she normally exhibited. Mallory chided herself silently thinking she sounded like she was sizing up a horse.

"I do apologize. I was on you before I realized it. I didn't know you also came up here to think and ponder," Genevieve noted.

"Well, I don't know that I do on a routine basis. I didn't know that you still did. What are you doing here at the barn at this time of night?" Mallory quizzed. The barn had been shut down for several hours. That did not mean that patrons were not free to visit their horses at all hours, but staff would not be on duty.

"Oh, felt the need to feel the horses and smell the hay. I have been so incarcerated with this book I have missed the barn and the horses," Genevieve responded.

"This book, Mom, how much longer are you going to be consumed with it?" There was a silence as Genevieve contemplated the question.

"Until it is finished, Mallory." Again, silence as both considered exactly what that meant.

"So, have you heard from Spence?" Genevieve changed the subject and the tone. She was skillful at avoiding and deferring in conversation. As a world expert she had been cornered many times and had to finesse her way around a position or philosophy.

"Yes, last night. He is in love with Egypt, the Zabr's are postponing the business, so he is seeing the sights, horses are magnificent, and I suppose he misses me. He doesn't even respond when I speak wedding lingo. I think he has forgotten who he is," Mallory said with a frown.

"I doubt that Mal. He is in a foreign country doing foreign things, eating foreign food, and hearing a foreign language. Think about it. Everything from the moment he opens his eyes till he closes them at night is different than anything he has ever known or possibly imagined. You have months to decide on his tux. Let him live in the moment. He'll soon be back, and all will be well. Egypt will be a fond memory. Don't be responsible for sour grapes because you chose to stay behind."

"Ouch! That was direct!" Mallory raised her eyebrows in shock.

"I have never been known to cut corners. He'll be home in a few days. Don't make a big deal out of nothing into something to overcome," Genevieve warned.

On that note they both left the barn, turning lights out as they went. They hugged in the moonlight and bid good night. Genevieve left happy she went and pleased she could help Mallory get through this difficult time while at the same time she wondered who would when she was gone. Mallory left thinking how her mom was good at putting things in perspective. She needed to lay low and let things happen instead of trying to facilitate outcomes. Spencer will come home, her dad will have his horse, and her mom will be okay. But deep down as much as she tried to ignore it, a feeling was struggling to materialize, a feeling that it was truly not okay.

Chapter 16

Spencer had time to unpack and explore his surroundings before he was expected for dinner. Mohammed told him that they would meet in the living room at eight. The gardens and home were beautiful. The garden, though overflowing with palms and flora, was not tropical. It was an Egyptian garden, green and luscious but not tropical. Spencer could not explain it. One of the many mysteries of Egypt.

Dinner was held in a private dining room. There were six others besides Spencer and Mohammed. Spencer was introduced to all. He noted there were several that also bore the name Mohammed, a favored name in Egypt. He was able to pinpoint Saad, the friend of Cav's. He felt he had at least two allies in the group, Mohammed his guide and Saad, Cav's friend.

He realized all the gentlemen spoke many languages including fluent English and they were able to converse comfortably about many topics. They were extremely curious about Texas and asked many questions about the culture, politics, the horsemanship, this thing called a rodeo, and other queries that brought a smile to Spencer's lips. He almost laughed out loud when they expressed an abiding interest in seeing the Alamo. Spencer could not help but note with pride that they were sitting here with some of the oldest archeological ruins on the earth and they would be excited to visit a 1700's Texas fort.

The dinner went well with little conversation regarding the actual reason for the meeting and Spencer's visit. But he left assured that soon the agenda would be fulfilled, and he could go home. He wasn't exactly sure how he felt about that … going home. He knew in his heart that he wanted more of Egypt before he returned home to Texas. He wasn't sure what would or could quench his ceaseless desire for more.

Mohammed found him the next morning at breakfast. He told him that they were planning lunch and then a tour of one of the stables. He suggested coming prepared to ride although he was not sure if that was the plan.

Spencer spent the morning in the library at the house researching Egyptian history as it related to what he had already seen. He discovered that in Luxor he was in the bed of Egyptian antiquities with Valley of the Kings and Queens nearby, the Colossus statues, and other Egyptian historical sites that he wanted to at least get a glimpse. He looked up just as a large clock in the dining room struck noon.

He headed for the dining room expecting people to have arrived, but no one was there. He thought that odd because he was sure Mohammed had said noon. He was not comfortable taking a seat because he had no idea who would sit where. He was confused as he again recalled his conversation with Mohammed, and he was certain he was in the right place at the right time.

"Well, I see you are on time and everyone else is on Egyptian time!" Spencer was startled. He thought he was alone in the room and out of nowhere came this sultry voice. He turned towards the sound and saw no one. Then she stepped out from behind the scrolled screen that provided a backdrop for a palm. Spencer thought he was going to wet his pants. He thought he would never see again this mirage of beauty and perfection that had galloped up yesterday in dust and seemed to disappear in the same.

Sekhmet was surprised by the silence and look of sheer terror of the gentleman before her.

"I'm sorry I thought you were the American," Sekhmet began to speak in French then Russian.

Spencer finally found his voice and tongue, "I am American, and I do speak English. Only."

"Well pleased to make your acquaintance. I am Sekhmet Zabr. I apologize for the others, but we operate on Egypt time which is pretty much when you show up."

Spencer did not care that not another person was visible. All he could see was this dark-haired beauty who stood before him in riding breeches and boots. In his previous sighting of her he had made out the dark eyes that sparkled like gems and the red lips that were naturally heart shaped and even the extraordinary figure that she presented. But up close he could see her perfect complexion, her olive skin that framed beautiful black animated eyes. He could smell her cinnabar and storax that radiated to him like pollen to a bee. Spencer was stunned but if a man could fall in love at first sight, he had fallen in love. Sekhmet was unlike any creature he had ever come close to, and he was fixated and consumed with desire and passion. He had been right all along. Egypt held much more for him than he had ever imagined.

In his room that evening before dinner, Spencer reflected on the afternoon. It had been hard to not concentrate all his attention and conversation on Sekhmet. She totally distracted him, and he fought with himself all afternoon to stay focused and conduct himself appropriately for the task given him. He enjoyed the tour of the stable. The stalls were outside with half walls of white stucco, with murals painted on them and plants beside each stall door. From the stalls hung heads of fantastic horses. One after another. The necks, the eyes, the ears, and nose, all that you could see was perfection. But Spencer intuitively knew he had not met the legendary bloodline that the Zabr livery was famous for and was keeping under wraps. But he supposed that the horses he met today would be the stallions from which Texas posterity would originate. However, he would have to see some demonstrations, movement, temperament, confirmation before he decided. Head confirmation was extremely important in Arabians. But he was here for the whole package.

He became restless, lacking entertainment from the television in another language. He thought he would grab a drink and maybe walk the gardens. They were luscious with dazzling floral designs and fountains that gave way to Zen. He went by the bar and then wandered down the walkway maze. Ground lights were arranged on the path to allow for viewing of the gardens and safety for walking. Spencer looked up to the moon, although not full was big and bright with stars shining brilliantly. Here there were not the millions of artificial lights to drown out the stars. They were so close it looked as though you could reach out and touch them.

"Well, if it is not the American cowboy out for a stroll?"

Spencer almost dropped his drink. What was up with this woman that seemed to pop out of nowhere all the time and totally catch him with no composure.

"Oooops, losing the liquid there, cowboy," Sekhmet reached out to help him steady his drink that he almost dumped in his surprise at seeing her.

Sekhmet found herself once more looking at this western cowboy who had lost his voice again and had eyes that were once more filled with absolute stark terror. What had she done to evoke such energy from him? Spencer was looking at this vision of scorching beauty and listening to her velvet voice trying not to give way to his knees of jello.

"Spencer, my name is Spencer," that was all he could think to say? He could have cut his tongue out.

"So, you are offended that I call you cowboy. I thought cowboys come from Texas."

"No, cowboys come from all parts of America. I happen to come from Texas. I am not offended but I prefer my name to cowboy. You can call me Spence my nickname."

"No, I like Spencer better. I shall call you Spencer, Spencer. So, Spencer what are you doing this balmy evening in the gardens of Sur Adir?"

"Well," Spencer started to reply but she interrupted him.

"Sekhmet. My name is Sekhmet. You may call me Sekhmet."

Spencer looked at her and thought to himself, "Smartass. I should call you Smartass." But he did not say it.

"Well, Sekhmet, I had a case of cabin fever, and I thought refreshments and the gardens would be relaxing and enjoyable." Spencer went on to think in his mind, "and running into you will certainly increase the chances."

"I see. Then we are of the same accord."

Sekhmet reached behind one of the shrubs and pulled a bottle of gin and a glass out. He had obviously interrupted her plans for a discreet evening with Tanqueray.

Spencer clicked glasses with her, and they sat down together on one of the benches provided for those that might want to sit or meditate in the garden. They shared the bottle of gin as they also began to share stories of who they were and what their life was about. Spencer learned that Sekhmet had been educated in England at an elite private school for girls which explained her fluent although with an accent, English. She spoke five languages which left Spencer in awe since he was still trying to master English.

She had been married at the age of thirteen to a man close to fifty years older than her. He had a heart attack and died when she was fifteen which is when she went off to school and she had refused to marry since. Instead, she found her purpose to bring worry and anxiety to her family as she lived her life as much as she could with her own rules and boundaries which seldom agreed with theirs. The young marriage had forever made her rebellious towards the male dominance in her culture. She was the exception. And if her father and mother and others in the family did not love her so, they would have had her head cut off and thrown her into the desert.

Spencer looked at her and asked, "This is true. I mean cutting your head off and …"

"Yes, why would you doubt it?"

"Well, it is a bit barbaric for these times," Spencer judged.

"And what times are these, Spencer?"

He thought for a moment. In Texas cutting someone's head off and throwing them in the desert would be against the law and unthought of. But here, family is everything. Offend the family there are consequences and obviously the law looks the other way. "Well, in Texas we don't cut heads off and throw people away no matter what their offense."

"What do you do when a family member offends or betrays?" Sekhmet puzzled.

"Most the time you are told and expected to work it out. Our family members do not commit violence as a rule against each other," Spencer clarified.

"I like that. You are a family of love, and not of obligation."

That sat on the bench for hours talking and sharing their differences and their commonalities. Spencer found her to be the most interesting woman he had ever encountered. He had always put Mallory and Genevieve in that column first. But Sekhmet was funny, allusive, vulnerable, nonjudgmental but certainly not afraid to criticize and comment. In Spencer's estimation she was almost perfect. They formed a friendship based on their differences and their likeness. They said good night finally when both were exhausted beyond reason, but they were not the same people that originally sat down on the bench.

Chapter 17

Spencer did not see Sekhmet the next day. He presumed perhaps she was sleeping off a hangover due to the consumption of gin the night before. He spent the day at the stables becoming acquainted with the Arabians offered for his inspection as studs. The decision was hard because all of the horses were certainly stud worthy in America. The fine points of the Arabians he was evaluating made such a difference in the overall function and beauty of the breed. He not only had to evaluate the actual horse, but he had to review the lineage records to determine what traits might come thru in another generation. It took time and patience to review all the factors and make decisions.

One day was not enough to complete the job. He needed another if not two to be thorough. He was making videos that he was sending to Cav in preparation for a future conversation on which horse to choose. He wanted Cav to be part of the decision. It was for Cav the most important horse deal he would ever do. Spencer was sensitive to this and wanted to include him as much as possible.

Mohammed came to him close to the end of the day. They discussed the days progress and Mohammed offered some advice based on his knowledge of Arabians. He told Spencer that Spencer was an invited guest at the Zabr compound for dinner that evening. Mohammed would not be accompanying him. Mohammed also divulged that it is highly unusual for a guest to be invited to the compound. Spencer speculated that the invitation had something to do with Sekhmet and their evening the night before. So now he had three allies. Mohammed his guide, Saad, Cav's friend and possibly Sekhmet Zabr. His fan club was growing.

A driver was sent for him, and he arrived at the compound dressed in a western tux. He debated on whether to don his cowboy hat but thought better of it. He knew he must be low key tonight and listen very carefully to both oral and body language. He was a little perturbed with Cav because Cav made it sound like this was a done deal and all he had to do was come over and pick a horse. He was not finding that the case. All indications are a deal was still to be made. He hoped he was up to the task.

He was escorted on arrival to a room that overlooked a garden area. Both the room and the garden were lavish in his opinion which was usual Egyptian motif. He was served hibiscus tea which is the Egyptian custom. Although charmed by the Egyptian furnishings and artifacts and abundant gardens, Spencer was acutely aware that he was not down the street at a block party. Guards, soldiers, sentries, whatever you want to call them were posted on the outside of the compound and throughout the courtyard. He was confident more security was within the walls of the palace he currently stood in.

"Here we go again," Spencer thought, "I am standing in the reception area of an Egyptian palace to sit down to dinner with one of richest, most influential families in the world. Cav, I may never forgive you!"

His thoughts were interrupted as members of the family began to arrive and introduce themselves. As usual, the majority were named Mohammed which made it easier for Spencer to carry on personal conversation. He only needed to remember who did not bare the first name of Mohammed. He was amiable and charismatic as he filtered through the attendees. There was a dozen to fifteen people attending, he estimated. But as it closed in on dinner time, he became immensely disappointed that Sekhmet did not appear. He was looking forward to her company more than he wanted to admit.

Dinner was announced and Spencer realized that not only was Sekhmet absent, but so was Leader Mohammed Zabr. He thought he would meet him tonight having been invited to the compound, his home, for dinner. Eventually double doors were opened and to the music of an Egyptian quartet, they took their designated places at the table. Spencer's card indicated a seat in the middle of the table, and he found it quickly. Others began to sit but he noted the head of the table was vacant and so far, a seat directly across from him was also empty.

Pleasantry and chatter began among those seated as they caught up on trivial matters. Spencer found himself engaged in a conversation with whom he discovered later was Sekhmet's oldest brother, Mohammed Ahmd. The conversation had shifted from questions regarding the recent Texas blizzard to oil production policies in the Middle East. Spencer was aghast because politics was the last subject he wanted to discuss here. His conservative viewpoints are not particularly popular in America currently. He could imagine how they would be viewed here. But just as the conversation became sticky, everyone at the table stood as Leader Mohammed Zabr entered the room with his daughter, Sekhmet on his arm.

Both took seats. He was at the head of the table and Sekhmet sat in the empty seat across from Spencer. Dinner began with the first course and conversations resumed. He looked at Sekhmet across the table and he had to close his eyes and look again. As beautiful as she was in riding attire with wild hair and little makeup, tonight, she was an Egyptian queen. She wore a long Egyptian gown in shades of red, adorned with beading and gems, that sparkled when she moved. Her untamed hair was coifed perfectly on top of her head with waves of gold and gems laced throughout.

She was beyond anything he had ever imagined sitting across the dinner table from him. And she was watching him as closely as he was watching her. Spencer could feel his blood racing contemplating forbidden thoughts. As the evening progressed, their eyes would lock, and he was dumbstruck trying to concentrate on others. He found himself half believing that the lava rushing through his veins might have the opportunity to be quenched. The dinner was spent both in ecstasy to be close to her and agony to know this was a close as he would ever be.

After dinner, the guests were entertained on an outside patio with coffee and dessert. Business had not been discussed to Spencer's disappointment. He fully expected to be ensconced in an arduous negotiation by this point, but the occasion was apparently purely social. He excused himself to the men's room and on his walk through the ancient twenty-foot columns he heard angry voices in a foyer off the main vein.

"What do you think you are doing Sekhmet? Inviting a stranger, an American to the compound! It has never been heard of!" Mohammed Ahmd was obviously infuriated.

"I sought permission before the invitation was extended. I am not a fool," Sekhmet replied defiantly.

"Oh, but you are! You are infatuated with this Texan! It is obvious! What did you do to talk Father into this? Do you have any idea what you have done? What are you doing?" Mohammed Ahmd went from angry to exasperated.

Silence for a moment.

"Sekhmet he is here on business to make a deal on a Zabr horse! We cannot be viewed as weak. Your friendship with this American will not be tolerated," Mohammed Ahmd commanded.

"Brother, you insult me. Sometimes it is wiser to be cordial than to be intimidating," Sekhmet defended herself.

"Stay out of this and do not consort with the American! I warn you!"

"I warn you! You will not dictate who I befriend! I will take you before Father if you continue with this demeanor. You are not the Leader of the family yet! And no matter, I will never bend to your will!"

Sekhmet met his challenge with no hesitation. Spencer dashed to the men's room so he would not be seen. He did not like Sekhmet taking flack for their friendship, but he did find it uplifting that Sekhmet was his ally and defended their friendship.

The night began to wind down with Spencer having made several friends during the evening. They found Spencer engaging and charming. He had not seen Sekhmet for some time, so he concluded she had retired after her argument with her brother. Guests began to say goodbyes and leave with Spencer among them. But he was delayed by an Egyptian guest named Amir Zabr. Amir was a cousin to Leader Zabr. Spencer and he did not sit near each other at dinner, so they had not had an opportunity to visit. The same held true during the evening. Amir was not going to let the evening pass without telling Spencer he had been to America and to Texas. They were in deep conversation as Amir related his experiences in America when Sekhmet popped out of nowhere to startle him but again.

"I'm sorry Amir but father wants to speak with Spencer," with that she took Spencer's arm and whisked him away to the obvious dismay of Amir. "Come with me and greet my father personally."

"Okay, do I do anything special," Spencer inquired a bit rattled by the abruptness.

They advanced towards Leader Zabr and a small group saying their goodbyes. He had his back to them but turned to address him and Sekhmet.

"Father, Spencer Ewing from the United States of America and in particular Texas."

And Spencer found himself facing one of the richest and most influential men in the world. The reality that he was here in this company was overwhelming. The conversation, albeit short, went well. The highest ranking Zabr turned out to be much less stiff and formidable then Spencer would have thought. Zabr seemed to know about Spencer and his mission for being in Egypt and he also exhibited interest in American Arabians and the King Equestrian Center.

Before it was over, Sekhmet had artfully arranged a meeting for the day after tomorrow at the compound stables to meet personally with Leader Zabr to talk horses. Spencer noted that Sekhmet had made it possible for him to circumvent many of the impediments and created a shortcut from point A to point B for him. He was not certain how many generals he would have had to go through before he would have reached a four star. He would have to thank her and maybe a small gift of appreciation. "So, what do you gift an Egyptian queen?" He would have to think about that one.

He was also concerned not overly, but notably, that Mohammed Ahmd, Sekhmet's brother had stood by while they visited with Leader Zabr. He looked none too happy about the conversation and appeared angry at the outcome. Spencer decided that his ally list was growing within the family, but he felt sure that he had one big adversary. By the time he returned to his quarters, it was too late to call Mallory. He would call tomorrow and let her know that his return was delayed once more.

Chapter 18

Mallory opened her eyes at her usual early hour with her first thought being she had not heard from Spence the previous day or night. She was instantly perturbed but reminded herself he was in a foreign country. The guest of an Arabian family and his time was probably not his own. She tossed around in her head the different scenarios of what might be happening on the African continent as she dressed and headed towards the barn.

Her day was full. She had her own training to attend and then several classes that she taught. She was also picking up a couple of her mom's students. She was thankful to see Carson at the barn taking care of the daily functions, so she could concentrate on training and classes.

She arranged for Murdach Frazier to audit her and Sky and offer a critique. She usually depended solely on her mother. But Japan was going to require the absolute best and her mother encouraged her to reach out. Murdach was probably the closest to being equal to Genevieve in the equestrian world. He had been an associate and good friend of the family for many years. His opinion was one of the few that Genevieve trusted without question.

The morning started without incident. She worked with a couple of students then retired to the office for a break and hydration. She was surprised to look up and see her Uncle Gil standing at the door.

"Good morning, Mallory," he greeted.

"Uncle Gil, what brings you here?"

"I was driving by and thought I would stop in. Is your father or mother here?" Gil asked looking around.

"No, haven't laid eyes on either. At the house I suspect," Mallory replied wondering what would bring Gil to the barn.

"Good, it isn't them I came to talk to." Mallory looked at him uncertainly.

"I came to talk to you, Mallory. I am hearing rumors and thought perhaps you might be kind enough to include part of the family in the loop. I am part of the family."

Mallory continued to stare questioningly.

"Tell me, Mallory, why is Spence in Egypt?"

Mallory's heart sank. She knew sooner or later this question would arise and she so hoped that someone else would be cornered by her uncle. She was sworn to secrecy, but her uncle was like a dog with a bone when he wanted answers. This might be the only moment that Mallory truly regretted not going with Spence.

"He is there on business. And obviously sightseeing since he continues to postpone his return."

"What business?" Gil continued to delve.

"Why I'm sure horse business. But Uncle Gil, you need to talk to Dad. He and Spence have cooked this up and I am too busy with Sky and Japan to worry about what they are up to," Mallory half lied. She hated to put him off to her dad. But her dad was behind this deception. He should be coping with her uncle, not her.

"I knew when I brought that filly home, that Cav would go nuts trying to surpass me. Off to Egypt to buy an Arabian I suppose! But I guarantee you that he will not find any bloodline on the open market that will surpass what is in my barn. It annoys me to no end that he would go running off to try to top me, but it doesn't surprise me either," Gil was noticeably annoyed.

"Uncle Gil, your filly is exceptional. I too would be surprised if Spence is able to purchase a better horse. I wouldn't worry too much." Again, Mallory only half lied. She honestly did not know if Spence would be successful in his mission.

"Well, I will be interested to see what Spence comes back with. When is he due back?" Gil was almost grilling Mallory.

"He was supposed to be back on Sunday, but his stay has been prolonged for some reason," Mallory was slightly annoyed but let it slide.

"Hummmp! Tell your dad I stopped by. And you must come meet my new prize!"

"I will, Uncle Gil! I promise! I am just overwhelmed with Spence being gone and getting ready for Japan and the wedding."

"Yes, next summer! I will look forward to your occasion, dear niece!"

Mallory walked Gil out to his truck and said goodbye. She immediately focused on her tasks at hand and did not notice the time until mid-afternoon. She paused to take a break and after checking her phone, pondered why she had not heard from Spence. It would be about midnight in Egypt which means he has gone two days and now two nights without calling or texting. She was not sure if she should be annoyed or worried.

Chapter 19

Spencer's day started with breakfast in the dining room. It was located downstairs by the pool. You did not order breakfast. You simply came and sat down and the waitstaff served you. He was surprised to see the breakfast table was full. Mohammed, his handler was present along with Mohammed Ahmd, Sekhmet's brother, and several family members. Sekhmet was also dining with the group. He concluded the group had plans and congregated here at the bed and breakfast. He sat down and in general conversation he was asked what he would do with his day. He replied that he would like to do some sightseeing.

Mohammed, his handler, spoke up, "I did not realize you would be free today. I am obligated elsewhere. I will arrange for another guide for the day."

"I can probably handle this by myself. I'll just do the tourist thing." Spencer said with a shrug.

"No, Egypt can be perilous if you are not accompanied. We insist to make arrangements for you," Mohammed was adamant.

Sekhmet spoke up, "I will take Mr. Ewing to see the sites." The table quietened. Mohammed Ahmd, Sekhmet's brother, looked up with a jerk. Spencer took it all in not knowing what to say. "I will take him to the Luxor palace, the Valley and Hatshepsut's tomb. We'll make a day of it. After all it is the least, we can do for our American guest," Sekhmet met the stares boldly.

"I don't want to be a bother. I really believe I can hit a tour bus and be just fine," Spencer spoke up in case the obvious disapproval at the table had Sekhmet rethinking her invitation.

"Nonsense! You will spend more time sitting on a bus than actually seeing the sights. My day is free, and I insist," Sekhmet had no intentions of letting her brother's clear displeasure along with the perplexed company deter her.

In the uneasy silence that followed, Spencer excused himself and went to his room to get ready for the day. He was emotionally divided between being concerned that sightseeing with Sekhmet would wreck his chances of achieving his mission and being overly excited that he would be spending the day with her. He chastised himself for being elated that he would have this opportunity, but he could not help himself. She was unlike any woman he had ever known. He had the same feeling you have when you connect with a wild animal. She was so removed and foreign to him and his curiosity and interest were overpowering.

He gathered up his belongings, turned off the fan and hit the light switch, "Damn, I haven't called Mal! I will have to do that when I get in this evening." Spencer shut the door.

****

Mal came in from the barn hungry, tired, disappointed in her day and highly aggravated that Spence had not contacted her. She tried to call but it was midnight in Egypt, and she assumed he was asleep. She was hopeful that he would return the call the next morning. She didn't care that he would wake her up in the middle of the night.

That thought jarred Mallory. She missed Spence. She missed him terribly. She realized that she took him for granted. She reflected on his being here for years no matter what. He had supported her for years with his attentiveness to her needs, his ability to run the barn and ranch profitably and with her father's endorsement, most of all, his being beside her through her manic dramas for years. He understood and accepted her OCD and her obsession with her riding and competing.

He was respected as a businessman and as a rider and trainer in his own right. However, he always took a back seat to Genevieve and her. She missed him so much. He would cheer her up even though she and Sky's performance today had been lacking. Even Murdach was critical of the lack of execution. She could count on Spence making her feel better and move on to a better day tomorrow. But he wasn't here, and she thought she would go nuts if she had to stay here alone with her thoughts. A visit with her mom always helped, so Mallory called her mom.

"Mom, you don't sound like you are home."

"Mal, I'm not," Genevieve said.

"Where are you."

"Well, your father and I are in Dallas. We are at the Omni. We had dinner and decided not to drive in."

"Oh. Ok. Well, I was going to run up for a visit. But I guess not. Y'all have a good evening," Mal responded but sounded disappointed.

"Mal, are you ok?" Genevieve did not miss the signals.

"Sure, Mom. Just missing Spence and thought some company would be good. I'll see you tomorrow when you get home."

Mallory and Genevieve hung up. Genevieve sat her phone on the hospital nightstand looking at Cav. Both knew that time was not on their side. Mallory immediately looked up the number for the Omni and dialed it.

"Omni Hotel Dallas"

"Yes, I need Cavanaugh King's room, please."

"Cavanaugh King, please hold and I will ring," the operator responded. But in a few seconds. "Ma'am, I do not show a Cavanaugh King registered. Could it be under another name?"

"No, that is fine. Thank you."

Mallory hung up. Her mother was lying to her, she and her father were disappearing on a regular basis, her fiancé was on the other side of the world and not heard from for days, she and Sky were falling apart when they should be at their best, the barn had been nothing but issues and problems for Carson without Spence. She felt like a dust storm was swarming around her and she could not see what was in the dust. She did not sleep well that night, waking up to look at the clock throughout the night hoping Spence would call.

Chapter 20

When Spencer joined Sekhmet downstairs, she was talking to her brother. His disapproving demeanor was obvious, and Spencer was embarrassed for interrupting, but he also felt he should have Sekhmet's back.

"Your criticisms are not necessary or welcome!" Sekhmet's voice was raised as she responded to her brother's unheard statement.

Mohammed Ahmd turned and looked at Spencer turning his angry eyes instantly into a pleasant expression. Spencer almost had chills and was reminded of a snake shedding its skin. Mohammed Ahmd was not his friend and what is more, he was a foe to his purpose of the trip and the new-found relationship with his sister.

"Spencer, the car is waiting. We are off to visit King Tut and Queen Nefertari," Sekhmet was dismissive of her brother.

"When will you return?" Mohammed Ahmd asked politely but the inflection was menacing.

"I have arranged an early evening hot air balloon ride over the Valley and probably dinner. We will be too hungry to wait to eat on returning home. All that need to know is in the know," again Sekhmet was unresponsive to her brother's obvious disapproval. Spencer nor her brother missed her insinuation that he was not on her need-to-know list.

"Well, in that case, have a good day enjoying the spoils of Egypt," Mohammed said looking at Spencer. He continued, "I am sure Sekhmet will be an excellent tour guide."

Mohammed Ahmd made a lame attempt of insulting Sekhmet. She made a scowl and shrugged him off and headed toward their waiting car. Spencer followed with a goodbye nod to him.

The first stops were Karnak and Luxor temples. Both were beyond amazing to Spencer as he walked where ancient Egyptians had once walked. The walls and columns were full of hieroglyphics relating to the stories of Ramses and Tut. Colossal statues of both rulers and their wives were around every corner. Being his first experience of wandering among ageless ruins he was full of wonder and a reverence for a past that was real here but so unreal in Texas.

Outside Luxor proper they visited Essa Temple which lies in the middle of Essa city proper. Spencer found it interesting that the temple was sunk in an excavation that was in a deep hole. You approached it by forty or so rickety wooden steps down the side of the cavernous hole. Temples like Luxor and Karnak consisted of colossal columns and immense walls with hieroglyphics adorning all surfaces. Spencer was in awe as he calculated the manpower and the skills required to construct the mammoth structures.

Sekhmet had knowledge of hieroglyphics and shared some of the common symbols with him. She was a wealth of Egyptian knowledge, but she had him laughing when she told him she acquired her knowledge of Egyptian history studying in England. He loved her humor, her wit, her worldliness. She was becoming more endearing and, yes, to his dismay more desirable with every word and gesture.

Spencer was a good-looking Texas cowboy. He more than once had to thwart female clients from romantic notions regarding him. He had experienced some real beauties trying to tempt him with their charms, but he never paid attention to them. He was one hundred percent dedicated to Mallory. To desire another woman in itself was astonishing to Spencer and was messing with his mind.

When he looked at Sekhmet, he could not imagine being intimate. It was almost like he doubted his ability to perform without the automatic mode that he and Mallory had adopted over the years. Deep, thirsty, aching, craving lust was not an emotion Spencer had experienced or dealt with in a long time if ever. He was perplexed trying to sort out his head and emotions. He was falling in love. He knew it. Maybe for the first time in his life. He could not stop himself. She was enchanting, enticing, and would be the end of him as he knew himself.

She floated through the ancient columns in her blue billowing sundress and gilded sandals, coal black hair swinging, talking in that deep velvet voice that seemed to reverberate through his body to his groin. He fell harder and deeper. He had no idea if she had any knowledge of how she was affecting him. But by the time they reached Valley of the Kings, he was becoming confident that the dynamic was mutual. The eyes, the smiles, the body language, they were not flirting, they were connecting.

Valley of the Kings turned out to be very physical, which helped Spencer get control of his emotions and thoughts. Visiting ancient burial sites and hearing the stories that accompanied the sites absorbed his thoughts as they trekked between the tombs. Some tombs were deep in the mountain and the entries were anything from holes you crawled through to somewhat spacious ramps. They visited the colorful King Tut's tomb. One of the many sites that he would pinch himself to remind himself that he was actually seeing this ancient wonder.

And in all of it, the wonder of it all, Sekhmet. She had traded her gilded sandals for combat boots to hike the terrain of the Valley. Spencer found himself fantasizing about taking those boots off and raising that blue sundress. Then he would admonish himself again for having such lusting thoughts. She was extending a friendship for a guest in her homeland. He was being a disrespectful, rude, lustful, elitist American thinking of her in those terms.

They continued on to Hatshepsut's Temple where again they wondered among the walls and columns of the ancient Egyptians. She was a female pharaoh that dressed as a man and was known to be as tough and barbarous as any ruler. Everywhere you look ancient stories unfold on the structures. Sekhmet was full of expertise. He was continuously surprised at how well spoken and intelligent as well as beautiful she was. Every moment with her was special and full of surprise and wonder.

Lunch was on the balcony of a local hotel overlooking the Nile. The Nile was the most beautiful river Spencer had ever seen. The banks were luscious with greenery and palm trees standing tall against the backdrop of the brown, barren desert. The Nile escorted large vessels as well as small fishing boats that came from another era. In Egypt the old and the new exist together side by side harmoniously.

They finished the day with a hot air balloon ride over the Valley of the Kings. Spencer felt the magic of <u>Around the World in Eighty Days</u> as he stood by this breathtaking Egyptian beauty framed by the setting Egyptian sun. Because of the close proximity in the basket, Spencer was able to touch Sekhmet ... his arm around her waist to steady them on the ride. Feeling her close was torture because he knew without a doubt that he wanted more. He was angst as to what and how much would be enough of this exquisite lady.

It was late before they reached the guest house where Spencer was staying. Sekhmet had a private room at the house for convenience when riding. Both were very tired and agreed to have food sent to their rooms, a shower and bed. Saying good night was extremely hard because as tired as Spencer was, he hated to see her go. He had glancing thoughts of dinner, a shower and then bed with Sekhmet. But again, banished the thoughts. He was racing into a brick wall. He knew they were friends, that she liked him and found his different background interesting, but dinner, shower and bed were a fantasy.

"Thank you, Sekhmet, for a fantastic day. I have seen things I will never forget."

"You are most welcome, Spencer. It has been a delightful excursion has it not?"

Her smile was almost as captivating as her dark brown eyes were mesmerizing. Spencer loved everything about this woman. As he climbed the stairs to his suite, he sighed and shook his head. He was falling in love. He could not help himself. She was absolutely the most compelling female he had ever met. He had to get out of Egypt, and he had to get out soon.

His head hit his pillow feeling every bone and muscle in his body after a day of climbing in and around a mountain all day. Food and shower had helped ease his muscles. But he was amazed, after working physically almost every day of his life, that sightseeing would wear him out. But it wasn't just the physical that had him feeling like a wet washrag. It was the emotional roller coaster he was on. He wasn't even sure he remembered Texas, his home, or Mallory, good grief, his fiancée. He drifted to sleep tired and with a kaleidoscope of Egypt spinning in his head. Images of the beauty, the Nile, the ruins with hieroglyphic columns, the history, the food and music, Egyptian gods, the magnificent horses, and Sekhmet flashed through his consciousness as he became gratefully unconscious. He fell asleep with dreams of Egypt and expectations for the next day and failed to call Mallory.

Chapter 21

Mallory was at the barn at her usual 5:30 AM although she had slept fruitlessly the previous night. Carson had already been in and gone to take care of a current crisis but had left coffee on the burner. Mallory stopped by Sky's stall on the way in and he was munching on morning hay, so she had time to start a little slow. Her mind drifted to the myriad of worrisome thoughts from last night, but she forced her attention to other matters.

She went through the mail, the notes left by staff, messages taken, and printed the emails. When she finished tending to what she could resolve, she looked at the desk and in front of her were three stacks of issues requiring another's handling. One for her mother, another for her father, and a third for her fiancé. All three were not there. Somehow the stacks made it real. Something was going on for sure and her worst fear was that they were keeping it from her. They were distracting her with barn duty while they did what she did not know. Her thoughts were interrupted by Murdach.

"Good morning, Mallory."

Murdach Frazier was a recognized international trainer and competitor that had been part of the barn team for several years. He and Genevieve had competed and judged events together all over the globe. They were casual friends, fierce competitors, and respectful of each other as renowned trainers and judges. He was a tall and lithe which allowed him to appear graceful and statuesque on his steeds. His skills for training horses in certain disciplines were unmatched.

But Murdach had a major shortcoming. He was not a people person. He was the perfect cross in Mallory's mind of "smartass and nerd." He did not have a natural friendly bone in his body and rarely smiled genuinely. Mallory often wondered how he possibly could be as cold as marble and yet have a connection with horses.

But horses were amazing creatures. They made up for the shortcomings of their rider both physically and emotionally.

"Hello, Murdach. You are up and at it early."

"Yes. Well. I wanted to visit you, Mallory. I considered going directly to your parents, but it is obvious that they are busy with things other than the barn."

Mallory did not miss the jab by Murdach at her parents being missing in action. Her feathers were instantly ruffled at the insinuation. "Well, talking to me is the same as talking to my parents or Spence. So, what say you, Murdach?" Mallory was totally expecting to hear Murdach whine about the arena not being dragged, or lights not working in the arena, etc., etc.

"I feel a certain loyalty to your mother. Otherwise, I would not say anything. I would make my decision and abide by it. But if I make the best decision for myself, I feel there will be a question of betrayal. I do not choose to have that label next to my name. So, I am here."

Mallory looked at him totally bewildered. She felt he was gaslighting, and she was ready to diss or reject anything he said.

"Your uncle requested dinner with me last night. He has made me a most lucrative offer to train his new Arabian filly," Murdach announced.

Mallory was again instantly ruffled, but this time, at her uncle. How dare he try to steal a trainer that had been part of this barn for years. But then again, Murdach was not under any contract to not train horses from other barns. He had traveled the world doing so. So, she was a bit perplexed at the gravity of Murdach's demeanor. Although she did get that working for the two brothers might be a bit stressful in itself.

"He not only is expecting me to train the filly. He has a further demand," Murdach took a deep breath, "He wants me to change barns."

Boom! There it was. The final insult, the ultimate rung for one upmanship! Buy the horse and steal the best trainer from his brother … when you consider he could not ask her mother. Uncle Gil at his best. Mallory was instantly furious.

"Now as I mentioned. Our meeting was held confidentially, so a response from any of you to Gillespie might affect his offer. So, I am asking at this juncture that you not contact him as I am considering the offer. But I do feel the honorable thing to do is be as transparent as possible without bringing harm to my future possibilities," Murdach continued.

"Do you mind my asking exactly what my uncle offered you that you do not have here?" Mallory knew that her mom had been more than fair with Murdach over the years. She felt his name at the barn was worth a lot more than any fees she might charge him to board, train, and home at the King Center. Mallory knew there was financial consideration regarding shows, endorsements, and other interests but she was not privy to the details. So other than the opportunity to train what may end up being the number one Arabian in the US, which she had to admit was big, what did Uncle Gil have to offer?

"I will not quote the exact offer because it is confidential. I will allow that the big difference, the only difference that I find attractive, is he has offered me a percentage of the barn and ranch revenues."

Mallory was stunned that her uncle would offer a part of the King Ranch to Murdach. She could not wrap her mind around his allowing an outsider to own part of the King Ranch. Her father will be devastated. This would make Murdach a partner on the ranch.

Mallory looked Murdach directly in the eyes, "Murdach, you and I both know that this is Uncle Gil's attempt at trying to up my father in this seven-decade civil war. I appreciate your coming to us with this. But I do not see a competing offer coming to the table. My father would never sell or offer part of the ranch to anyone but posterity. I am shocked and grieved that Uncle Gil would."

"I understand. Now you must understand my decision," Murdach said firmly.

"We do. If we part, let us not part on anything but the best of terms," Mallory said much more stiffly than she meant to.

Murdach left Mallory staring at the three stacks sitting on the desk. She reached out and swiped across the desk knocking them down and scattering the items across the desk and floor.

Chapter 22

Spencer slept in the next morning. Even the broadcast of morning prayers did not disturb him. A knock on the door about ten o'clock did.

"Spencer, Spencer … this is Mohammed."

Spencer rose, opened the door, and let Mohammed in. He instantly became anxious as he thought he had overslept and missed the meeting with Leader Zabr at the Zabr stable. Mohammed read his thoughts.

"No, no, my friend. I am here to take you. I would not let you miss such an important meeting, nor would I want to explain to Leader Zabr that you had. But here we go by Egypt time and being a bit tardy is not frowned upon. However, it is time to go so don't delay. I believe you will have to skip breakfast, but lunch will be served."

Spencer arrived at the Zabr stable to find himself sitting on a sofa for over an hour in an outside pavilion waiting on exactly whom he was not sure. As Mohammed mentioned, Egyptian time allows for one to be late. Spencer was thinking that you could spend all day trying to make one appointment in Egypt with both parties feigning ok to be late.

He did have the opportunity to observe the activities around an Egyptian stable. The first thing he noticed was how many workers were busily tending to horse business. It seemed each horse had two to three handlers. One would be bathing, one would be feeding, and one would be mucking preparing each horse for the day. The stable itself was beautiful. The walls were white stucco open so horses could visit. The stall doors were wooden painted black with the name of the horse in gold on the front. Most boasted blooming hibiscus plants at the stall door. Everything was meticulously clean, and the horses were impeccably groomed.

The round tack room was stunning. It was aesthetic with different colors of velvet saddles decorated in silver and gold sitting on the pristine saddle trees that hung on the wall. The ornamental headstalls and breast collars hung below the saddles adding to the color and aesthetics. And in the middle of the room from the ceiling hung a sparkling crystal chandelier. Spencer had to admit to himself that the tack rooms at home with a few shades of leather and assorted leather accessories did not make for a colorful, picturesque tack room.

Finally, the party began to arrive. Spencer was surprised on two fronts. First, he thought he would have a meeting with Leader Zabr and his generals. He thought he was at the stable to choose the horse and then they would negotiate a price and seal the deal. But this was anything but a private audience. At least twenty maybe twenty-five people were in attendance. The second disappointment was that Sekhmet was not among them. He hoped, even expected, that she would be there to help him navigate the waters. But not so.

The party as a whole moved to the outside arena with old wooden bleachers as seating except for the Leader Zabr who had a special tent and seating. Spencer found himself sitting in the hot sun on the top bleacher far from any personal contact. But he settled himself in and accepted the water served in a cup that was passed among the crowd to stay hydrated as he watched the show.

And it was a show. Handlers brought the different horses out and presented them to the crowd. Seeing the horses in the exhibition gave Spencer a different perspective from his evaluations earlier of the horses. But it was about the second horse presented that Spencer began to understand. It was never a private audience. It was an invitation to join others who were looking, hoping to acquire a Zabr horse also. But it appeared the Kings were nothing special as he had thought coming to this land. Just another patron to increase the price and value of the bloodline. This was not the done deal that Cav had led him to believe.

Spencer could not help but ask himself what the hell was he doing here? He was most likely not going to even come close to achieving the purpose and would disappoint his soon-to-be in-laws. He was totally ignoring the barn and barn business. He was cavorting all over Egypt with another woman that he was insanely attracted to regardless of his love interest since he was in high school and happened to be his fiancé.

He made himself focus on the horses being displayed. He was duly impressed. The breeding, the lineage, the bloodline was full blown in all exhibited. The colors were deep and vibrant and varied. The manes and tails were abundant and groomed to perfection. The horses were perfect without scratches, bug bites, or any imperfections in the coat. Heads and muzzles were exaggerated Arabian with eyes that were clear, quick, and alert. Their movement was more graceful and poetic than a prima donna ballerina. Light on their feet was a total disservice to their movement and fluidity. Spencer knew that any of these horses were potentially a number one Arabian in the US. The US had nothing to compete with these horses.

But there was one particular horse that caught his attention. He wasn't sure if it was the horse or the young handler that was showing him so well. He rode him soft and hard, slow and fast. And on the ground, he handled the horse impeccably. The horse exhibited its best points due to the expert handling and showmanship of the handler.

The exhibition ended with twelve horses having been displayed. Spencer tuned in and realized that not all in attendance were Egyptian. Again, confirming what he had concluded. He was not the only buyer in the marketplace. He left his seating and as he reached the walkway, Sekhmet's brother approached him.

"Mr. Ewing, did you find the exhibition to your liking?"

"Yes, the horses are exceptional. However, I am not sure who I should direct my questions or offer."

A voice came from behind Spencer as he and Mohammed Ahmd were walking and conversing. Spencer turned to find Leader Zabr addressing him. "Your communications will be with me or my emissary, Mr. Ewing," Leader Zabr responded.

Mohammed Ahmd looked a bit green that his father had interrupted their conversation.

"Thank you, Leader Zabr. I will look forward to that opportunity. When might we conduct our business?" Spencer boldly asked.

"I will make arrangements to have your requirements met as a guest of my daughter. There was an empty chair in my tent for which you were intended at her request. I have an interest in Texas and would have entertained a visit with you. We will meet again soon."

Spencer realized very quickly that Sekhmet's brother had circumvented Sekhmet's plan to have him personally meet with Leader Zabr. And he also believed that perhaps Leader Zabr knew that Mohammed Ahmd had manipulated events. But the Egyptian gods had favored him, and it appeared as though he might get through this after all. He immediately chastised himself that he would give credit to ancient gods. He was a Texan with one God not an Egyptian. He needed to get out of here.

Chapter 23

The day did not improve for Mallory. Sky was showing signs of colic. Mallory was beside herself that if this was the case, they would certainly miss Japan and she could very well lose him. A horseman's nemesis is colic. It strikes mercilessly with no warning or apparent reason resulting in serious illness at best and death at worse. She had a ranch hand walk him and called the vet. Sky would not eat or drink. He couldn't go long like that. She appeared calm as she worked through the crisis but inside, she was a wreck. She needed Spence.

To her surprise when her mom heard the circumstance, she appeared at the barn to personally check on Sky.

"Mom, he is not eating or drinking and hasn't all day."

"Where is Delzel?" referring to Spencer's father, their vet.

"He is out of town and driving in but had car issues and is running late. It will be nine or ten before he can get here."

"How long has Sky been like this?" Genevieve questioned.

"Started this morning or during the night. He just won't eat or drink."

"How long since he has consumed anything? Have you taken his temperature?" Genevieve was examining Sky as she asked questions. She listened to his belly. She looked at each hoof.

"It was normal, but I don't think he has eaten or drank water in twenty-four hours."

Genevieve walked away and went to the feeder scooping up a handful of feed. She walked over and offered it to Sky. Sky aggressively grabbed at the food. "Whoa! You are definitely eating! You are starving," Genevieve exclaimed!

"What!" Mallory equaled her mother's exclamation.

"Mallory fetch a pail of feed and water," Genevieve directed.

Once fetched, Genevieve had Mallory set them on bales of hay high where Sky could reach them without bending his neck down. Sky had a strained neck or shoulder.

"Oh, Mom! I would have driven him into colic if he had not received water and feed. Thank you so much for figuring this out."

"Mallory, I am certain you would have figured it out if it had not been Sky. Your emotions got in the way. Not to mention, you have too much on your plate to think clearly. But had Sky ended up in colic and in danger, well the consequences could have been unpleasant."

With that Genevieve kissed Mallory on the forehead and left the barn. Mallory called Delzel and told him the pressure was off and to come in the morning. She directed the overnight crew on how to treat Sky for strained muscles. Carson came by and updated Mallory that some of the big equipment was having mechanical problems and the day's work was not completed.

Mallory just looked at him with dull, tired eyes.

"Okay then, nothing we can't address tomorrow. You look like you are on your last leg Mallory. Go home. The day is done."

Mallory went home without argument which was surprising to Carson. She walked into the house and began shedding her clothes at the front door all the way to the bedroom. She crawled into bed in her underwear and crashed. But not before a tear drifted down her cheek. Her mother was paper thin and had big deep dark circles around her eyes. Her skin was ashen grey, and her hands trembled. Her voice was shaky and soft. Her gait was slow and thoughtful. Mallory knew. Her mom was apparently terribly ill. Mallory fell into an exhausted, deep slumber as she left her day of problems behind her and escaped to dreamland.

Chapter 24

Spencer returned to his room and took a shower immediately. He dressed and then sat down to call Mallory. It was about five in Texas so he felt sure Mallory would be winding down and available. But there was no answer. As he was listening to the continuous ringing, there was a knock at the door. A busboy handed him a note which turned out to be invitation from Sekhmet to meet her in thirty minutes for a late evening ride in the desert.

An hour later Spencer was entrenched once again in his love of Egypt and its charms. They rode through corn fields with the Nile flowing close beyond and shades of green flora flourished. They rode through small town streets with kids coming out of the windowless and roofless structures to greet them. Women in black Muslim stood in the doorways. They rode to the Colossus, and she took pictures of him on his horse at the base of the mammoth Egyptian monuments.

They concluded the ride with an amazing crossing of the Sahara Desert. Their horses galloped full out across the endless sandbox. Sekhmet was bewitching as she raced him across the desert with pealing laughter. Her black hair blowing in the breeze, her regal figure sitting proudly and perfectly in her seat. She was not only an expert rider, but she was also a moving motion picture of beauty and grace. The ride ended with a sight he will never forget. She beat him to the top of a desert hill. When he looked up, she and horse were silhouetted against the setting Egyptian sun. She was beyond breathtaking sitting proudly on her Arabian stallion.

As he made his way up the hill to join her, he thought of the many pictures of Sekhmet he would take home with him, his first image of her riding up the first day he was here; arriving at the dinner in exquisite gown, hair, and make-up; and the day at the Valley of the

Kings sightseeing in her sundress, flitting around Luxor Temple and later looking sexy and desirable in boots climbing around the mountain. And now … she looked like an Egyptian goddess. He rode up beside her to watch the Egyptian sun set over the desert, he felt like an Egyptian god that belonged with her.

After the ride they returned to the compound and had dinner with wine in the courtyard. Later the conversation was on him as he told her about Texas.

"What does it look like?"

"Texas? Well, it depends on where you are. We have lakes, forests, coastlines, rivers, mountains, desert …"

"Where you live … what does it look like? What does your house look like?"

"Well, I live in central Texas. We have a lot of trees, pecans, oak, elms, and many more. Green fields, corn fields, cotton fields. We live in the country. I live on a large ranch. I live in a house on the property and run the barn and ranch."

"Do you own this ranch or does the government?"

"No … neither. The ranch is privately owned but not by me."

"So how did you become boss of big ranch?"

Spencer was becoming increasingly uncomfortable with the questioning, trying to avoid telling Sekhmet the truth. He lived on his future in-law's land, who had handed him this wonderful existence including the approval to marry their exceptional and delightful daughter. The daughter he had in the last few days cheated on with his lust for this woman who sat across from him. And what really scared him was why he felt the need to hide his status from her. Because she might not succumb if she knew of Mallory? He was ashamed.

"Well, Miss Zabr that is another story that we will take up another time. I have phone calls I need to make to the US, so I need to excuse myself. I presume business will take place tomorrow?"

"Yes, Spencer I will visit with Father early tomorrow to accommodate you. Did you enjoy your visit with Father today at the exhibition?"

"Well, do you mean the time spent visiting inside the tent during the event?" Spencer coyly asked.

Sekhmet nodded yes.

"I sat in the bleachers and missed out on that opportunity."

"What? Why? I arranged for you to be near Father. He is interested in Texas and has questions before he sends our bloodline to Texas. That was your time to persuade him!" Spencer just looked at her. It did not take her long. She squinted her eyes in knowing and set her jaw in anger.

"I know who is responsible. I apologize. I felt it better that I was not there to distract the conversation for either of you. I did not realize I needed to police the event."

"No problem. We did have a moment afterwards and he assured me I would have my day in court."

"Day in court? You are going to court?" Sekhmet expressed confusion.

"No, no … that is a saying in America."

"A saying in America … you are going to court? And jail maybe."

"No … another saying might be … it's not over till the fat lady sings."

Sekhmet shook her head in total disbelief and misunderstanding.

"Ehhhh, court and fat lady mean the same in America?"

Spencer laughed and Sekhmet joined in as they realized the miscommunication had become hilarious!

"Spencer, we should say good night so the singing fat lady can have her court day tomorrow!"

Both laughed at her misinterpretation of the words, stood up and before either realized they were in an embrace. It wasn't a prelude to more, but it was closeness, acceptance of touch and personal presence.

"Good night, Sekhmet."

"Good night, Spencer."

Chapter 25

Mallory crashed about four that afternoon and slept for ten hours waking up about two in the morning thirsty, hungry, and rested although groggy. She took care of immediate needs and then trotted to the kitchen noticing her mess of shedding clothes as she went. Amazingly, Mallory would normally stop everything to pick them up and keep the house perfect. But she looked at them numbly as though they belonged there. They were a symbol of how she was feeling and thinking.

She looked at her phone and noted that Spencer had tried to call earlier. She had missed his call after waiting two days to get it. The day was definitely a bust in all columns! She fixed a veggie plate with ranch dip and crackers with iced tea and sat down at the table to call Spencer. It would be about nine at night his time. He should be available. But if he was available, why wasn't he calling her back. Then it dawned on her it was nearly three in the morning here. He was not going to call her this time of night. She picked up the phone.

"Hello."

"Hello. Mal is that you?"

"Spence is that you?" Mallory asked almost sarcastically.

The phone connected and they were looking at each other. Spencer was in an upheaval. Seeing Mallory and hearing her voice catapulted him into reality. Texas did exist and he was engaged to marry the woman on the other end of this line.

"Mal, how are you?"

Mallory wanted to scream at him that she was anything but all right. She wanted him to feel the misery of what the day had been like. She wanted him to take the burden, the fear, and the anger away. She wanted him to know that she was exhausted and needed him to come home. "I'm okay, how about you?"

"Fine. I'm fine," Spencer responded.

"Good that's good." Mallory was thinking, "what is this conversation?" Was she talking to Spence? She felt like she had interrupted a stranger's dinner.

Spencer felt the awkwardness too. "How's the barn? Are you and Carson making it okay?"

This was her chance. This was her opportunity to dump it all on him. She could tell him she knew! She knew they were keeping secrets. She could demand to know what was going on and in turn demand he know what was going on at home. "Yes ... we are making it fine. How's the Egypt project going?"

"It has been difficult, Mal. The Egyptians work on their time, and I have had to wait to actually make a deal. It wasn't quite what your father presented to me."

"Well, that is not a surprise. His schemes usually have obstacles. So, what do you do? Waiting around until whenever you are summoned?"

"Well ... I did some sightseeing. Saw King Tut's tomb among other things."

"Really," Mallory said uninterested.

"Huh-uh ... a lot of temples, ruins, history."

Awkward silence.

"Look, why are you up at this time in the morning?" Spencer asked.

"I fell asleep earlier and woke up looking for dinner. Looked at the time and thought I might catch you since I missed you earlier."

"Good. I thought for a minute something might be wrong. You don't seem like yourself."

Mallory almost choked, "You come across like a cousin twice removed and tell me I don't seem like myself!"

"Well, I am. It's probably the time of night. I'll let you go and try to get a little shut eye before I have to get up."

"Okay … well sweet dreams, Mal."

"Thanks! Same to you! Good luck with the deal!"

Both hung up the phone wondering what had just happened. Never in the years they had been together had they had a conversation like they just had. Both felt loneliness, a hole in their fabric they had never felt before. They prided themselves on always being on the same page and both felt they were not even in the same book at the moment. Mallory went back to bed and had a fitful night. She would be grateful to get up and go to work. Maybe Sky would be better and would welcome her.

Spencer felt claustrophobic in his room after that dreadful conversation with Mallory. He wasn't sure how it had gone so wrong. He just couldn't think or relate to Texas right now. And unfortunately, he couldn't relate to Mallory either. He decided to get out of the room. He walked out and instead of going down to the courtyard, he went up. He went all the way to the top of the stairs to the lookouts that were at each corner of the compound. Spencer assumed at one time they were lookouts for protection purposes. The lookouts were similar to what you would see at forts in America, but their only purpose now was to enjoy the view.

It was a picturesque evening. The moon was bold, and the stars glittered in the sky. Both seemed close enough to touch. The night was cool and fragrant and seemed to calm the storm that raged inside of Spencer. It was dark so the landscape was a parade of lights here and there ending at the river. Spencer was hypnotized by the sight and the realization that the water out there was the Nile River. He could remember being in the sixth grade and studying Egypt in social studies. Egypt was yellow on his map when he colored the world. He recalled studying about the Sphinx, the pyramids, King Tut, and much more. Never believing that one day he would stand before all. He turned to look the other way and almost jumped out of his skin. Sekhmet broke out in laughter!

"Whoa, Spencer! I am not a mummy!"

"Sekhmet, you have a way of just popping out of nowhere that leaves me in startle mode!"

"I'm sorry Spencer! You were in such deep thought. I did not want to interrupt. But I did not mean to frighten you!"

Sekhmet continued. "So, what brings you to the parapet?"

"Needed some fresh air before bedtime," Spencer replied.

"Are you homesick, Spencer?"

"Homesick? I guess I hadn't thought about it. But I probably am. I mean I love Egypt and I have seen so many wonderful things and would not give for the experience … but … it's not home, Dorothy."

"Dorothy?" Sekhmet looked confused again.

"Another American saying," Spencer replied seeing the look on her face.

"Again, puzzling American sayings. Do you ever talk in complete, coherent sentences?"

"Not unless we have to!"

They both laughed at the joke. That broke the ice. They just seemed to click. No matter what, Spencer could not deny that. In his wildest dreams, he would have never thought that the love of his life would be an Egyptian daughter of the richest man in the world in the oldest country in the world.

Much later into their conversation. "So, are you single, Spencer? You have not mentioned a lady at home." Spencer sighed. He had to make the choice to lie or tell her about Mallory. Either case he risked losing whatever it was he seemed to be seeking.

"Yes, Sekhmet. I do have a lady at home. Someone I have been with for years and we live together in the house I told you about. Her parents own the ranch." The brown eyes penetrated him. He wasn't sure what she was thinking or feeling.

"I see. I was certain that a good-looking gentleman such as you would have a lady waiting on him. You have not married in years? Is there reason for that?"

"We have just never been in a hurry. We have had other life plans such as finishing school. That came first."

"Well, I congratulate the lady on snagging a most desirable cowboy. I'm sure you make her happy with your thoughtfulness and patience."

Spencer could feel her withdrawing. He could not stand that. They had been so perfectly blended and now he could feel the separation. "Sekhmet. Sekhmet, I ..." he stood reaching out to her.

She stood looking at him. He could feel her. He could feel her acquiesce. He could not stop himself. Under the Egyptian moon and stars, she came to him. They extinguished the desire to touch each other and ignited a flame that would consume them both before they were through. Their kiss was long and hard, filled with passion and desire, and more importantly, promise. Both were confused because they knew they were forbidden fruit, and this tsunami of feelings and passion could come to nothing in the long run. But this kiss was unlike anything experienced in the arms of others. It exploded their minds, their bodies, their souls, and hearts. When they pulled away, Sekhmet met his eyes with almost fear. And before he could say a word she disappeared. He stood there with the breeze coming off the Nile cooling the night and giving him a much-needed breath of air. Because he was drowning. He was drowning in desire, lust, and love. His fate was sealed.

Chapter 26

Mallory went to the barn and began to work like a trojan so she could get the conversation that had transpired last night out of her mind or at least try to. There was always work to do at a barn for two hands and strong shoulders. The cleaning, the replenishing, the watering, the feeding, the mucking, the grooming, and the list goes on. Never will you walk into a barn where big animals are housed and cared for and there is nothing to do.

But the uncomfortable conversation with Spence the night before kept coming back to her. She was perplexed as to who was not being genuine. She knew she had not been forthright, but she also felt Spence had not either. His demeanor was totally unlike any she had ever seen before, and she had known Spence a long time. He was rattled. He was stressed at having to talk to her.

There was a secret, she was certain. He did not know if she knew and did not want to let the cat out of the bag. That had to be what was going on! The general questions, never mentioning her parents, waiting for her to talk, he was being coy on her parents' behalf. She needed to talk to her parents. They must come clean. Whatever the problem they would work it out together.

Mallory felt much better having resolved that major issue or at least a plan to resolve. She also felt much better about the conversation with Spence understanding his position between her and her parents. But she wished that her parents did not promote secrets between them. She was certain that he had no choice or would have confided in her long ago.

She ran into Murdach in the barn aisle. He was observing the groom with his next ride. They simply looked at each other and acknowledged each other. Mallory was in a stew as how to handle this situation. She wished Spence would come home. He might be the one person that could broach the subject with Uncle Gil and get him to change his mind. She had thought about sharing with Carson. But he had so much on his plate in Spence's absence she did not want to burden him. If she did influence Uncle Gil to retract his offer, how would Murdach feel? Cheated? But then why did he come to her if he did not want her to act on the information? The questions were swirling in her brain when her phone rang.

"Miss King? This is Amanda at All About You calling to confirm your appointment coming up on the twentieth, a couple of weeks from now."

"Yes, I believe it is on my calendar," Mallory replied.

"We look forward to working with you to design the perfect gown. As a matter of fact, we will have designers in the shop that are also looking forward to meeting you and your mother. We hope you will consider doing a photo shoot in your gown with your horses for a major publication."

"I don't know about that. I do not photograph well," Mallory stalled. She was accustomed to pictures on horses in her riding habit not in a wedding gown.

"Miss King, I assure you, we will see that you photograph well. Please keep the proposition in mind and we will see you that Saturday with bells," she giggled.

"Yes, well, we will see you on the twentieth." Mallory hung up thinking she had totally forgotten the appointment. The past couple of days had erased any real thoughts of wedding planning. All she wanted was for Spencer to come home. And then she promised herself, she would never let him leave her again. The phone call brought home all that had changed since Spence went to Egypt.

A few days ago, her only thoughts were taking blue in Japan and gold at the Olympics and planning a lavish, glorious wedding to her beloved Spence. Now she had fires all around her. She felt isolated from everyone by a secret. Spence was nowhere in sight or sound. Her uncle was on the verge of giving part of the ranch away. Deep down she was mortified at what her dad might do in retaliation. Her world was imploding, and Mallory was alarmed at what a world in fragments would look like.

Chapter 27

Spencer was anxious the next morning as he dressed for breakfast. His night had been full of dreams of Sekhmet in his embrace. He lived the kiss over and over in his mind. Was it as mind blowing as it seemed at the time? He remembered her stroking his hair and the back of his neck while her breasts pressed against him as she breathed heavy with want and lust. She was enchantingly fragrant, and a perfumed scent hung in the air around her. Not overpowering but a lingering delicate scent saying she had been there. Her body was strong and powerful. Her lips were soft and supple and found his perfectly as they wrapped themselves in the moment and the feelings. He remembered every detail of that kiss. And he knew if he never kissed her again, he would never forget one detail.

But he was nervous about seeing her in the daylight. Continuing as though last night had not occurred would require his best acting skills. He wanted nothing more than to pull her into a corner and coax her to a day in the desert with their horses and other such fantasies. But he also needed to conclude the business he was there to conduct. He had after deliberation chosen the stallion that he felt would establish the definitive pedigree of Zabr Arabians in the US. His plans were to have a Skype call with Cav at one his time and seven Cav's time to discuss his decision and seek agreement to move forward. But first he needed to determine from the Egyptian power base if he even had a deal at all. He had several obstacles to clear at this breakfast, so his anxiety was valid.

The open dining room was clear when he arrived. The room had arches on three sides overlooking the gardens and pool. It had a tiled floored with Egyptian décor. A huge electric fan with bamboo blades waved above to ward off insects and cool the room for eating. He was served coffee and juice and a soda without ordering. The staff always remember you and what you like. Sometimes you could eat a whole meal without having to ask for anything you might want. Almost like they read your mind. The staffs in Egypt were phenomenal. You were never treated like a paying guest in any establishment, but instead like a guest of honor at all times.

Mohammed entered the open cavern and sat down across from Spencer. Spencer sensed that he was there to have a serious conversation and not pass the time.

"Good morning, Spencer," he greeted.

"Good morning, Mohammed."

Mohammed waved to the wait staff to bring him a cup of coffee. Spencer continued with his breakfast. Mohammed spoke first. "Have you chosen your stud?"

"Yes. I think I have. I will confirm with Cavanaugh King this afternoon and make my offer if that is appropriate."

"Hmmmmm," Mohammed seemed to be stumbling for words. Fear invaded Spencer that there had been a change of mind. Mohammed went on to say. "I think your plan to choose your final candidate is a good one. But I do not believe you can present your offer today."

"Why not?" Spencer again could feel that there was as much being unsaid as being said.

"Let me say delicately, you should extend your offer to Leader Zabr only. It would most likely breed failure to conduct your business with anyone else who might put themselves in charge in the Leader's absence."

"And is Leader Zabr absent?"

"Yes. He is taking his thirteenth wife and there are private ceremonies for the next forty-eight hours. He is unavailable."

Spencer's thoughts bounced between thirteen wives and who was in charge. "And who is in charge in his absence."

"Mohammed Ahmd."

Spencer understood immediately. Sekhmet's brother would never make a fair deal with him if any deal at all. He would have to stay another couple of days to meet with Leader Zabr. He would or might have a couple of more days to enjoy Egypt. "Okay, so I hang till he comes off his honeymoon."

"I feel I must inquire about something, Spencer. You may feel it is not my business to ask, but I assure you it is. It is in your best interest and the best interest of your purpose here."

Spencer felt sure he knew what was coming. Mohammed Ahmd probably had spies or cameras on the parapet, and he was going to be beheaded for kissing Sekhmet. Mohammed continued.

"I overheard Sekhmet and her brother this morning in disagreement. He was accusing Sekhmet of you and her having eyes for each other and affecting any deal adversely that might be made with you." Spencer felt his chances of beheading going up fast. "I ask you if this is true? Are you and Sekhmet in a romance shall we say?"

Spencer wasn't sure what to do. If he told the truth, he would be in trouble, if he lied and was found out, he would be in worse trouble. His concern was for Sekhmet. He would leave Egypt, but she would have to stay. This Cavanaugh scheme was turning into a bed of fire ants. But Spencer was an honest man at heart and did not like being on either side of deceit.

"Sekhmet and I are certainly friends and yes, I find her immensely attractive. You would have to ask her how she sees me because nothing of consequence has occurred. Mild bantering and sincere friendship."

"But you would like to see … shall we say … more?" Mohammed cocked his head and raised his eyebrow when he asked.

Spencer was not sure if he was just interested man to man … "hey ya think the girl is cute?" Or if he was a hitman for Zabr and when he answered wrong his head would tumble to the floor. All

Spencer knew was that the dynamics were turning weird. "I'm not sure what to say, Mohammed."

"Spencer, I am here to extend an invitation for Sekhmet. I am Sekhmet's confidant and I hold all secrets in my heart. But I wanted to know if you would be honest with me. And you were. Evasive, I confess, but honest. Sekhmet would like to invite you to Aswan for the night and day while her father is out of Luxor. She feels that being out of sight will allow more freedom and less questions. I am to get you to the boat. You will travel on the Nile and then a car will drive you to Aswan."

"Will the Zabr's suspect when we both disappear? Or Mohammed Ahmd?"

"Mohammed Ahmd is expected for ceremonies and will be otherwise occupied for the most part. But Aswan will give you and Sekhmet the blanket of protection to continue your friendship. I will be back for you in an hour."

Spencer took the opportunity to call Mallory when he returned to his suite. "Good morning, are you up yet? "Mallory, Mal are you there?"

Mallory answered the phone, pushing on the phone lights thinking it was the alarm. "Spence. I thought you were the alarm."

"I'm sorry to call so early and wake you. But I will be on a boat later and not sure I can call from there."

Mallory was blinking and rubbing her eyes when Spencer saw her. He obviously had disturbed her. "Okay," Mallory was trying to wake up, process Spence was on the phone, and how he is on a boat in the middle of the Sahara Desert.

"Mal, I have to delay my return again. We are close, awfully close. I am Skyping with your dad this afternoon to make the final selection and then I can make an offer."

"So why can't you catch a plane tonight or tomorrow morning?"

"Because Leader Zabr is getting married for the thirteenth time and not available for a couple of days to make the deal."

Again, Mallory was trying to process thirteenth marriage and a boat in the desert. "What is this place called Egypt?"

"So, you are having to wait for him? How long is the honeymoon? Another two weeks?" Mallory was done with Egypt. She had fires all around her and Spence was floating across the desert on a boat while the other party was celebrating his thirteenth marriage.

"Mal, I will meet with him as soon as he makes himself available. Shouldn't be more than a couple more days. Hang in there. Your father will be ecstatic if I pull this off."

Mallory thought to herself, "I hope you know what you are talking about, Spence. We need some good news here."

There was a knock at Spencer's door.

"I gotta run, Mal. The car to take me to the boat is here. I will call you when I can and be home in a few days."

"Okay, then. I will talk to you soon."

"Mal."

"Yes."

"Mal, I love and miss you. I will be glad to be home."

"Good, Spence. Good. I will be glad to see you. Bye now."

They hung up. Mallory got up to ready herself for her day. Spencer followed the boy with his luggage down the stairs for a tryst with his newfound Egyptian friend.

Chapter 28

Mallory faced the day with newfound energy and motivation. Carson came by early and assured her that all repairs had been made from the storm that occurred last week. Mallory was amazed that the blizzard happened a little over a week ago. It seemed like centuries had passed. After tending to immediate business, Mallory decided to visit her parents. She had not talked to them in several days now and neither had visited the barn.

"Hello," Genevieve answered.

"Hi, Mom."

"Mal."

"Yes, it is me. You don't sound like yourself are you ok?"

"I was sleeping."

"Good. We can have coffee together. I'm on my way up. Is Dad there?" Mallory asked.

"Mal, your father left a few minutes earlier. But you can't come up. We are not home. We are in Houston."

"When did y'all go to Houston?" Mallory was stunned.

"Your father had business here, so I came along," Genevieve explained.

"Well, I wish you had told me."

"We should have. It was at the last minute, and we'll be home tomorrow. Just didn't see it as a big deal. But I do regret not having coffee with you this morning. Is everything okay? Do you need help?" Genevive inquired.

"Well, if you mean do I need you to come tutor me in the difference between a strained muscle and colic, no I got that down now. But I do need time with you when you get back," she added, "as soon as possible."

"This sounds urgent. Are you sure we do not need to talk about the matter now?"

"No, Mom. Holler at me when you get back and I'll come up."

Genevieve clicked her phone off and she and Cav proceeded into the M.D. Anderson Cancer Center in Houston.

****

Across the world, Mohammed and Spencer boarded a felucca, a sailing vessel, named the Titanic. The boat had quarters below that was a cabin for sleeping and a galley. Spencer was surprised and disappointed that Sekhmet was not on board also for the trip. But he deduced that it was best he was not seen leaving Luxor with her as she and Mohammed had obviously arranged.

Two chaise lounges were on the bow that he and Mohammed settled into. A waitstaff brought them beers and they settled back for the trip. Conversation was light and easy, and periods of silence ensued as they watched the moving river and observed the beauty on the banks on both sides.

"Are you confident of your choice, Spencer?" Mohammed inquired.

"Yes, I think so, the dark horse with flaxen mane. Never seen anything like him," Spencer said sincerely.

"Yes! Yes! … excellent choice. He is a spectacular Arabian. And Yousuf does an excellent job of showing him."

"Mohammed, funny you would say that. I noted the young fellow seemed to really have a connection with the horse. He truly knew how to exhibit his finer points."

"Yes, I am proud of my grandson."

"Your grandson! I did not know! He is a talented young man!"

Spencer said this remembering the boy rider tearing through the arena on his chosen horse. He was rearing and looked like Roy Rogers on Trigger. Except the boy had no saddle nor rein. He controlled the horse entirely by seat and leg. He certainly received the approval of the crowd.

"Yes, he has found his happy place with horses. We have been fortunate that I know the family that can offer him the best to work with."

In time, they reached the Aswan area, docked, and took a car to the hotel. Spencer was not ready for the ride to the hotel. They were in a van seemingly on a narrow one lane road. Sometimes it was no more than a path going up the side of a cliff with hairpin turns and always a drop off on the cliff side. Spencer was sweating and a nervous wreck by the time they pulled into a small driveway at the evening's accommodation.

The hotel was Nubian style with painted doors and matching shutters on windows. It appeared to be built on the side of the cliff with steep stairs going up to an open vestibule. If you turned to the left, you walked up steeper stairs towards the adobe rooms built up the side of the cliff and to the right you walked downstairs into a large cave-like room that served as a sitting room and dining room. A long stone bar was carved out of the mountain in the middle of the room although obviously not in use. There was no furniture. The seating and tables were all carved out of the mountain. The room was extraordinary, unlike anything he had ever seen before.

The doors to the quarters were arched, painted colorfully in blues, yellows, greens and reds and Spencer had to duck when walking into the room. Again, in Nubian style everything from furniture to curtains and bedding were in vibrant, primary colors. The key in his hand looked like a key from the 1800's that collectors valued. The bathroom, although a bit primitive, was functional.

Spencer was quite taken with the little hotel carved out of a cliff overlooking the Nile River. But he was single-minded as to why he was here. He had not seen Sekhmet since he kissed her last night. Last night seemed like a million years ago. They were right. Time in Egypt was like time in Vegas. It doesn't exist for the most part. There was no dinner time. It was when you were hungry. Should you have an appointment at two, show up at three. Egyptian time. But he knew he needed to Skype with Cav very shortly and he only hoped that this cliffside hotel would accommodate his electronics. And where was Sekhmet?

He sat his computer up on a small table by a small window, the only window in the room, raised the window shade to a view of the pool area and the Nile. The pool was street level and across the driveway on a ledge overlooking the Nile. The hotel was literally carved out of the cliff and supplemented with large stone blocks. It was totally unique and quaint. He waited patiently for the connection. Finally, Cav came on the screen.

"Hi, Cav."

"Hi, Spence. How is Egypt?"

"Boy, do I have stories to share, Cav. Believe me, this has been like pulling teeth. The Egyptians do not believe in expediting anything. How are things there, Cav?"

"Well, I am in a conference room at MD Anderson in Houston. Genevieve is looking for an alternative treatment. She is with doctors now."

"Does Mal have any idea?"

"No, I don't think so. But she has had a rough time since you left. Carson has reported that there has been one calamity after another for her to deal with. He also is concerned that Gil might be up to something and that is worrying her. But she has not questioned Genevieve's or my activities so far."

Spencer was astonished at how far away all of this seemed. He felt so removed from them and their lives. He was part of them, but at that moment he was in another world.

"Okay, let's talk horses," Cav got down to business.

Spencer began to debrief Cav on his experiences and shopping for the right horse. He described several that he had viewed at the exhibition, but then finally singled in on what he felt was the one.

"The horse is a direct descendant from the Al-Maanaki bloodline, one of the three original Arabian assets. He is rich in color and bountiful in mane and tail. His movement is high stepping, forward moving and proud. A beautiful, refined neck and flaming nostrils! Here is the video."

Cav viewed the video.

"What is his name, Spence?"

"Al-Marah"

"Yes, Spence! He is marvelous! He will turn the American Arabians on their ears including Gil's latest acquisition. The handler … is that Yousuf Zawahiri?"

"Why, yes, it is," Spencer responded thinking it was an odd question from Cav.

"Do the deal and come home! Mal needs you and will need you more shortly. I don't know how much longer we can keep this from her," Cav abruptly ended the conversation before Spencer could ask how he knew this young horseman.

"Good to see you, Cav. I'll see you soon."

"Bye Spence! Bring the goods home!"

Spencer looked out his window at the setting sun. The panoramic picture was outstanding with mauve hues. The sky was a deep orange with the bright yellow ball peaking over purple shaded sandstone mountains. The lush flora that adorned the bank reflected in the water as it rippled gold from the sun. The palm trees created a filigree effect against the setting sun blush. Egypt was beyond beautiful. He decided he needed a drink, if not dinner, and again wondered when he might see Sekhmet.

He went into the large room that served as a sitting room and dining room. It was actually a cavern with benches in the sitting room carved out of the stone mountain and made comfortable with cushions. The back wall was solid mountain, and the outside wall was mountain with cavities cut for windows. He was served at a long granite table again carved from the mountain. His dinner consisted of bar-b-que chicken and corn on the cob with roasted eggplant and beer. And it was delicious! He wasn't sure what to expect from this primitive place, but delicious gourmet chicken was not it. Again, he wondered about Sekhmet.

After dinner he decided to visit the pool that was across the one lane that served as a street and parking lot. The pool was located on an overhanging ledge overlooking the Nile. He had spotted it when looking out his window earlier. The sunset began to fade into darkness as he took his seat. But he could see sailing vessels with lights passing by on the Nile below. The tranquility and stillness were comforting.

"Well, hello, I thought perhaps you had fallen off the cliff."

He did not have to turn to see who was surprising him. Her silky, throaty voice floated over him like an aphrodisiac. She had arrived finally. "Hi, come join me," he invited.

"So, was your passage here comfortable and entertaining?" Sekhmet inquired.

"Yes! Mohammed is always great company and has become a friend. The waterway was magnificent. I can't get over the luscious green on the banks backing up to the brown sands of the desert. An amazing sight, but of course Egypt is full of amazing sights."

Both knew that he was not only referring to Egyptian sights, but to Sekhmet herself. He instantly wondered if that had been too cheesy a comment. It had been so long since he had flirted or courted, and he couldn't believe he was attempting it now. But Sekhmet was a beautiful sight. Her black mane was tied back with strands hanging and bangs perfecting her deep dark eyes. She wore a sundress that seemed to match the color of the evening. He wondered how you could accidentally match the colors of a sunset while dressing. But in the darkness that was enveloping, Sekhmet was as beautiful as the sky with the falling sun.

She smiled at his comment. An awkward moment occurred as Spencer dwelled with his thoughts.

"I have a spectacular day planned for us tomorrow," Sekhmet broke the silence.

"Will it be a busy day?"

"Yes, it will be! And then I have a surprise for you!"

"A surprise?" Spencer looked questioningly.

"Yes, I think you will be pleasantly surprised!"

"I am looking forward to it," Spencer volunteered.

A waitstaff from the hotel brought Sekhmet a drink along with the makings of more gin cocktails. She refreshed Spencer's drink and settled back in the pool chair.

"Tell me about your life, Spencer. I know nothing of who you are except you live in Texas on a horse ranch. Who is your family? Have you always lived in Texas? What do you like to do as a pastime? I want to know all of you, Spencer."

Spencer became instantly uncomfortable as he processed her questions. Who was he? He had never until now really thought about it. And what really bothered him was he realized that for over a decade his whole life was wrapped up in Mallory. It was hard to remember anything about him. It was Mallory's graduation, Mallory's college, Mallory's ranch, Mallory's horses, Mallory's house, and Mallory's wedding. Egypt had offered for the first time in years, almost since he could remember, his journey, his thoughts, his actions that were not based on Mallory.

"I am not an interesting person, Sekhmet. I grew up in Texas and have lived there all my life. I have wonderful parents. My father is a second-generation veterinarian. I went to school, graduated, and began managing the King Equestrian Center. I deal with horses, boarders, trainers, clinics, horse exhibitions, manage the ranch and try to do some riding and training in between."

"Okay, but what do you do when you are not working?" Sekhmet dug further.

"Wow! It seems I work most of my time. Even my off time is spent in a horse related activity. It's my life."

"No, Spencer. I suspect that you have another life that you are not sharing with me," Sekhmet said wisely.

"Sekhmet," Spencer looked at her almost helplessly. Could he speak of Mallory? What would that do to this furnace that was burning inside him?

But one of the qualities Mallory loved about Spencer and had witnessed many times over, was his absolute honesty. Spencer had a philosophy that you should live your life where you do not have to worry about being honest and forthright. You simply do not put yourself in a position to do something different. And here he was! In the quagmire of all quagmires, having to choose whether to be forthright or secretive. A position he did not like.

"I see worry lines on that handsome face. It is acceptable to be revealing. I would not expect you to have no romantic ties in your homeland. My goodness, Spencer, we live on two different continents. Nothing matters here. Just two people whose stars have crossed."

"I hesitate because I do not want to disrespect either of you. And talking about Mallory to you seems disrespectful." Okay, he chose honesty. But why would there be the question? He asked himself was that statement based on being honorable or being manipulative? Was he backpedaling because he wanted, he needed to extract himself from the situation? He knew it led to dishonor no matter what? Or was he spinning her so he could appear honorable while secretly lusting and desiring her? Spencer was confused at best with himself.

"Tell me more about this fortunate lady that has you to call her own," Sekhmet wanted more details.

Spencer hesitated, speaking of Mal to Sekhmet seemed gauche. "Well, as you know her name is Mallory, I call her Mal most the time. She calls me Spence. We have been together as friends and a couple since we were kids. She is a nationally recognized equestrian in English dressage and hoping to compete in the next Olympics. She is training a Thoroughbred gelding named Sky. She puts her heart and soul into her horses. She is successful in everything she attempts. Is a meticulous planner and a bit of a perfectionist. And her mother is currently dying of a brain tumor and Mal does not know per her mother's wishes."

Sekhmet took all this information in, but she felt like she had put a puzzle together that was missing some pieces. No mention of romance, love, or affection? And then drop the bomb that her mother was dying? Sekhmet realized that Spencer was in more pain than she originally thought over their emerging friendship.

"Spencer, that is heartrending and certainly a burden to bear."

"Yes, I don't think I really recognized how much it was weighing on me until I said it to someone. Mal and I have always been truthful with each other and now I have this major secret weighing on me that I am sworn to keep knowing how much it will hurt her," Spencer lamented.

"I understand, Spencer, and I sympathize. Keeping secrets from someone you love is hard and usually a disastrous decision. But I also understand keeping a dying person's covenant and I believe Mallory will too."

The dynamics had changed. What Spencer thought would or might end up as a romantic evening that he would live to regret, instead, he felt he had found a friend on this starry night. Someone he could talk to, confide in, share anything, and she would understand. She was about him. He had never experienced that before with Mallory. Mallory's self-interest, although Spencer believed she loved him fiercely, always precluded him. It was always about her. Her dreams, her fears, her wishes and he were just part of the package that Mallory had put together as her life.

"You are an amazing woman, Sekhmet. I am so glad our stars have crossed, and I can call you, my friend."

Sekhmet smiled. "Yes, Spencer. We are friends from two continents, but we share the same sun!"

"Here, here," Spencer said holding his glass up to meet her toast.

"I have great plans for us tomorrow. It will be a long, exhausting day. We should go up and rest. Breakfast will be early in the main dining room."

She stood to take her leave. Spence stood. He could not believe after just concluding that they were friends, how much he wanted more. He did not have another secret to keep from Mallory. His honor was intact on all accounts. But as he looked at this magnificent woman with beauty, charm more alluring than gold, he had to accept that he desired her. With every bone, every muscle, every cell in his body. So, he hugged her. He wrapped his arms around her and felt her near him and he felt like he had fallen into a pit of fire.

"Good night, my dear cowboy," she whispered in his ear as they embraced.

"Good night, Sekhmet," he said overcoming the urge to say, "don't go, stay with me Sekhmet".

They left the pool and star filled night holding hands and when it came time to part, simply nodded a good night and went to their separate rooms. Rooms that were filled with dreams of cowboys and Egyptian beauties and unfulfilled lust.

Chapter 29

It was later that day that Murdach sought Mallory out. She was watching one of her students braid her horse's mane for show and offering tips, when she saw him coming down the corridor. Her spirits instantly sank as she recalled the looming issue surrounding Murdach and his future. He approached them.

"Hello."

"Hello, Murdach. How are you today?" Mallory exchanged pleasantries.

"What do you think of this braid?" Mallory continued.

"Very nice. Could be a bit tighter were I to be judging."

"Ok, Sara, from an expert. Need to pull tighter and slicker," Mallory offered to the student.

"Mallory, can you and I visit for a few minutes?" Murdach asked.

"Sure, we'll be back to see your final presentation," Mallory informed Sara.

She and Murdach retired to an outside seating area at the barn. It was a patio area with an awning to protect from the sun or rain. Tables and chairs were available, and it overlooked a paddock that was quite often the location of beautiful horses grazing. They sat and faced each other. Mallory found the moment awkward and wished again that Spence was here.

"Mallory, I want to let you know that I have accepted your uncle's offer. I have also told him that I made you aware of the offer previously."

"Oh," was all Mallory could muster.

"I truly regret leaving this barn and Genevieve's organization, but I must consider where opportunity lies. Your uncle has made me truly an offer I cannot refuse," Murdach continued.

Mallory cringed inside as she reprocessed that offer included a percentage of the King birthright. Her father would be beyond furious and revengeful.

"I recognize that here I will always be just one of the trainers, an elite trainer I grant you, but none the less. This organization has a built-in celebrity trainer that I play second to, it has a ranch CEO in Spence and includes a third-generation owner of all when the time comes. I will never really meet my financial goals here and probably not my professional."

Mallory listened to his reasoning, and she had to admit he was correct. He would never surpass her mother as the elite trainer at the barn. Spence will be managing the business long after Murdach is retired, and she would certainly inherit all of it.

"Your uncle has none of these complications. He needs a second hand, someone to bring prestige to his barn and organization. He needs a trainer for the filly that will soon rule the Arabian world. He needs experience, reputation, and class. I can provide all of that for him and he in turn can provide me a financial future that I aspire to."

"What are your plans?"

"I will be moving my horses at the end of the month and phasing my students out over the next thirty to sixty days."

"You will not be taking your students?"

"I will take my private and long-term. But recent students, say in the last six months, will stay here where they belong. I do not want my departure to affect the balance sheet too adversely."

"Mom and Dad will be disappointed. Do you plan on telling them or are you looking for me to take care of that?" Mallory decided to ignore the previous comment. She knew her father had a written contract and she planned on following any departure from the barn to the letter.

"That is your call. I have not seen either here at the barn in recent weeks," Murdach replied.

"I know. I too have had trouble tracking them down. But I will. They need to know."

Mallory made the last comment wiping her brow and looking deeply troubled. Murdach was instantly sympathetic.

"Mallory, I am sorry."

"Business is business."

"But I realize this agreement with your uncle may be a family issue. I do not like being the catalyst for this type of discord."

Mallory instantly felt the hair on her neck stand up as she thought, "then don't damn it! You may be second fiddle here, but it was in my mother's shadow and her support and putting you in the limelight that has made your reputation. And you repay them by deserting them and to all people, Uncle Gil!"

"Discord in this family is a way of life, I assure you. There will be some fireworks, then everyone will go back to doing what they do. I will relay the news to my parents. I believe, Murdach, there is a written contract that addresses breaking the contract. I will be reviewing it to be sure we both adhere to any previous agreements."

"You will not find such a document, Mallory. Your mom tore the contract up in front of me as a gift at the Moscow Olympics when I took gold. She has always been generous," Murdach stated.

"I see. Well, excuse my lack of knowledge. I will talk to my parents."

"Very well. Please relay my best wishes and my hope this will not destroy our friendship. After all," Murdach immediately caught himself.

Mallory finished his thought silently, "after all I'm going to be a partner in the King dynasty."

"I will, Murdach," Mallory looked him square in the eye and he knew she was dismissing him.

He had delivered the news. It was time to take his leave.

Before the door shut, Mallory dialed her Uncle Gil. He would face her wrath before anyone else. At least she would have that satisfaction.

****

The sunrise the next morning in Egypt was astonishing. It rose as a dark orange ball over the darkness of desert mounds. The Nile in the foreground with banks of rich greens and luscious foliage adding to the portrait and a contrast of colors that melted together like an artist's pallet. A pallet of deep richness and spectacular beauty. Spencer admired the picturesque scene drinking coffee on the balcony of the small brightly colored Nubian hotel. It wasn't long before Sekhmet was waving to him from the parking lot to join her in the car.

The day was full of sights and sounds of Egypt today and yesterday. The first point of interest was the Low Aswan Dam. The British built the dam beginning construction in 1899 and completed it in 1902 to control Nile flooding and facilitate irrigation. The dam was the first of its kind and nothing of its scale had ever been attempted. The dam served its purpose until the 1960's when construction on the High Dam downriver began. The Low Dam, although raised a couple of times, could not hold back the Nile, and fulfill its purpose.

The High Dam, as it is referred to, was built on Lake Nassar, one of the largest man-made lakes in the world. The High Dam was complete in 1968 between Egypt and the Sudan and replaced the Low Dam. The High Dam built on Lake Nassar which was supposedly home to thousands of alligators. Spence then understood the deference to alligators in hieroglyphics, statues, mummies, and paintings he had seen since touring Egypt.

They visited a papyrus factory where Spencer chose a depiction of a decorated Egyptian horse that he thought he would have framed and hung over the mantle for Mallory. It was large so it was rolled and put in a tube and mailed to Texas. He would have to remember to have someone retrieve it so Mallory would not see it.

They visited a mummy alligator museum. Spencer became educated on how common alligators were in Egypt. They were depicted in Egyptian hieroglyphics and antiquities. He also became more educated on the Egyptian mummification process. He could not help but be in awe that he was walking among artifacts, mummified alligators, that had been created by ancient Egyptians centuries ago.

They ended their day together with lunch at an eatery with a dining room that was a balcony overlooking the Nile. It was casual and simple. But again, the food was delicious!

"I hope you have enjoyed your day, Spencer. We are now leaving for Hurghada!" Sekhmet shared with Spencer.

"May I ask why we are off to Hurghada?" Spencer inquired.

"I have a very special morning planned for you before you fly back to Luxor for collection."

"Will you be joining me for the ride to Hurghada?"

"No, I will go separate from you. There are several checkpoints, and it would not be prudent for us to be seen together. But I will join you for a late dinner. Enjoy your quarters and the Red Sea. A driver will come for you."

The ride to Hurghada was a highway that threaded through the Sahara Desert. The desert, although desolate, was beautiful in its own right. Spencer did not realize the different colors of sand and dirt. Much like a green landscape full of shades and textures, the desert is a brown landscape full of shades and textures. Tall mountains made of mounds of rock and packed sand cast shadows across valleys and crevices accented by the sun. They drove for miles without any movement in the Egyptian wasteland. But Spencer's mind was active with thoughts of who might have viewed this same terrain or wondering what might lie beneath the dunes that created the panoramic vision.

Spencer had repeatedly thought to himself that Egypt is full of surprises. Hurghada was one of the surprises. After leaving the ancient Nubian environment of Aswan, Hurghada was like Miami but on the Red Sea. The coastline was a resort haven with actual shopping on a main street much like in the US. Hurghada seemed new compared to Cairo and modern compared to Aswan or Luxor. He only caught glimpses of the Red Sea driving in but the biblical history of the Red Sea being parted by Moses could not help but cross his mind.

His quarters were in a small beachy condo that was part of a small complex. He was steps from the shoreline and beach. The only people that he encountered were the waitstaff. He mused if the privacy was planned by Sekhmet on purpose. Then he chided himself for thinking that she would consider what he was fantasizing about.

The driver knocked and Spencer accompanied him to the car that took him to what he would call a boardwalk. It was a street that paralleled the coastline and harbor. The street was lined with bars and restaurants and people walking as all boardwalks are. But what captured Spencer's attention was the harbor across the street that offered refuge to one magnificent, unbelievable yacht after another. He had seen big boats anchored in the Gulf or California or Florida. But these yachts were mammoth and magnificent beyond belief!

He followed his driver up a set of stairs which were located between two buildings. He entered a small lobby with two elevators. The driver motioned to one of them and after Spencer entered, he pushed the button for him and stepped out. The elevator opened into a second lobby of what appeared to be a restaurant, albeit a small intimate restaurant. He was escorted to a table for two sitting in a private alcove with windows overlooking the street, the harbor, and the Red Sea.

The restaurant was sumptuous in Egyptian décor including beautiful tapestries, gold accents, rich colors, and plush seating. He was relaxing, taking in the beautiful sights from the window when Sekhmet appeared. He could not believe his eyes. She was breathtaking in Egyptian attire that was magenta in color with jade brocade and gold trim. Spencer was amazed that her modest dress could be so sexy and alluring. Her dress covered and concealed. But Spencer found himself speculating what secrets the fabric held. He stood when she came to the table and although his instinct was to hug her hello, he knew touching her was forbidden, especially in a public setting.

"Sekhmet you are absolutely lovely," Spencer offered as he seated her.

"Shukran," Sekhmet responded in Arabic.

"How was your journey here?" Sekhmet started the conversation.

"It was pleasant. I enjoyed the desert."

"Fabulous!"

As Sekhmet spoke three waiters appeared carrying food. The meal was the gourmet of Egyptian fare. The main course was stuffed quail, various vegetables, fruits, cheeses, breads, pasta dishes and salads. Spencer settled in for a meal to be remembered.

"This is delicious Sekhmet," Spencer commented a few minutes into the meal.

"I'm pleased you are pleased," she replied.

"And those yachts out there. They are really something! I have never seen million-dollar boats sit side by side like jet skis," Spencer noted.

"Really, you do not have boats in America?" Sekhmet said in surprise.

"Yes, we have a few yacht harbors. But not sure, I have ever seen a boat like that black one with gold inlaid trim all over it! Never have seen anything like that in America."

Sekhmet laughed in merriment at his statement. "That boat belongs to the family," Sekhmet smiled.

"Of course, I should have known," Spencer replied shaking his head.

"Would you like a tour?"

"Well, I would not turn it down for sure."

"Then come, let's go!"

They stood to leave. Spencer looked around in confusion. "Do we not need to pay for our food?"

"No. The family owns the restaurant," Sekhmet answered.

"Of course," Spencer said sarcastically.

They crossed the street to the yacht that was anchored peacefully and quietly. Sekhmet made a call from her phone and within minutes a sailor came to the bridge and put the plank down for them to board. The lights came on and Spencer was stunned by what was before him.

Opulence, luxurious, richness, lavishness was all that came to mind. Spencer had been in some really nice equestrian ranch homes that were in the millions easily. But this boat was over the top with black, padded, rolled, and pleated seating and wood accents trimmed in gold. The main cabin offered a fully stocked 8-foot custom bar of black cherrywood, three large screen televisions, any and all amenities one could imagine. The room itself was huge with windows on both sides overlooking the water. The room had two living areas and a dining area, all expensively, tastefully, and professionally decorated.

There were several bedrooms all with their own bath, sitting rooms, balconies with a wall of windows allowing a view from the bed. As they continued into the interior of the yacht Spencer became even more in awe. There was an exercise room with spa, a media room, and a huge kitchen with all modern commercial appliances. The yacht was more than amazing. Not a detail overlooked, not a penny pinched. Spencer was certain he would never see such splendor again. He was certain the yacht he was walking through was probably in the hundred million or more range.

They finished their tour and settled on one of the lookout decks.

"I see you bring the gin again," Spencer noted when Sekhmet sat two glasses and the bottle down.

"Yes, but we must not overdo!"

Spencer immediately reacted to her comment thinking that she was insinuating that if they found themselves in a drunken state who knew what might happen. Sekhmet never missing any cue realized what Spencer was thinking.

"We have a ride early in the morning. I am not at my best if I consume alcohol to excess the night before. That is when I wear my hijab and remain silent," Sekhmet joked.

Both laughed at her humor. Then a silence fell as they looked across the sea at the bright reflection of the moon, the soft waves in the harbor, the stars twinkling temptingly close. The scene was pastoral and romantic at the same time. It was Sekhmet that broke the silence.

"Spencer …before we ride, I have someone I want you to meet."

"Really," Spencer was intrigued. They stowaway like thieves to not be seen and now she was into introductions.

"Yes, but it will require you dressing in Egyptian attire."

Spencer looked at her quizzically.

"You will need to wear jibbahs and cover your hair with a keffiyeh."

"Okay and why am I in costume?"

"Well truthfully, you are not in costume, you are incognito."

"So, I'm going where I should not go?"

"Well, yes and no. It would be best if you were not in boots, cowboy hat and silver belt buckle. Were you to be described in that manner, there would be no doubt that we spent this time in each other's company. Blending will help with no memory of who accompanied me."

"This sounds very mysterious."

"Yes, perhaps but well worth it, I assure you. Do we have your contact information, so we know to whom to send your head?"

"Cute! Real cute," Spencer and she were laughing with merriment at her jesting.

Spencer was having feelings that he was having trouble keeping under control. The gin and the day with her had his head spinning with illicit thoughts. But after another drink, Sekhmet called for transportation. They exited the magnificent yacht to the street. There were no hugs, not on the busy public street. Only a bid of good night and both entered their respective vehicles to be delivered to their quarters.

****

Mallory was visibly upset after her conversation with Murdach. She continued with her morning calendar, but it was early afternoon when she realized that she had something that needed to be said to Uncle Gil. Regardless of what her parents would say or do or feel, she was an adult, a bloodline King, the bloodline heir of the King property. He owed her an explanation and an apology as

147

much as anyone. She took a break and headed around the bend to Uncle Gil's place.

"Mallory! Mallory! What do I owe this pleasure?" Gillespie met Mallory in the barn drive when she pulled up and greeted her when she exited her truck.

"Uncle Gil," she greeted as they gave each other a hug. Gil had enjoyed Mallory coming over to see him since she was a little girl. When she was little, she would ride over in secret to spend time. He cherished his friendship with her and admired her as an equestrian. He was definitely her cheerleader in her aspirations. But he knew today would be demanding at best. He led the way to a paddock behind the barn where his prized Arabian filly was in turn-out. She was putting on quite a show prancing and strutting back and forth across the paddock.

"Wow! She is a beauty," Mallory sincerely complimented watching how light and balanced she was on her feet.

"Yes, she is! The hopes and dreams of the Gillespie King Horse Ranch lie between those hooves," Gil stated.

"So, you steal an elite trainer from us to reach your dreams?" Mallory said accusingly.

"I presume you have spoken with Murdach," Gil responded.

"Spoken? He spoke to me and gave notice at the barn. He tells me you have not only offered him lead trainer and barn manager but a percentage of the ranch." Gil said nothing while Mallory stared at him with her big blue eyes accusingly.

"Hello! Is that how you have enticed him to leave a successful career at our barn? Or did I get it wrong?" Mallory sarcastically asked.

"You know, Mallory. This filly is almost two years old. She has a long, successful career in front of her. She will be renowned before she retires to pastures. Her legacy will be extended with not only her achievements but that of her progeny," Gil paused.

"Okay." Mallory's impatience showing.

"Mallory, I will be gone long before this filly accomplishes even half her life's triumphs. At best I will be retired, still mobile I hope, but certainly not overseeing the ranch. At worst, I will be on a hill somewhere providing a mound for grass," Gil continued.

"Either way my time is limited now. I must think about the future of my ranch, my business, my barn. I need a second in command, Mallory. I need a Spencer or you. I have no one to continue operations and management should I get kicked in the head tomorrow. I never concerned myself too much until," Gil motioned to the proud, regal horse that occupied the paddock in front of them, "her. I can't let her down. She deserves her future." Mallory was taken aback by the emotion and sentiment her uncle had just shared. "I know that your dad and possibly even your mother will look at this from another perspective. They will think this is just another chess move. But Mallory, I looked, I interviewed, I sought another individual, but it always came back to the second to your mom, Murdach."

Gil nodded at the filly running the paddock, "I owe that bundle of promise and potential nothing less than a Murdach. When I first approached him, he refused. I could offer nothing more and somewhat less than his present situation. So, I had to bite the bullet and make him an offer he could not refuse."

"But Uncle Gil, you are giving away part of the ranch. My grandparents never believed for a minute that anyone would give away the ranch!"

"First of all, I am not giving it away. There is a five-year contract prior to any ownership by Murdach of the ranch. If he performs as expected and needed, then with that tenure, I am comfortable on making him a partner with a small percentage. If you are, shall we say, in charge, I'm sure you will be able to buy him out. He will be close to my age by that time and looking for a different life than riding horses ten hours a day. I truly am not trying to take another shot at your father, Mallory. I promise you."

"But I will be there for you, Uncle Gil."

"Mallory, Mallory. I do love you so and appreciate your loyalty to me. But the future could be tomorrow. It may not be five, ten, fifteen years from now. Could you drop everything and take over here? Would that horse get the attention and training and investment that she deserves? If I stroke out walking to the house today my affairs would be a mess. I am planning for the future that is on the horizon and cannot be circumvented."

****

When Spencer returned to his condo as late as it was, he could not sleep. He walked the coastline of the sea finding the waves to be soothing in his chaotic state of mind. He was fascinated and possibly in love with Sekhmet. He could not deny that. But he also could not deny that it was futile and hopeless. He would be leaving Egypt in days and somehow, he had to let this go. He decided to call Mallory. He felt it would help ground him to hear her voice and see her.

"Hi, Mallory," Spencer FaceTimed her, so he was waiting for her face to appear.

"Spence …. Hello!"

"How are you doing, Mal?"

"I'm okay. Missing you. Missing you a lot, Spence," Mallory acknowledged.

Spencer cleared his throat. Suddenly he had a frog that was choking him. Seeing Mallory made home seem real and Egypt like a dream.

"Missing you too, Mal. How are things at the barn?"

"I'm saving all the problems till you get back."

"Really ... lots going on?"

Mallory could not begin to tell him about the last few days since he left. She felt like he would not relate to how perturbed she was with her uncle. Normally, he would be the person she would pour out her heart regarding how poor training was going with Sky, how scared she was with whatever was going on with her mom, and the overall craziness that seemed to engulf the barn since his departure. But the words would not come out.

"Nothing that can't wait till you come home. Speaking of ... do we have an ETA? Like maybe tomorrow night and that is why you are calling?"

"No, not tomorrow night, Mal. Two days I will be there. Just delay what you can delay."

"So where are you on the deal? Have you even chosen a donor yet?"

"Yes, the collection will occur in about a day."

"Then home?"

"Yes, Mal, then home."

The call ended with little comfort to either Mallory or Spencer. Once they had been each other's safe harbor. But now it felt like they were not in the same ocean.

Chapter 30

Spencer met Sekhmet for their drive early the next morning. Breakfast was on the go. Sekhmet was beautiful as always. She was in riding clothes which revealed her almost perfect figure. He was dressed in the Egyptian attire she had left for him. He was not sure if he felt like a total joker or if he felt mysterious and covert. The head accessory was difficult for him, so he carried it to Sekhmet for help to complete the attire.

The drive to where he did not know was uneventful. Both were quiet and rested from the previous late night. Spencer was in his usual mental turmoil dealing with his emotions and whims. He was looking forward to the day with Sekhmet, but he knew their time was coming to an end. He felt a physical ache when he thought about the end.

He could not help but notice the terrain was becoming more barren and desolate. They had turned off the main highway and seemed to be crossing the desert without a road. The driver apparently knew where he was going, but Spencer was uncomfortable just heading directly into the desert abyss.

In actuality the driver knew exactly where to go because although there was no apparent road, the ground was packed so that a vehicle could pass. To veer from the narrow path would mean being stuck in the desert. Spencer looked at his phone which indicated no service. He became more uneasy wondering who would come get them if a problem arose. As far as Spencer knew, no one knew their location. And he certainly didn't.

But just as his anxiety hit another level, civilization appeared out of nowhere. The structures seemed to materialize out of nothing. One minute he was looking at nothing, but a bleak desert and the next, an oasis of blue water, grass, palm trees and pink buildings were before his eyes. As they drew closer, he realized the buildings were actually a line of stalls in "L" shape. He could not imagine why the color pink. There were several corrals with a couple of main buildings. But the scene overall was primitive.

Pulling into what served as a courtyard, a rather intimidating sentry waved the driver down. They exchanged greetings through the open window. Then a conversation ensued in which he heard Sekhmet's name several times. The greeter walked to Sekhmet's window as the driver rolled the window down. They had a brief conversation and then he motioned them to a parking place.

They exited the car and were escorted into a tent that had pillows for seating on rugs spread over the ground. Sekhmet gestured to sit, and she took a seat across from him. An Egyptian groomsman soon entered the tent and he and Sekhmet conversed. Spencer did not understand a word, but when he left, Sekhmet told him she had asked that horses be prepared for a ride.

In the meantime, they were served tea from a brass tea set. Several men that Spencer determined were locals here at the complex came in and visited briefly with Sekhmet. They finished their tea and Sekhmet stood.

"Come Spencer. Our horses are ready. But before we ride, I want you to meet someone." Spencer stood and followed her out of the tent up a path that seemed to lead behind the complex. The area was beautiful. It was just a bit of green and water plopped down in the middle of the desert.

"This is beautiful, Sekhmet," Spencer commented as they walked to where Spencer had no idea.

"Yes, I come here occasionally to ride. We are actually very close to the Red Sea. We will ride there, and you will be glad you are wearing dishadasha."

"Really, why?" Spencer asked. Spencer felt a bit ridiculous in what felt like a dress. But he knew it must be important or Sekhmet would not have insisted. They walked a bit further and a rustic wooden fenced paddock came into view. At first Spencer thought the paddock was empty.

"You will know why soon. But in the meantime, I want you to meet Tawfik."

Then Spencer saw him. At first Spencer was speechless. "What in the world is that Sekhmet?"

"The crown jewel Spencer. The crown jewel," Sekhmet replied.

Spencer was looking at a horse that was beyond astonishing. He found himself holding his breath as he absorbed the animal that now after seeing humans seem to be putting on a show. Powerful was the first word that came to Spencer's mind. His torso was muscular and rippled when he moved. And boy could he move. He looked like a prancing ballet dancer he was so light. Spencer watched as he romped back and forth across the pasture showing off. The fluidity was unparalleled from any horse Spencer had ever seen in Egypt or the US. It was as though his hooves did not hit the ground but touched lightly. The four legs seem to operate as easily as a wheel turns, a perfect forward move.

His spirit was tangible as he paraded back and forth in the paddock showing off every gait known to man. His tail hung high like a flag flowing down his back legs while his mane was lush and full and hung from the long neck that carried the pronounced Arabian profile. His head and ears were impeccably placed with flared nostrils and black muzzle. His eyes appeared to be enhanced with make-up. His color was unique and unmatched. He looked like white and grey marble with a snow-white mane and tail. Tawfik was truly a horse like no other. He could not have been more perfect if Disney had created him.

"Crown jewel is right," Spencer commented after a minute. He went on, "I suppose the horses that I chose from are not from this lineage?"

"No, you certainly were able to choose from the very best. The family has several outstanding bloodlines. But Tawfik posterity is kept only within the Zabr family. A fresh collection routinely occurs in case something was to happen to him. His progeny is limited and protected by the family. He is the pure horse descendant from Skowronek and they will not allow the posterity to be less than their standards. Every Zabr descendant for hundreds of years have understood and know they are charged to protect this legacy," Sekhmet shared.

"He is truly magnificent. Thank you for sharing him with me," Spencer said.

"Oh, you must meet him more closely," Sekhmet said as she began to climb over the fence.

Spencer followed her over the fence and across the pasture towards Tawfik. At first, he was agitated. He wasn't sure about these two strange beings coming at him. But Sekhmet stopped far from him and began a low soft whistle. He turned his head immediately with ears forward and snorted. And although Spencer could never explain how a horse can saunter, Tawfik sauntered across the distance straight to Sekhmet and stood.

He remained stationary as both Sekhmet and Spencer petted and admired the horse. Spencer was beyond impressed with the conformation of the horse. He picked up the hooves and they were unflawed. The horse was textbook perfect.

They left Tawfik with Spencer feeling as though he had brushed shoulders with royalty, with ancient history, with a legend of the highest order. He was quiet and thoughtful walking back to their rides as he processed what he had just seen. And he was also processing that Sekhmet must think he was special to share such a family treasure.

Back at the stable, they mounted their horses and again, Spencer was taken aback by the spirit and heart the horses exhibited. It took three men to hold the horse that Sekhmet rode when she mounted. Her horse was a black Arabian stallion that could not keep his feet still. His horse was a dark Sorrel with a flaxen mane and a handful himself. At first Spencer was uncomfortable with the robe he was wearing. But as they rode out, he found himself feeling like Lawrence of Arabia. They rode hard and fast. The desert is like a never-ending arena or paddock. He was feeling total euphoria.

They crossed the desert and came over a hill and Spencer was looking at the desolate coastline of the Red Sea. They stopped on top of the hill to take the sight in. Spencer looked across the sea and processed that the Red Sea was biblical and part of ancient, recorded history. He was in awe.

Sekhmet jumped off her horse, pulled out her blouse which turned out to be quite long and offered coverage because she also took her riding pants off. "Spencer, get off. Take either your pants off or your dishadasha. You will wear one or the other on the return ride."

Spencer dismounted and shed his jeans that were under his robe. Sekhmet was taking the saddle of her horse, so he followed suit. They walked their horses down the hill onto the beach into the water and when the water became waist high climbed on their swimming horses.

The experience was memorable. Swimming in the Red Sea with his horse and Sekhmet. She was prettier than a mermaid atop her black stallion that she rode bareback. The water glistened all around her with a deep blue sky and billowy clouds behind her. He could not help but notice her shapely legs that gripped the horse. He filed the image away knowing that someday he would draw on images of Sekhmet to comfort himself. But it wasn't just the visual that was picturesque, it was hearing Sekhmet's genuine laughter and joy that he would always treasure.

After swimming with the horses, they raced each other down the coastline. Spencer had never ridden so freely. Bareback and uninhibited. Sekhmet let go of her reins and spread her arms like an eagle as her horse galloped full out down the coastline. He followed suit and although an excellent rider, Spencer could not believe the elation almost rapture he felt bareback with no reins with a horse full out. Spencer had never felt that exhilaration in his life and time would show he would never feel it again.

They walked their horses back to where they left their clothes. The conversation was basically Spencer expressing gratitude to Sekhmet for all she had shared with him in a matter of a few days. He had seen and done things that he never dreamed he would do. He thanked her for her influence that ensured a successful outcome for his business there.

They returned to their clothes and finished dressing in dry clothes for the ride back. Standing on a sandhill overlooking the Red Sea they stood holding their horses, realizing that it was over. Spencer reached out, took her beautiful face in his hand and gently pulled her to him. And in the privacy of the desert and the sea they shared a kiss that shook the universe. The ride back was slow and deliberate with both coping with the impending goodbye. Sekhmet finally spoke.

"Spencer, when we return to the stable, you will take one car that will take you to Aswan where you will be delivered to a boat which will take you to Luxor. When you reach Luxor, Mohammed will be there to meet you. It is important that you be seen with Mohammed and that others think you have spent this time with Mohammed."

"You mean in a matter of minutes this is goodbye," Spencer exclaimed thinking he was going to panic, "you won't be leaving with me? Going back with me?"

"No, Spencer, we must bid each other goodbye when we return."

"Wow! I did not realize that our time was so close to over," bemoaned Spencer.

"I know, Spencer. I feel the same way. Our friendship has been remarkable, and I will miss you very much."

She let her voice drift away as she finished her thought, "maybe the rest of my life."

Chapter 31

Spencer's head was spinning. It was like he had been in a time warp wherein he would stay in Egypt forever always going home but never leaving. He wanted to go home, but never wanting to say goodbye to the mystery, the beauty and enchantment of Egypt. He would return to Luxor tonight, meet with the Zabr clan in the morning to complete the transaction, and fly out that day. This was goodbye to Sekhmet and his heart was broken. He would never see her again.

He spent a few moments looking at her and taking in her dark hair hanging straight and long with bangs framing her face, her dark eyes that boasted long lashes with pigments of gold. He had fallen into the depths of the liquid gold. Her face was perfectly angular with a Roman nose and full, inviting lips. When she smiled, she exhibited beautiful teeth, and her eyes actually took on a different shade of darkness. Her skin was the color of honey and the sun. Sekhmet was unlike any woman Spencer had ever encountered and in a matter of minutes, he would say goodbye. He thought he was going to throw up or cry or both.

Neither knew how to say goodbye. They had bonded but they would never explore the bond. They had connected on many levels, but the connection would never be honored. The chemistry was stronger than attracting magnets that would never meet.

Instead in the blinding heat and light of the Egyptian sun, Spencer gave her a hug and they whispered goodbye, and she left. Spencer stared as she walked away and continued to stare at the empty space when she faded from sight.

Within minutes a man came to take him to the boat to sail for Luxor. He stared out of the boat at the dark waters of the Nile with lights dotting the riverbank. He reran the tapes in his head of his experiences since coming to Egypt. More often than not, he reviewed his time with Sekhmet wishing he had said this or done that. He knew he would never forget her. It was like he had met his other bookend, but they would never hold books. Their fortunes and fate did not include each other.

A couple of hours into the trip, Spencer went below to use the facilities. He noted while occupied that the boat seemed to stop, he heard voices but could not make out the foreign conversation. He came from below and standing on the bow of the boat was a vision. For a moment, he thought he was hallucinating. But there she stood. Sekhmet, in a white dress blowing in the wind, holding on to the sail ropes with the lights on the shore of Luxor sparkling behind her. She looked like a Nile queen, or an angel dropped from above. Most importantly, he was not delusional. They had not said goodbye earlier.

"Sekhmet!" he exclaimed.

"Spencer, I know this is startling but after I left you today, I realized that … that I," Sekhmet stopped seemingly not knowing what she was about to say. But she continued, "We … our time together has been exceptionally rewarding."

Sekhmet stumbled as she tried to communicate her deep feelings without giving herself away. Spencer noted the small dinghy type boat attached to his larger craft. He deduced that was how Sekhmet came and that would be how she would go. She would not be staying long. He was instantly disappointed.

"Sekhmet, no explanation is necessary. I understand why you are here."

She took his breath away. She could be a fairy princess light and airy, or a goddess of nature. Nile waters framed her reflecting a halo of lights, but he saw in her eyes none of the aforementioned. In her eyes he saw passion, lust and wanting. And he was just as sure she saw the same in his.

He took a couple of steps toward her, but she held her hand up to stop him.

"There can be no embrace, Spencer. Too many eyes and ears that might betray our confidence for coin. I did not have time to buy total privacy. This must be a business meeting and brief. But I needed to know that what I was feeling in my heart was also in yours."

"Sekhmet … how I wish … how I wish we were of another time, another place … I will never be able to forget you or Egypt. I have been changed forever. And I grieve never seeing you again," Spencer spilled his heart.

They were standing close but not touching as they submerged in each other's eyes. "I cannot believe that is our fate, Spencer. Emotions such as ours cannot go forever unfulfilled. We must have another chance … maybe in another life … this cannot be our goodbye."

"Sekhmet, I hope you are right. When I imagine living the rest of my life and never seeing you again, I feel hopeless, blighted, and cheated. Being cheated for the rest of my life was not how I was meant to live," Spencer mourned.

"We are close to the dock. I must go. Spencer, I believe in my heart I will see you again. If not in life, in dreams. You will always be there in the shadows, the deep purple."

With that she quickly boarded the dinghy, and they motored off. He watched as her white dress faded away and he fought the desire to jump in the water and go after her. It had to end. There was not a tomorrow for them. The blanket of despair fell over him as he watched the compound dock come closer.

This was his last night in Egypt. He felt like he had been here for a long time, and that a lifetime of history had unfolded in a few short days. What he told Sekhmet was absolutely correct. He was forever changed and when he finally reached his quarters and sunk into his Egyptian sheets for the last time, he wondered. He wondered how he would feel back in Texas. How would he feel when he was home? Home … no Sphinx, no pyramids, no temples, no Nile or Sahara, no Arabians, no Sekhmet. After much turmoil he finally slept his last night in Egypt.

****

Mallory was mulling over her visit with her uncle when she walked in the door that night seeking a hot bath and glass of plum wine. The day had turned into a long one after her visit with her uncle. Her phone rang and she looked down to see Spence on the other end.

"Mal, are you there?"

"Yes, yes. Coming in the door, let me set my stuff down," Mallory replied.

"How are you, Mal?" Spencer asked almost awkwardly.

He had just left Sekhmet minutes before with nothing but lust and cheating in his heart and soul, and here he was asking his fiancé in a faraway land called Texas how she was doing like he was not a world away, but down the road.

"Okay," Mallory said freeing her hands and perching on a bar stool to talk to her fiancé who had been missing in action for days now, "I am fine, how are you, stranger?"

Spencer noted the reference to stranger. But instead of feeling the barb, he agreed with her. He felt like a stranger, a time traveler in another realm. "I am doing okay, Mallory. I am waiting to meet with the Zabr elders tomorrow to witness withdrawal of the specimen. There is some issue regarding an acceptable mare, but your father and the Zabr's are negotiating that personally."

"Really, I didn't know. I have barely seen Dad or Mom since you have been gone. I could claim abandonment based on the three of you and the last ten days," Mallory let her loneliness and desperation come through.

"Mallory, I am finishing the contract in the morning and catching an afternoon flight. I will be in New York at eight tomorrow night and in Dallas at midnight," Spencer hoped to comfort her. As the words came out of Spencer's mouth, he realized he was talking about going home. Going home to Texas, to the barn, to his fiancé, to the pending loss of Genevieve, to a wedding. All of it came crashing down on Spencer. He was not sure he actually belonged there. He chided himself silently for saying he didn't belong at home.

"Yeaaaaaa! Seems like you have been gone forever. I will sleep better tonight! It sounds like everything is a go for tomorrow! That should make Dad very happy! This has been hell without you, Spence, but I thank you for doing this for Dad."

"I know, Mal. I know a lot has been dumped on you. I'll be there soon, within hours actually. Hang tight."

"I think I can make it now knowing you are right around the corner. One more day … just one more day. I will never let you do anything like this again, though, Spence. No more across-the-world excursions. I miss you entirely too much!"

Spencer was astonished at how demonstrative Mallory was expressing her feelings of missing him. He felt instantly ashamed that he had spent the last week being totally enchanted by another woman while Mallory had kept the home fires burning and obviously, it had not been easy.

"Hey, see you tomorrow! Have a safe flight and get through customs so you don't miss the red eye to Dallas," Mallory gave last minute instructions.

"Will do, Mallory. See you soon."

They both hung up realizing neither again had expressed love or even affection. They took each other for granted, both knew it, and both accepted it. Tonight, it made them sad although neither knew why and neither slept soundly due to the combination of melancholy and excitement.

****

Sekhmet had taken the small dinghy to a private dock where Mohammed, Spencer's handler, and her devoted friend, met her. "Mohammed, thank you for meeting me," Sekhmet greeted him.

"Sekhmet, are you okay?"

"Yes, a bit sad, but okay. You know what I want done, right?" Sekhmet inquired.

"Yes, are you sure? This will anger your elders and your brother beyond repair. You are risking the Zabr reputation and legacy. You have weighed this against your gains, have you not?" Mohammed chanced questioning Sekhmet which he rarely did.

"You know, Mohammed. I don't know! I probably have not thought this through. I just know that never seeing Spencer again is unacceptable. Go forward with our plans and I will accept my consequences."

Cleopatra and Julius Caesar

Gaius Julius Caesar, a ruler and statesman before the times of Christ. A general who led Roman legions to victory in the Gallic Wars. And continued his rise to power by defeating Pompey in a civil war and rising politically in the leadership of the Roman Republic. Only to become absolute dictator of the Roman Empire for five years before his assassination.

Who was this man that was barbaric enough to win brutal wars but suave enough to sway the opinion and influence of the most prestigious of the times? Who was this man that ruled Rome with an iron hand with the mighty falling at his heel, but compassionate enough to contribute to society by offering citizenship in far regions of Rome and initiating land and building programs to benefit Roman citizens? Who was this man interested in progressing mankind by pursuits such as the creation of the Julian calendar and was a recognized author?

Julius Caesar was proclaimed "dictator for life" because he was the most strategic of the strategist, he was the bravest of the brave, he was the strongest of the strong, he was the most ruthless of the ruthless, and he was a political genius. He was a man's man. But most of all he was man of beauty.

He found beauty in strategically fighting and winning wars. He found beauty in influencing and leading men to his opinion and viewpoint. He found beauty in ruling and domineering the Roman public. He found beauty in building and creuling. And he found beauty in a woman named Cleopatra.

What woman, when he could have his choice of any woman of the times, could capture the interest, the admiration, and the love of such a man? What female of the age could possibly match his intellect, his savvy, his power, his experience? What must a femme fatale possess to keep the attention and attract such a formidable man? Was it the proverbial young woman and older man entrapment? She was 21 and he was 52. Or just two mere mortals unlikely to ever meet and unite, but together became willing to topple Rome in the name of love.

Their love, their passion, their devotion was legendary even at the time. They become the power couple of the age combining talents, knowledge, politics, Cleopatra's fair of face and Caesar's authority to charm and conquer the world.

Although not in Egypt, Cleopatra brought the mystery, the allure, the magic of love from Egypt to Rome. One can only ponder what really occurred. Did Caesar become so distracted by lust and passion that he failed to see the game changing on him? Did he find such comfort and solace in the arms of Cleopatra that this tried-and-true statesman could not feel the tide turning against him? Did Caesar mistake Cleopatra's adoration and love for the obedience and adherence of the Roman Senate? Or did love simply just make him stupid?

It is well known that on March fifteen he lost his life in a successful assassination by members of his peer group. The day has been noted in history as a day of treachery, deceit, and betrayal. A phenomenal man in history was murdered due to jealousy of his life, his power and even perhaps his happiness, happiness in the aura and rapture of Cleopatra. Egypt, the land of dreams, love, lust, and loss. Caesar fell victim to all when he fell in love with Cleopatra, Queen of Egypt.

Chapter 32

The next morning Spencer found his way to the parapet to say a final goodbye to Egypt. The early morning Egypt seemed to know they were bidding adieu and put her best foot forward. The rising sun created a yellow halo above the mountains that form Valley of the Kings. Vibrant colorful hot air balloons were out early dotting the sapphire sky, and melodic prayers reverberated across the atmosphere. Spencer could hear the noises of a stable waking up as the horses began to rustle and look for morning feed. Egypt waking up to another day. My how he would miss it. He packed and prepared for the day. He was going home and would be home tonight in his own bed. He turned to say goodbye to the room that had become his home in Egypt and blew a kiss.

The morning went fast and without incident. He arrived at the Zabr stables. The collection occurred with him as a witness and was placed in special packaging and placed in a carry on for Spencer. Mohammed Ahmd, Sekhmet's brother, was the only witness from the Zabr side. He was less than cordial and displayed an attitude that Spencer was leaving, so he really did not have to be gracious anymore.

However, Mohammed, his friend, did come to the car before it left for the airport to say his goodbye.

"Mohammed, I'm so pleased you made time to say goodbye."

"Spencer, my friend, I would not let you leave without a farewell."

"You have indeed been a friend, Mohammed. I thank you for guiding me through the ups and downs of my visit. I value your friendship so much." Spencer handed an envelope containing money as a gift to Mohammed for his assistance. "And I also need to tell the staff how much I appreciate them," Spencer declared.

"No problem, I will see that your belongings are loaded while you care for that," Mohammed graciously offered.

When Spencer returned the men shook hands and half hugged. Spencer found himself despondent as he realized he had said his last goodbye in Egypt. Within a short period of time, he was deposited at the airport only to reach Cairo for another flight home. He went through the routine like a robot. He did not feel like himself. He watched the desert disappear through the airplane window and his heart sank. It was over. He closed his eyes and forced himself to sleep as the plane flew fast and hard to take him home.

****

Mallory also took the day fast and hard. Knowing Spencer was on the way gave her renewed enthusiasm to make sure all was well when he arrived. She checked with Carson to be sure he was on point, which of course he was. All classes and lessons were covered. Horse and barn maintenance were on schedule. Groomsman were showing up to ready horses for their riders and training. Paperwork was organized and ready to be addressed. But she had not seen nor spoken to her parents. She felt she should tell them of Murdach's plans rather than leave it for Spencer to handle.

"Mal, come in," her father greeted, "your mom and I are having coffee on the patio. Spencer is on his way home. That should make your day!"

"Yes, with your little specimen. That should make your day," Mallory retorted.

"Hi, Mom!"

"Hi, Mal! What a nice surprise! Cav, get her a cup."

"Not necessary," Mal replied flashing her bottled water. She had finished with coffee some time ago.

Everyone took their seats. Mallory was trying not to show her shock at her mother's appearance. Although, she wore make-up, it did not hide the dark circles under her sunken eyes, or her grey, ashen color and although always thin, she was skeletal.

"So, are you ready for Spencer's arrival?" Cav inquired.

"Yes, I have missed him terribly," Mallory stated.

"How is wedding planning going?" Genevieve asked.

"Have an appointment coming up. I thought I put it on your calendar. Three designers are meeting with us."

"I wonder if they would care to meet here?"

"Why, Mother? Are you becoming a recluse?"

"No, no ... just thought it would be a more relaxed environment. We will go there. Let me know when we need to leave."

"I think your mom might be right, Mallory. Have the meeting here. Just stagger the appointments," Cav spoke up.

Mallory looked at her father and she felt he was sending her signals. She wasn't sure why, but she felt the need to go along with him.

"Sure, Mom! It really is a great idea! We will invite everyone here, serve lunch, then have a designer present. It will be a marvelous event and the who's who columns will be all over it!"

"Well, I don't know if your mom was planning a mega party, Mallory," Cav questioned.

"I will take care of it all. She won't have to do a thing but show up and look beautiful," Mallory volunteered. "Spencer will be here, and I will have time. If you prefer, we can have it at our house if up here is too much."

"You do as you want, Mallory. I will let our housekeeper know she will need more staff. I presume you will cater."

"Yes ... I'll give that some thought and order." Mallory began a mental list of bases to be covered. But she realized she needed to address the reason for which she had actually come. "Okay. I will keep you posted on plans as they unfold. But I really came to talk to you about something else."

Genevieve held her breath. She knew they were close to telling Mallory her situation, but she wanted that one special day. She wanted a day of joy with no clouds as they chose the dress.

"This is barn business," Mallory let that settle in on her parents.

"Murdach is leaving the barn and the business."

"Really!" Genevieve reacted.

"Yes, he has given me his plans for his exit. He says he does not have a contract. Is that so?"

"Yes, I tore it up in Russia."

Cav said nothing. No eruption, no frustration, no reaction. Mallory could not help but note.

"So, I guess he gets what he wants on the way out," Mallory said dejected.

"Where? Where is he going?" finally Cav spoke.

Mallory cleared her throat.

"Uncle Gil's. He is going to be second in command," Mallory answered.

"Really!" again Genevieve exclaimed.

"Yes. Uncle Gil has made him an offer that Murdach cannot refuse."

"How much?" Cav queried.

"He will be the barn and business manager at the normal rate. Will be the elite trainer and of course, train the filly."

"No. I mean how much, what percentage of the business?"

Mallory was shocked that her father knew the punch line before she delivered it. "I have not heard a number."

"Well, he will certainly regret this decision when he realizes what Spencer is bringing home in his back pocket," Genevieve interjected.

Mallory had not really thought about this perspective. Uncle Gil's ace was the filly. The package Spence was bringing will boast a Zabr Arabian which should be the final card played in that deck. That explained part of why her father was not more reactive to the betrayal. But he was not ruffled at all. "Spill it, Dad! Tell me what you have up your sleeve besides baby Zabr," Mallory insisted.

"We have another trainer lined up. I caught wind of Gil's intentions a while back. Does he think someday he will move on and have no one to leave his legacy to? Did he cry about the future of the filly that he won't be around to reap the rewards or as he put it, guide her to her stardom?"

Mallory instantly became embarrassed and mad that her uncle had pulled one over on her. He had not shared his heart and soul. He had simply recited a speech he obviously delivered on the drop of a dime.

"Do not fret, Mallory. I have been staying one step ahead of your Uncle Gil for a lifetime. You concentrate on dresses and parties and marrying the man of your dreams. I will take care of Gil and his devious plans," Cav directed.

"Yes, darling! Do not let this silly rivalry affect one minute of your happiness right now. Nothing matters … nothing … but you and Spence having the wedding you deserve," Genevieve echoed.

Mallory thought she picked up on a hidden agenda behind the emphasis on nothing in her mother's declaration, but she felt enough had been discussed for the day. She still had her fiancé returning tonight and now she had a party for thirty people or more in a few days. She began a mental list as soon as she gave hugs and left her parents.

Spencer exited the plane in New York in a daze. It was late in the day with grey skies which was all he saw as he made his way through customs. He barely made his connection to Dallas but settled himself and began to realize he was in America. He was home. When he landed in Dallas and the cold and freezing rain hit his face, he looked up as if he thought the sun would suddenly appear at midnight and warm his face. But he was met with icy wetness. The everyday warmth and inviting glow of the sun across the Sahara blanket was gone. He was home.

Chapter 33

Spencer sat in his office with his boots on the desk leaning back in his chair with his hat over his eyes. He had been home from Egypt for several weeks and he still had not acclimated. He found himself taking moments to remove himself and sink into his memories of Egypt. Sometimes he was in a temple reading hieroglyphics or on a boat sailing the Nile sitting across the table from Sekhmet admiring her from afar. It was a private world he could go to that gave him comfort and pain at the same time. He missed Sekhmet immensely. His dismay at not seeing her or Egypt again was deep and real.

He was making himself scarce. It turned out that Mallory's affair last Saturday when she shopped for her wedding gown design had made the Dallas society pages and national media. As a result, a national magazine was on the premises with a full crew doing a photo shoot of the bride in her natural surroundings. Mallory had not made or at least announced a final choice yet. He came home every night to find gown designs spread across every flat surface in the house and on several easels. Keeping the gown, a secret from the groom did not hold water here. He would know every stitch of her gown before the actual event. Mallory had asked his opinion several times. In all honesty when he looked at the drawings, the gowns all looked alike. Some had more skirts than others, but they were all long and white.

The wedding planning was beginning to take on a life of its own. He was entrenched in his thoughts of Egypt and dread of the pending wedding. He instantly felt guilty that he would be so selfish knowing that Mallory had the hardest days of her life in front of her. He had to admit that when he learned how meaningful the dress day had been for not only Mallory, but also Genevieve, he recognized it was huge for them to have these moments.

He was concerned when he returned from Egypt and saw Genevieve. She had become visibly weaker during his time in Egypt. He would be surprised if she was able to attend their wedding in June. That fact seemed incomprehensible. He made a promise to himself he would bite his tongue, shelve his feelings and frustration and support Mallory no matter how silly he found the wedding affair to be. He also knew he would be there for her when it all came crashing down.

His phone rang and he saw that Cav was calling.

"Hi, Cav."

"Spencer, I'm on my way down there. We have a problem."

"Okay. Anything I need to look at before you get here?"

"No, stay put. I am around the corner," Cav stated.

Spencer clicked off and went to meet him in the barn in case he wandered into the photo shoot. He knew that would not bode well with Mallory. As it turned out, he met Cav outside the barn.

"I just got a call from your father's office. We have a zero-count collection," Cav immediately stated.

"What?"

"Nothing is swimming in that tube!"

Spencer was stunned. He was there and witnessed the collection. The horse was a vital, healthy stallion of breeding quality. He did not understand. The specimen had only been in his and his father's hands. He knew his father would follow protocol for storage until time for insemination. Spencer asked the obvious question. "Have you spoken to Egypt?"

"No. I need to think this through. They may say we contaminated the specimen."

"There is no way. It never left my hands till I gave it to Dad. He put it immediately on dry ice. I saw him do it. The specimen was positive before it left Egypt bottom line. I am sure."

"Well, I will call Saad and give him the news. He will be a good ally to have if this becomes an issue. But the financial transaction is complete. I need to know that this was not done with intent."

Spencer searched his brain, and he believed the Zabr family, although ruthless and unyielding in some matters, to be honorable. He could not imagine them pulling a scam such as this. Spencer knew they highly valued their reputation and this devious activity in the international horse community would not be acceptable or tolerated. It made no sense.

"I am requesting a meeting tomorrow. It will be nine in our time. Be in my office."

Spencer had a restless evening thinking about the turn of events. No matter how he turned the kaleidoscope, he could not see the Zabr family guilty of such dishonesty. The only bad blood whatsoever was between him and Sekhmet's brother. But it was just a general dislike of each other. Spencer could not see Mohammed Ahmd throwing away reputation and standing because he did not care for Spencer's cowboy hat.

Mallory was full of endless chatter regarding the photo shoot and reliving the dress party.

"The producer of the shoot shared pictures of the party. She had about twelve hundred so I could not look at them all. But there were shots of everyone. Several were of Mom and I looking at the drawings. Of course, pictures of all the dresses they brought as samples. Today Sky stole the show! He was groomed to perfection, and he did live up to his image. The bridesmaids' dresses were pretty much chosen at the party as it turns out. I spoke to Maryam today. You know she is a maid of honor. She polled the girls and they all voted on an Anna Marie Fairbanks design. I guess I am ok with it, but they made a quick decision. As did Mom. She chose and ordered her dress. I was surprised that she did not want to do more shopping, but she insisted this was the dress. Your mom has ordered her dress from Christy Lane. So almost everyone is dressed but me. I don't know how I will ever make up my mind," Mallory finally drifted off into silence.

And just in time. Spencer had so much on his mind and a damn dress was not his priority. Someone had betrayed them. Someone he knew that he probably ate with, or rode with, or had beers with … someone he called friend had stabbed him in the back.

Mallory was standing in front of him holding a drawing of a gown in each hand when he realized she was expecting him to respond. He had totally missed the question.

"Spence, Spence what do you think … for goodness' sake … what zone are you in?" Mallory looked exasperated that Spencer had not given her his total attention.

"Better yet, where have you been since you have been back?" Mallory rephrased her question.

"Mal, don't pick a fight just because I can't choose a different dress every night to pacify your fancy."

"Wow! That was rude," Mallory stepped back sitting the drawings down.

"I do not mean to be rude. But you must know that if you walk down the aisle in jeans and a sweatshirt, I will be happy and think you are the most beautiful bride in the world. Choose a dress Mallory. It will be the perfect dress because you chose it. But this torment every night needs to end."

"Well, I do believe you do mean to be rude. Thinking that I could make the decision of what dress would be the dress to honor you and our life together requires a little more than the heads and tales of a coin toss," Mallory refuted and continued, "besides this isn't just about my indecision on my dress. You have been distant and remote since you returned from Egypt. Don't think I haven't noticed your lack of enthusiasm for anything going on around here. It's like you left your brain in Egypt."

Spencer almost said, "not my brain, Mal, but maybe my heart." But instead, he responded. "I apologize if you mistook my logic for rudeness, Mal. I do not intend to hurt your feelings whatsoever. I am serious that you will be breathtaking no matter what you wear, so it is a matter of level of breathtaking. Only you can determine that. I am sure you are unaware that we have an issue with the specimen. It turned out to be negative. I have a meeting with your dad and the Zabr's tomorrow at nine. That is why I am distracted."

He did not need to explain the seriousness and complexity of the specimen being negative. Hundreds of thousands of dollars had been expended and if the Zabr's were trying to run a scam ... well ... Mallory could not imagine such an occurrence.

"Wow! I get it now! How? How could the specimen be negative when you witnessed the collection and storage and handheld it coming home? How?" Mallory was as confused and taken aback as anyone. This was unheard of.

"I don't know Mallory. It never was out of my sight or hands. Your dad is calling Egypt tomorrow to make them aware of the situation. We'll see what their reaction is. I do not see your dad backing down on this whatsoever. But that family is like royalty. They are unlike any family unit we have in this country. They rule their world, and they are never questioned," Spencer said.

He stood walking towards the bedroom, "I am beat. A shower and bed are in my immediate future." He leaned down as he walked by and kissed Mallory on the head. "The one over there on the table at the top on the left. That is the one I like. But I will take you in riding gear riding an ass carrying an umbrella as long as you come down the aisle to me."

Mallory sat looking at the print that Spence had referred to. She smiled thinking to herself. "Of course, that would be your pick. It is my pick too. I just hated to end the fun. But I will order and announce next week."

Mallory felt relief that a decision had been made. But she found herself in a twisted maze wondering why she had to hear Spence validate her decision. They were so bonded. After all these years and the ups and the downs, living together, living apart, then back together, why was she doubting her beloved fiancé. She picked this man out as a young girl and had groomed him into the perfect man for her. He had never given her any reason to doubt him. But her gut, the gut that she shared with him on almost everything, was telling her. He has secrets. She had always been his confidante. But she could feel a part of him was someplace else.

She rose went to the table picked up the Sally Keene design and removing the current occupant put it on the easel. She turned off the lights and went to bed.

Chapter 34

Spencer awakened to a continental breakfast complete with mimosas. "I wanted to thank you for helping me make my decision. So, a little celebration before work was called for," Mallory explained when he entered the kitchen. She apparently chose to forgo her usual 5:30 am schedule.

Spencer was both aggravated and pleased with the greeting. He had a lot on his mind, and he wanted to get to the barn and take care of things so he would be ready for the Egypt call. But he also appreciated Mallory listening to him. He knew he needed to buy into this celebration, and he reminded himself that in a matter of a few months it would all be over. Life could resume without the wedding looming.

He was at the big house in Cav's office at 8:45 am. Cav welcomed him, but Spence could tell that Cav was troubled. Calling the Zabr's in Egypt and accusing them of scamming was intimidating at best. The call was FaceTime and projected on a large screen in Cav's office. Seeing Saad in Egyptian surroundings made Spence's heart leap. He missed so much about the country. Cav and Saad exchanged greetings and then Cav delved directly into the problem.

"I hear distress in your voice Cavanaugh."

"Saad, I am in distress. It seems the specimen arriving from Egypt is negative."

"Impossible! He has sired several great horses! I am not sure to take this as a joke or to be insulted Cavanaugh."

"Saad this is neither. This is a fact. The vet who happens to be Spence's father tested the specimen before storage and it is negative."

"Whose father?"

Spencer spoke up. "My father, Saad."

Saad looked perplexed. He began to speak very fast. "But you are responsible for safe transport. You must have let something happen. There is no way that the horse provided a negative collection. There has to be an explanation. We have never in the history of the Zabr family provided a negative specimen. Never!"

Spence spoke up. "Saad, we know and believe that the specimen was valid. I witnessed the entire process, and the specimen was under my control until I handed it to my dad. He has handled inseminations for over fifty years. I assure you I too am confused and baffled."

"Cavanaugh, have you spoken to any other family member regarding this dilemma?"

"No, Saad, my first call is to you. I would like you to use your influence to negotiate a mutually beneficial outcome for all parties. I don't need to remind you that payment in full has been deposited in the Bank of Egypt."

"No, I am mindful of the position all are in. I will request a meeting with Leader Zabr. I cannot speak for him. I can only relay the information."

"Ok, but I would appreciate a callback with intentions or resolution suggestions."

"Your call is forthcoming. I favor the opportunity to speak with you Cavanaugh, but I regret the circumstances."

The screen went black, and Spence looked at Cav. "What do we do now?" he asked Cav.

"We wait. We wait and give the Egyptians time to figure how the fuck I give them hundreds of thousands of dollars and receive a vial void of any swimming tails. How the fuck does that happen? We wait."

Knowing that her dad and Spence were occupied with the Egypt call, Mallory had a break and decided to visit her mom. She made a quick stop at her house and grabbed the pictures that had been taken at the wedding dress luncheon.

She found her mom upstairs in her bedroom resting. Mallory had never known her mom to take a nap early in the morning in her life and wondered if she was resting or had never arisen for the day at all.

"Mallory, you caught me napping! I'm embarrassed. I was up very late last night writing and still felt tired after breakfast. But I'm glad you are here! What brings you by?"

Mallory smiled and put the pictures in front of her mother. But inside she was gearing herself for what she knew was coming. What she knew had to come.

"Mallory! Let me see!"

They sat together on Genevieve's bed looking at the day through the lens of the photographers. The dining room and living room area had been set up for the designers to present their designs. The designers sat up in the nooks and crooks of the rooms with chairs in the middle for participants. As different presentations were made, the chairs could easily be positioned to face the presenter. Easels with designs were numerous and everyone enjoyed being able to amble through and see them up close.

The agenda was short but full. The designers and their representatives introduced themselves and their designs. The gowns that Mallory would choose from were custom and not available to actually see. But a fashion show of samples for each designer to showcase their styles offered an opportunity for Mallory to try on several gowns. She modeled in between the professional models.

After the runway show, everyone retired to the patio for brunch. Several tables were set up for guests. The tables were set with sky blue linens and silver and crystal tableware. Each table boasted a different centerpiece, but all were unified by the theme of sky blue and paper dolls adorned in beautiful gowns.

While dining, a second fashion show occurred with models strolling between tables wearing wedding styles for bridesmaids, flower girls, mothers of, etc. The event ended with a photo shoot of Mallory and guests.

The event provided a turf fertile with photo opportunities for the local and even the New York socialite media. The fashion pages were full of news of the designers that attended, and the affair was deemed a triumph for all involved.

Genevieve and Mallory perused the pictures noting different aspects. They reveled in sincerely approving of all and congratulating themselves for the last minute but highly successful predecessor to the upcoming showers and wedding events.

But the elephant was in the room. The photographs of the event reflected all ages of beautiful, healthy, in full bloom women. Genevieve photographed with her grey, waxen complexion, long sleeves and skirt which camouflaged her skeletal frame, dark circles under sunken eyes, and patches of thinning hair in what once was a lush crown. It was all there in front of their eyes.

"The picture of you and Maryam is so sweet and beautiful," Genevieve commented as she viewed a shot of Mallory and her best friend since they were young girls.

"Yes, Maryam has been supportive and helped out so much on all this. I appreciate her very much."

"She is a good friend, and she will certainly be there ..." Genevieve interrupted her thought as though she were about to say something she did not want to say, "will be there for you when I am not."

"Mom, are you going to tell me?"

Mallory looked sternly at her mother. Genevieve raised her gaze to meet her stare.

"Yes, I am going to tell you."

"When?"

"When would you like?"

"Mother do not play games with me. You are sick. I know that. My question is how sick?"

"The answer to that question would be serious. Terminally."

Mallory almost passed out. She was not expecting the word terminally. She had imagined her mother might not ride again or maybe even end up in a wheelchair. She had considered any number of what she considered the worst of options. But terminal never came up in her horror picture show.

"How long have you known? Who else knows? Dad?"

"We have known a few months. I have been in various treatments. I did not want to share until I knew the answers to your questions."

"And your answer is terminal?" Mallory searched her mom's face.

"Yes, I am afraid so, Mal," Genevieve felt the weight of having the conversation she had wanted to avoid. She had even selfishly hoped she would just pass in her sleep and never have to have this conversation. But it's hard to die without people close to you noticing.

Mallory could not believe how she was feeling. She thought she should be crying, sobbing, screaming. But all she could do was look at her mom and realize that in a short time she would never have that privilege again. She had been so blessed to have called a woman mom that the world saw as phenomenal, but none not even her, saw as mortal. In her perfect world Mallory had never considered her mom not being part of it.

"Mallory, I want you to take this information and deal with it. I know you want answers like how long and the like. But remember, most answers will only come when all has passed, and you are looking back. So, let's not dwell on the what ifs and what abouts. Take some time and then come back to see me and we will talk about the future and what I would like to see happen during and after my passing. I love you and your father very, very much. Being strong and leaving you at this time is incredibly hard. But then I ask myself when would be better?"

Mallory hugged her mom as she spoke, and her mom rubbed her as if she were rubbing a prized horse. Most moms pat, but Genevieve rubbed which horses prefer. To know that the rub that she had known all her life would go away put a major lump in Mallory's throat and tears began to trinkle down her cheeks.

"Now, now, Mallory. I can only be so stalwart. We will be okay. You will be okay. I will certainly be in clover in heaven taking care of God's steed and waiting on your dad and someday you. You must believe that. We will be reunited in God's house. But first we must leave ours. Wipe your tears. We have a lot of living to do, and we will not do it somberly but with love and purpose as we always have. Now that I am not hiding from you come see me anytime, night or day. We have lots to do."

Another hug between mother and daughter that was as precious as the hug they experienced when Mallory was born. Then Mallory stood up to leave.

"The barn ... it is pretty much yours now, go take care of it. I am so fortunate to call you my daughter Mal because I know you will care for the ranch, your dad, and your family just as I would want. Gives me comfort."

"Mom, Dad knows, but does Spence?" Mallory turned and asked as she was exiting the door.

"Yes, Mallory and sworn to silence by my wishes. Do not be angry. It has been a burden for him. Free him from this burden."

Mallory removed all the pictures and covered her mom with a quilt before she left. She did something that they rarely did. She kissed her mom on the cheek. Genevieve reached up and touched Mallory's cheek. For a moment time stood still and they were little girl and mom instead of grown woman and dying lady. For a brief brisk second neither felt anything but the joy of the bond between mother and daughter.

Spencer saw her as he was leaving his office. She was walking down the barn aisle towards him, and he could see with every step a bit more of her crumble. When she reached him, he knew beyond a doubt that the conversation that needed to be had was now history. By the time they reached his office she was sobbing. He had rarely seen Mallory cry, much less sob. His heart was broken for her, and he held her until her weeping turned into sniffling and a zombie demeaner.

He took her home and put her to bed as she vacillated between bursts of grief and restless sleep. He did not sleep well either. His night was spent worrying about Mallory and what would be the response and outcome of the call to Egypt. He knew his credibility was on the line because only he had access to the specimen. But all he could do was wait.

Mallory awoke the next morning to the conversation occurring between Spence and her father in the kitchen.

"She had a difficult night, did she?" Cav asked.

"Yes, Cav. She barely slept between fits of sobbing. She is beside herself with grief."

Spencer looked at Cav and saw an old man with his head hanging, slumping posture, depicting a picture of defeat. Spencer had never seen Cav defeated. He was always up for the challenge and thrived on it. But terminal cancer was not an enemy he could outsmart or buy out. Spencer felt such empathy for him.

"Well, I will go and let her sleep. Tell her I came by. I will see you at the barn later."

Almost like Cav knew what Spencer was thinking, he changed his demeanor. He became the crusty, unemotional Cav that Spence recognized.

"I have matters at the barn. Murdach is leaving today. I want to personally bid him goodbye and good luck. He will need it being Gil's right-hand man. I don't guess Murdach has wondered why Gil hasn't had a right-hand for how many years now. Fifty maybe. There is a reason for that."

"Is that why you have not been worried about his leaving?"

"Nooooo ... noooo," Cav replied, "I have a plan and Murdach is a variable in the plan. I can and will succeed with or without him. But I will leave the door open when he tires of Gil and his antics." With that farewells were said, and Cav left for the barn.

Mallory pulled the pillow over her head as she considered how she could face the day after yesterday and forced herself to sleep instead. Spencer sat down with some paperwork and began a process that he despised. He began to wait. Right now, it seemed his whole life was on hold, and he was on pause. He had no idea how everything would unravel but he knew one thing. Life as they knew it was changing and he knew in six to nine months nothing would be the same.

Chapter 35

A fact of life is that no matter what happens, the sun comes up the next day. No matter the human condition or situation, the next day happens. The demands do not go away no matter the suffering or pain. The sun comes up and one must face the day and what it brings.

And so, it was at the ranch. Mallory began a brutal routine that included teaching her students and classes and assuming her mom's. She visited her mom every day and had dinner with her several times a week. What had been Mallory's agenda for so long which was training Sky for the Olympics, took a backseat to caring for her mom and the barn.

Spencer did not know whether to complain of neglect or sing Mallory's praises as she made every minute count with her mom. He respected and knew that the day when this would not be an issue would come too soon. Thus, he found himself immersed in barn and ranch duties and trying to absorb more responsibility to allow both Mallory and Cav to spend as much time as possible with Genevieve.

Even with gloomy prospects for the upcoming new year, December was upon them. Mallory and Cav were faced with planning Genevieve's last holiday. Normally the barn hosted a holiday party that included neighbors, clients, other trainers, and horse celebrities. The King Equestrian Center Christmas party was a traditional event for many. But neither Mallory nor Cav could muster planning such an event. Both were despondent as they considered participating in holiday decorating and other Christmas celebratory rituals. And to their surprise it was Genevieve from her sickbed that made the plans for Christmas at the ranch.

"What? Mother! How can we host a Christmas dinner in two weeks? I ... well I ... Dad ... we ... well .... we," Mallory stuttered.

"Are you two so into your own damn self-pity and self-interest to not continue our traditions whether I am here or not? Are you going to cancel the International Exhibition too? Please tell me next Christmas should I not be here that you won't cancel Christmas! We will do what we have always done! I want a Christmas party and I shall have one that I have the joy of planning. You and your dad need only worry about being on time. December 21. Put it on your calendar."

Genevieve spent the next few days hiring a party planner and going over decorations, food, and entertainment with her. As she promised Mallory, she chose everything for the party and was excited in her emancipated state that she would attend with God's grace one more King celebratory affair. She did agree that after the party she would be content with a small family Christmas dinner. Normally she would invite close friends and neighbors and of course extended family. But she knew the party would take a lot out of her, so she succumbed to Cav and Mallory's wishes.

Mallory was surprised and pleased at how her mom threw herself into the party planning. Genevieve had her home adorned with several Christmas trees decorated elegantly with different themes such as angels, snowmen, and other Christmas standards. But the huge tree that sat in the foyer was all about horses. Genevieve ordered hand painted horses of all colors and motifs. She used rope as garland and the top of the tree was her last trophy for international showing. Traditional garland and arrangements embellished all areas of the house representing every Christmas theme and turning the home into a Christmas paradise. Buffet food with specific food stations were throughout the courtyard gardens and pool area. Christmas lights were hung generously so lighting was plentiful. The barn was also decorated with each stall garnished in Christmas trimming and garland strung between. She had a false floor installed in the arena and a western band was hired to entertain and offered a place to dance. Christmas was everywhere you looked!

"Wow! Your mom did a fantastic job planning this party, Mal. No one would ever believe she is as ill as she is," Spence commented.

"I know. I think it has been good for her even with her failing energy. She has come to the barn a couple of times to observe. I love seeing her there, but it makes me sad that she can't ride anymore. She told me she rides through me. But she hasn't lost her eye that's for sure. She gave Sky and I a critique the other day that would have burned paper on the sidewalk. I think she wants me to remember what it is like to have Genevieve King evaluate your performance."

Both she and Spence laughed at her comment. Spence made a mental note that it was good to hear Mal laugh. Laughter had been scarce for the past few weeks. He originally thought it insane to throw a Christmas bash for two hundred people under the circumstances, but it seemed to have helped both Genevieve and Mal to live through this hard time. This hard time of waiting for the future to unfold.

The party itself was a complete triumph. The guests were overwhelmed with the hospitality and atmosphere. And although there were those that had their concerns confirmed that Genevieve King was very ill when she attended in a wheelchair, the overtone of the party was jovial and merry. Spence and Cav were both grateful that the party for a short period of time had interrupted the continuous grieving of Mal and that Genevieve had been able to concentrate on something besides living or dying.

It was late in the evening that Cav sought Spence out for a nightcap. Genevieve had retired long ago, and Mal was still socializing with guests that had not left.

"Nice affair, Cav. I think everyone had a splendid time," Spence offered as he sat down.

"Yes, I'm proud for Genevieve. This was quite an accomplishment. I was extremely touched when she posed so proudly for the media in her wheelchair. She is such a confident, secure person even in …" Cav stopped before he finished the thought.

Spencer picked up on the conversation. "Yes, Cav. She is an amazing woman. She has spent most her of life in the spotlight under pressure and she seems to thrive in it."

"And how is Mal doing? Really?" Cav questioned.

"She is living with the inevitable, Cav. Her heart is broken, and I think she lives the day that she loses her mother every day. Genevieve insisting that she continue to train for the Olympics helped in a way by giving her permission not to spend every waking minute at Genevieve's bedside. But she has fits of depression that I suppose only I see. She is much like her mom. Strong, confident and refuses to expose her pain publicly."

"Well, the party is over so I am not sure what will get us through the next thirty days," Cav moaned.

"The wedding activities should begin at warp speed which hopefully will have the same positive energy for them."

"I am considering reaching out to Saad. I have heard nothing from Egypt and my patience is wearing thin," Cav sounded exasperated.

"I feel you on that, Cav. This waiting is driving me crazy. I feel I need to defend my actions on the delivery, and I have no one to defend myself against. I know that I did nothing to compromise the cargo. It was still in the same dry ice that it was originally packed in. The thermometer reflected the correct temperature. I saw it packed and secured and unpacked."

"I know, son. I know. I do not believe for a minute this is your failing. Whatever happened, happened in Egypt, not here. I just hope they understand that."

"Well, if you decide to call Egypt, please let me know I would like to be there," Spencer requested.

"I will but I may do it impromptu because of the time difference. But you will know the outcome immediately after the call."

Spencer nodded his head in approval. But he was thinking to himself that Cav did not want him on the call. Cav was willing to be discreet behind his back to work this out and that felt like Cav was not totally supportive. It bothered him that Cav had contact with Egypt that he was not privy to. Spencer took his last drink and stood.

"Great party, Cav. My best to both you and Genevieve."

Cav nodded his goodbye with a toast in the air.

Spence found Mal and indicated his desire to leave. She told him to go without her. She would follow after everything was closed down. Spence took a golf cart and headed towards home. But he was concerned why Cav would not want him on the call to Egypt. He could not really fire Spence considering Spence was marrying his daughter in nine months. Spence always found Cav to be open and honest to a fault. But he had to be honest. Cav had hundreds of thousands invested in this venture. Spence did not.

Christmas Day came, and the Christmas dinner was small and somewhat rushed. Genevieve was unable to eat anymore and was having an unusually bad day. Cav did not mention if he had spoken to Egypt in the last week. The week between Christmas and New Year's came and went and Cav did not share any details of any call. Spence was beside himself waiting. Waiting was not his strong suit and he felt he was being tested.

Approaching New Year's Day, Spencer was in turmoil. Waiting to hear Egypt's response to the mishap was brutal. But in addition, his dreams, his daydreams his thoughts were filled with Egypt and Sekhmet. The beauty and mystery of Egypt haunted him. He could smell her, be blinded by her smile, mesmerized by her eyes, and spellbound by her kiss in his dreams. With these thoughts he was frustrated that he did not trust Cav and felt he should. And he was tormented by the unfulfilled lust he felt for a woman on the other side of the world when he had the perfect lady in his bed every night.

New Year's Eve was a quiet dinner without Genevieve's presence. She was physically unable to attend. So, it was family including Gil and Spencer's parents, and a few close friends. Cav was cordial and a pleasant host. But it was not a jovial gathering. It seemed all recognized that this year would be difficult for the Kings and celebrating it was futile.

The dinner conversation centered around Gil's unhappiness with Murdach. It was a small intimate group, so Gil felt comfortable expressing his displeasure of Murdach's training methods in particular with the Arabian filly.

"What exactly do you object to Gil?" Cav asked mainly to be polite.

"His so-called European methods. I don't want an Arabian prancing around the ring like a Lipizzaner. He is ruining her natural movement. I need an Arabian trainer with that filly that's all there is to it."

"Have you contacted the Arabian council? They would know who to recommend," Cav offered secretly finding Murdach in this situation self-satisfying after his desertion of them.

"No, I don't want someone who has spent years training Arabians their way and therefore the community accepts their theories as divine inspiration and carved in stone! No, I want a true Arabian trainer. I am currently talking to an elite Egyptian family about providing such a trainer."

That comment caught Cav's attention, but he did not want to show his hand to Gil in case Gil was baiting him. Spencer felt the tension and began to tune in to the conversation in dismay. It was New Year's and no one, especially Genevieve and Mal deserved a Gil – Cav episode.

"Really," Cav remarked.

Cav also was aware this was not the place to pursue this conversation. He knew how quickly things could turn bad with Gil. But Gil's connection to Egypt was more than intriguing. He would be investigating this development.

"Well, let us toast to Gil's outstanding filly with a stellar future and his endeavor to find the trainer that will carve the road for that to happen." Spencer caught Cav's eye across the table, and he knew instantly that Cav was hiding an agenda behind the smile and the sparkling champagne.

It was a little after midnight when everyone bid a Happy New Year's to each other with hugs and kisses. Although Genevieve had remained in her room, she did come down for the New Year commenting she would not miss it. And so, it was a bit somber, but yet very special as toasts were made and the moment with her shared. The few guests began to say goodbye and leave when Spencer saw his phone blinking a FaceTime call. His head spun, his heart stopped, and he dashed for privacy.

"Hello," he answered breathlessly watching as the screen cleared and there she was, Sekhmet in front of him. It was bizarre to be standing in the King's laundry room looking at the beautiful, alluring Sekhmet. Spencer was in total surprise because they agreed not to contact each other once he left Egypt.

"Hello, Spencer. I hope I have not disturbed your holiday revelry?"

"No, not at all. We are wrapping up. I am surprised to receive a call from you."

"I started to text, but I wanted to wish you a Happy New Year in person ... sort of."

They both laughed. Suddenly, he relaxed. It was Sekhmet. It was the lady he roamed Egypt with and discovered a part of himself he didn't know existed.

"Happy New Year to you too, Sekhmet! I'm pleased to hear from you! What time is it there?"

"It is sunrise here. Look!"

Sekhmet held her phone up and Spencer was looking at the Egyptian sunrise. His heart skipped a beat. You try to remember how breathtaking the Egyptian sunrise is, but memory did not begin to do it justice.

"Ahlan, Spencer! I have called to make your New Year shall we say brighter!"

"You make everything brighter, Sekhmet," Spencer flirted.

But he meant it. She sat in front of him like a living Cleopatra with her dark hair and dark eyes in that mahogany skin. She was easily the most beautiful woman in the world.

"And you are ... what is it you say in America ... silver tongued?"

Again, they both laughed. Spencer noted their banter came easy. They picked up where they left off.

"Spencer, I have another reason to call you besides glad tidings. You will receive good news regarding the negative specimen very soon. My father and I have consulted. He believes that whatever occurred to have such a devastating result, it was not your fault or the fault of your father-in-law. Spencer, I hope to see you soon again."

Spencer deduced that Sekhmet had gone to bat for him. He knew she was a favorite of her father, and her influence was invaluable. Silently he had depended on her to work this matter out. But he dared not share with Cav the reason behind his optimism.

"Be patient, Spencer. The news will come soon, and all questions answered. Inshallah, Spencer."

"I will wait for destiny to unfold, Sekhmet. Happy New Year!"

"Happy New Year Spencer!"

The screen went black. Spencer stepped out of the laundry room and put his phone in his pocket. He was trying to contain his feeling of elation. He was trying to process what this short conversation meant. It meant that the Zabr family did not hold him accountable. It meant that they recognized the honesty that prevailed regarding the handling of the specimen stateside. It meant they were going to make things right with Cav. It meant … he had to hold his breath … because it meant he was going back. He was going back to Egypt and back to Sekhmet.

Chapter 36

The initial elation turned into anxiety and apprehension. As Spencer watched Cav struggle daily wondering what the Zabr family's response would be. Spencer felt guilty knowing it would be okay. He trusted Sekhmet without question. But he knew when Egyptians say shortly it does not mean the same to Americans. Egyptian time was in good time and rarely right now.

But there was so much more on Cav's shoulders. His wife was dying and not expected to live past tomorrow but continued to fight the battle. Spencer admired Genevieve for her fierceness and courage, but he was watching Cav and Mallory suffer daily as they waited for the inevitable. In the meantime, the barn was suffering with Murdach's departure and Mallory backing off training to be with Genevieve. He had for all intents and purposes lost three national/international trainers at once and the barn was taking a beating.

Mallory could not absorb both Genevieve's and Murdach's clients and maintain her own packed training schedule. He was genuinely concerned for her and felt for her. She was grieving her mom, comforting her dad, trying to plan a wedding, and shouldering more than anyone could possibly handle at the barn. There was such duress at the barn it was difficult to keep the public from knowing the depth of the wounds. Spencer was watching the tractor drag the arena as all of this rolled around in his mind. Along with guilt that deep down even with all the empathy, sympathy and love he felt for Mallory, he was holding his breath wondering would he really see Egypt and Sekhmet again.

His thoughts about Cav's state of mind were validated as he watched Cav walk down the aisle of the barn towards him. Cav always had a presence. He did not strut, but his walk was solid and with purpose. Even horses seem to come to attention when he strolled by as though they knew he was the one that was responsible for their good life. But today, his walk was almost a shuffle, he was distracted, and his energy affected no one. He looked years older and almost unkept. He did not look like Cavanaugh King in any way. Spencer's heart broke as he greeted Cav.

"Hi, Cav. What brings you to the barn?" Spencer inquired.

"Spence," Cav acknowledged Spencer's greeting.

"How are things with Genevieve?" Spencer again inquired.

"She is holding her own but losing in the long run. I don't know how much longer she can hang on. The lady is tough as nails," Cav stated.

Spencer listened. There were no words that could express the sorrow he felt.

"I think I worry more about Mallory than Genevieve. At least we know Genevieve will not be here to deal with the loss. I have decided dying is quite selfish. She will be in heaven, and we are left on earth to grieve for her, to miss her, to live her absence every day."

"Mallory will be okay, Cav. I will be here taking care of her. We will have some tough days, but we will get through them. I will be sure she will never feel alone in her sadness. I promise."

"We have no choice, Spencer. For the first time in my life, I have no choices, no alternatives, no schemes, no way out ..."

Spencer remained quiet as Cav wandered off in his statement. He just didn't know what to say. Genevieve was going to die. No one knew when, only God. No matter what, it was a hard pill to swallow for all of them. She was like a superhuman in life. She was a respected, loved, admired, internationally known equestrian. In the international horse scene, she was an icon. And all the while running a distinguished barn training some of the most renowned horses in the world. But none of that mattered now. All that mattered was she was dying.

Cav looked up, caught the soulful expression on Spencer's face and decided to change the subject. There were other concerns that needed addressing.

"Spencer, what have you heard from Gil's place?"

"Not a word, Cav. I have been too slammed here to even check it out."

"Well, based on Gil's tirade New Years I would venture to say there is trouble in paradise. I would be interested to know Murdach's side of the story. As if I don't."

"I'll put my ears to the ground and see what I can gather. But Cav are you thinking of bringing him back?"

"Well, I am more interested in knowing what Gil's connection is in Egypt. I am beginning to put this and that together and I am suspicious that the Zabr's may be playing both sides of the coin and I'm the loser."

"What!" Spencer exclaimed.

"Well, I'm doing business with the family, and so far, they have my money and I have nothing. What a nice outcome for Gil, don't you think?" Cav explained. "And icing on the cake, they allow one of their trainers to come to the US to train the filly? Be a nice package for Gil, a nice package."

Spencer was flabbergasted. He knew that this scenario was not even close to the truth as far as the Zabr's being deceitful and stealing hundreds of thousands from Cav. What Gil might be up to regarding changing trainers, he did not know but was sure he could find out. And he was certain that Cav was jumping to conclusions regarding the Zabr's pulling a scam on him with Gil in the driver's seat.

"Cav, I see why you might go there. But I think you are overestimating Gil's influence and underestimating your influence. Think about it. You are always two steps ahead of Gil. You have said that yourself. You believed in that fully not too long ago. I know the weight of life is heavy now, but you are still Cavanaugh King no matter what. The Cavanaugh King I have always known, would not let Gil's rants shake his confidence in his orchestrated outcomes or in his partners that he had cultivated. I urge you to wait a little longer. Things take a long time in Egypt. An investigation must be like climbing Mount Everest for them. I found nothing but people I believe to be honorable in the Zabr family. Take heart that you will achieve what you set out to do."

Cav sat for a moment letting Spencer's words sink in. "How and when did you become so smart Spence?"

"I only know what you and my father modeled for me all my life. Integrity, straight forwardness, and common sense."

Cav stood to leave. "You are an outstanding individual Spence. Both your dad and I are very proud of you and who you have become. I know the barn business is in the tank right now. But I also know that you will it bring back and I need not worry."

"Cav, you are right. The training issues will have to be addressed. But I feel that it is disrespectful to worry about the next international trainer when we are waiting for another's demise. All of this will unwind and work out. Genevieve is our focus now."

Cav nodded his head in agreement and walked to the door to exit. Spencer could not help but note that he stood a little straighter and walked a little more like Cav's usual gait. But on his leaving Spencer felt guilty that he was so well thought of but hid a terrible, horrible secret yearning.

That evening Spencer arrived home before Mallory. He knew she was with Genevieve and would be exhausted. He started the grill and was in the midst of making a salad when Mallory made her appearance. He noted immediately how worn she looked. He had seen her up twenty-four hours nursing a sick horse or traveling all night to a competition and arriving fresh as a daisy to perform. But an hour with her mother now sucked up all her energy and stamina.

He agreed with Cav. He did not know how Mallory was going to get through losing Genevieve. He just didn't know.

"How is your mom?"

"She is status quo. She is pretty much on oxygen all the time now. So, it is hard to talk much. She doesn't have the strength to talk a lot anyway. The feeding tube seems to be doing its job. But no more getting out of bed."

"I'm sorry Mallory. I know this is hell for you."

"For all of us, Spence. For all of us. I love her so much, and it is so hard to watch her just deteriorate. And she is insisting that we go forward with the wedding. Who feels like getting married?"

"Mallory, she only wants your happiness."

"Well, she is also insisting that Sky and I go to Japan. Go to Japan when your mom is taking her last breath. I don't think so. We have lost too much time anyway."

"Well, I think you should compromise. I know you have not had time to train effectively with Sky but even if you miss Japan, you can still qualify for Olympics next year. Just one less notch on your belt. So, agree with her to continue with the wedding plans but dropping the pressure of Japan. Explain to her that you would need my support and presence and I cannot imagine leaving the barn right now."

"I don't know, Spence. I don't know anything right now. I am thinking of cancelling the wedding. I can't get married without her."

"Mallory, I will be there. I will be at the end of the aisle waiting for you to walk down it. Your mom will be everywhere looking on from above. I promise you we will all be happy that day. Let your mom pass if she does, knowing that day will happen. And on the outside chance that she lives to see the day, how would you feel if you had canceled everything and then she didn't live to see a second date? You must go forward with the wedding."

Spencer was amazed that he was talking Mallory into the wedding that he actually had never wanted. The justice of peace on a beach would suit him well. But he knew that Genevieve would be heartbroken if she thought the wedding had been postponed.

"Okay. I will talk to her. Better yet. You talk to her. Today she actually asked me to ask you to come see her. I told her I would ask you to come by on the way to the barn. She is usually better in the morning than in the evenings. You negotiate your own compromise."

"I will go by in the morning. Let's have some dinner. I have the wine on the table already."

Chapter 37

The next morning Mallory was up at her usual five and out the door before Spence had coffee and checked his e-mail. He wasn't putting off visiting Genevieve, but he wasn't rushing either. As much as he loved Genevieve, seeing her on her deathbed was disturbing. He was up to most things but watching her die was heartbreaking.

The King bedroom had been transformed into a hospital room. Two nurses in uniform were attending to monitors, medications and who knew what. The king-size bed had been replaced with a hospital bed and in place of the bedroom furniture stood hospital equipment for lifting and transporting Genevieve as needed. The only remembrance of the former beautifully adorned room were the curtains that hung on the floor from tall windows. He knew Genevieve loved them open to allow visibility of the sunlight and views of the barn. But today they were closed. The room was as solemn and dismal as it could possibly be.

"Genevieve, it's Spence."

She was lying in bed in an oxygen tent and appeared to be sleeping. She was a skeleton with little hair and black circles for eyes. He was instantly distraught when he realized that Mallory was watching her mom wither away to nothing. His river of sadness overran the banks.

"Spence. You came. Thank you. I wasn't sure if Mal would ask you."

"Well, I apologize for not being here more often."

"Apology not necessary. I know everyone has their hands full." Genevieve began to cough. The nurse came to help her with a machine that pulled the mucus from the throat. She wasn't strong enough to clear her own throat. When she caught her breath, she continued. "I recognize that you are under the gun trying to fill five roles, me, Cav, Mallory, Murdach and your own business. This is a hard time for sure I know."

"Genevieve, please do not worry or fret about barn business. It will all work out. The barn has been through hard times many times and we are still here."

"I trust you Spence. I trust you to see Cav and Mallory through this. Knowing you are there for them to lean on and depend on makes this sojourn so much easier." She coughed again and the nurse attended to her. Spence decided to take the moment.

"Genevieve, I do want to talk to you about Mallory if you are up to it."

"Mallory? Is there something wrong with Mallory?"

Spence could not help but think, "no Genevieve, her mom is dying, her barn and life are turned upside down, her father is basket case, why would something be wrong with Mallory?"

"She has too much on her Genevieve. She is trying to cover as many bases as me. She is working trying to cover your clients, Murdach's clients, and her own. She is beating herself up because she can't find time to work Sky and doubting her ability to show in Japan. And in between all of this she is trying to plan a wedding."

"And nurturing her dying mother. I see, Spence. I see why she looks like a raggedy mop doll when she sits before me," another coughing fit.

"Genevieve, I think it would be better if Mallory put Japan on the back burner."

"No, no!" Another coughing episode.

"I know Japan is important to her. She needs to compete to ensure that she makes it to the Olympics. You know that Spence."

"Genevieve, let me ask you. What if it is impossible for Mallory under the circumstances to compete successfully in Japan? What if the time and training she is able to put in, which is very limited now, isn't enough? She will be devastated coming in fourth or fifth. You know that."

"Is her time that limited? She should make a Japan a priority?" Coughing again.

"Genevieve, she can't. There is too much on her plate. Plain and simple."

"So, what are you asking of me Spence?" It seemed so callous to be asking anything of this dying woman. "Help her to make the decision to withdraw from Japan and concentrate on what you and she want most, a beautiful, romantic perfect wedding." Coughing once more. He could see that she was tired. "Is that what you think is best for her? Does she not need distractions from my circumstance?"

"Mallory will be better not having the pressure of Japan on her plate. There will be other alternatives and she will make the Olympics, I promise you. But give her your blessing if she bows out of Japan."

"If you think that is the wise thing to do, Spence, I shall follow your advice. You are an amazing, sensitive honorable man, Spence. Mallory could not find anyone on this earth so worthy of her love. Your lives will be blessed with understanding, compassion, and honesty. I could ask for nothing more for my daughter."

Spence instantly felt the knife in his chest. To have this failing lady impart her confidence in his love, his honesty and integrity when he knew that deep down inside, the love was not enough to keep lust for another woman from his heart. His honesty and integrity were in the dirt. He was a fake and he desperately needed to confess his transgressions. "Genevieve, I appreciate your feelings, but ..." Spence paused. He was in turmoil. The burden of his wanton desires was heavy and overbearing, "but I am not necessarily as honorable as you make me out to be."

"Shhhhhh, I don't know why you would make such a statement. And I do not want to know. But whatever the reason, Spence, keep it to yourself. Work it out with yourself. Be kind to yourself. But most of all be kind to those around you that love you and believe in you. Keep your confessions of inadequacy to yourself. I have discovered in this life, unrealized dreams are the demons that haunt us when we rest at night. Manage your demons, Spence."

With that said she laid her head back as a dismissal. A ten-minute conversation had totally taken her strength. A lady that would ride horses from dawn to midnight and never lose her focus or energy or enthusiasm could not converse but for minutes. Spence leaned over and kissed her forehead. He had never made such a gesture before. Genevieve had always seemed untouchable. He rarely over the years had an occasion to hug her. She was aloof in a friendly way but was obviously not fond of physical affection. She opened her eyes when he took the liberty and smiled at him. He instantly regretted he had not spent more time in Genevieve's company. He would miss her.

He returned to the barn to discover that two patrons had ended up in a quarrel that had become physical. Apparently, one did not appreciate the constructive criticism of their horse that was thrown their way. People were standing in the aisles, some in front of stalls, all gaping and gawking. Spencer was instantly angry that two adult men could let their tempers get out of control in an inappropriate place. What is more, he knew he would be expected to take some sort of action. Evict one or both from the barn. Be the judge of who was in the wrong. He was tempted to call the authorities and have both arrested. The drama never stops in a competitive barn. He had just defused the situation when he heard Cav.

"Spence, Spence," Cav had come out of the office and was calling him. Spencer noted he seemed excited, "Come in, sit, I have news."

Finally. Spence thought to himself finally. The waiting was over.

"Saad has contacted me. The Zabr's are certain the issue did not occur in mishandling of the specimen. Saad would not elaborate, but they are requesting to replace the dud. Leader Zabr will be contacting me personally to discuss the matter. In the meantime, you need to get ready to return to Egypt."

There it was. The invite, the demand, the license to do what he most wanted to do, return to Egypt.

"Cav, the barn is in straits right now. Mallory is thinking of giving up Japan to devote more time here. Genevieve is certain to pass soon. You are in no mental state to run the barn in my absence. How do you see this coming down?"

"Nonsense! I was running a barn when you were in knee pants, Spence. I can certainly keep a lid on things for a few days. I will have Carson to help me. The two of us with the crew will be fine. You are the only one I can count on and the only one the Zabr family will accept."

"When?"

"I will know after I talk to Leader Zabr. That should be very soon. Saad said that he is anxious to resolve this issue. Which considering he has spent almost two months to even contact us is a joke in my mind."

Spence immediately thought to himself, Egyptian time. *"Should I tell Mallory?"*

"Well, it is going to upset her. But she has to understand that we are just trying to collect what is owed to us. We are going to have our bloodline, Spence! We are going to possess the most valuable horse in North America. We are starting a legacy that will have profound influence on the equine industry. I was so afraid we were being defrauded. But we are not. The dream is alive and real! I am on my way to tell Genevieve. She will be ecstatic."

Spence could not imagine the lady he spent time with earlier being ecstatic. He felt a bit off balance. Dreaming about going back to Egypt and actually going was playing with his emotions and mind. He was on a path that would leave him no choice but to deal with his demons.

Chapter 38

"No! Absolutely not! Not now! Dad is crazy! We are falling apart, and he is sending you off for another fruitless escapade in Egypt! No! Is being a fool once not enough for him?"

Spence had never seen Mallory lose it so completely. He could tell her stress was overwhelming and his running off to Egypt again was the last straw. He walked over to put his arms around her. "Don't! Don't try to cajole me! You are in this with Dad! Both of you are chasing some damn dream that isn't going to come true! And in the meantime, good ole Mallory will hold the fort down all by herself! Forget the fact that my mother is dying! That I may wake up tomorrow or the next day and my best friend will be gone forever! And you are going to leave me! Don't even try to console me! You are both inconsiderate, selfish jackasses!" With that she flew to the bedroom and slammed the door.

The next morning did not find Mallory in much better humor. She was up at five and out the door before she and Spencer had any contact other than a muttered good morning. He felt he needed to give her space. He called Cav last night to warn him of Mallory's wrath. Cav said not to worry that Mallory would be handled. Spencer wondered about that statement. Is that how Cav perceived the people he loved so dearly, as being handled to suit his purpose? Was Mallory, right? Cav was manipulating him and her to get what he wanted. And what was worse was that Genevieve was on her deathbed.

He arrived at the barn with a full schedule. Carson was asking to work less hours. The man was nearly seventy years old and had been at the barn for over forty years. Spence had to honor such loyalty and dedication. Carson was more than just a good friend or long time hired hand. Carson was family. So, in the midst of the headliners fading into fog, he needed a new second in command.

He had interviews set up. He knew what he was looking for, but he also knew he would have to talk to a lot of people to find it. His day was full, but he felt his blood rushing through his body as he anticipated and begin to make plans for another journey to Egypt.

Mallory arrived at the big house that morning after her first early class looking for her father. As it turned out he was not home. He was being honored at a civic club meeting and would not be back until early afternoon. Mallory swallowed the anger that was boiling inside her and went upstairs to visit her mother.

Genevieve was lying quietly under her tent. Mallory thought she was asleep but was surprised when Genevieve spoke.

"Mallory, is that you?"

"Yes, Mom."

"Come and sit with me," Genevieve coughed.

"Are you sure? You were sleeping."

"No, I was actually lying here thinking of you."

"What are you thinking Mom?" Mallory sat down beside her mom on the side of the bed so Genevieve could see her. To help with her breathing, Genevieve sat up with support most of the time. It was hard to look at her mom. Her voice was weak, she looked so sick and frail.

"Mallory, I visited with Spence. He mentioned the stress you are under with so much on your plate. I know I have pushed you to work hard for Japan and insisted you continue with your wedding plans while you try to take over barn training pretty much by yourself. I think that is too much for any one person to manage especially with circumstances as they are."

"Soooooooo, drop Japan, don't marry Spence and runaway to Egypt." Mallory instantly felt guilty that her anger and sarcasm had

209

come out toward her mom, even as her mom coughed and required attention. She had to rein it in. She had to.

"Mallory, I am suggesting that you put Japan on the back burner. It is acceptable to recognize that you are unable to devote the time and work required for both you and Sky because of circumstances beyond your control. Rarely would I suggest someone give up a competition. But I am hoping to attend your wedding. I lay here and will myself to be at that wedding. So, I cannot ask you to change that date. And we cannot change my circumstance. So that brings you to training issues."

"Like there are no trainers, Mom?"

"Mallory, before you can remember this barn did not have the reputation or the success that it has had most of your life. Riders were not standing in line at the gate to be trained. Your father and Gil destroyed a lot of what your grandparents built with their endless feud! We were never destitute, but we were hopeless at times. I was over thirty before my star began to shine, Mallory. I was not born with the skills, the knowledge and the experience that took me where I ended up. You and Spence can and will do the same thing."

The constant coughing that occurred when Genevieve spoke was hard for Mallory to ignore. She felt so sorry for her and regretted getting her into this deep conversation. But yet hearing her mother's counsel one more time meant so much to her.

"The days that brought your father and I closer to being total confidantes were not, shall we say, the golden years Mallory. They were the years we both were struggling to become who we were destined to be. The triumphs were memorable, but it was the hard times when we depended on each other that we both cherish."

"Well, it is hard to depend on Spence right now when he is running off to Egypt to placate Dad's dream of the ultimate Arabian. I don't see either one of them being there for me."

The coughing was becoming worse. Both knew the conversation would have to come to an end soon. "Mallory, forget Japan. Marry Spence and build the barn back to what you want. Spence and you can do that together, I am confident. But think for a moment how much easier that will be with the top Arabian in the country and one of the most celebrated in the world in your barn. Think of the prestige that will bring to your breeding and showing. You and Spence have an unbelievable future in front of you if your dad satisfies this whim, you speak so carelessly of. Do not mistake your father's intentions. This is as much for you and Spence as it is for himself and me. We want to leave you with a legacy that you can carry forward to your children and their children." More coughing.

"But Mom, Egypt has changed Spence. He hasn't been the same since he returned. He is distant, aloof, out of body and mind. I am afraid of what it is in Egypt that has him so mesmerized. I am afraid and I don't even know of what. I just don't want him to go back."

"Mallory, what could possibly be in Egypt that could harm you? You are afraid of ghosts. No matter Spence's attraction to Egypt, Egypt will stay just that, a place across the world that he once visited on barn business. Egypt will never be in Texas and Texas will never be in Egypt. You and Spence will marry and live wonderful, fulfilling lives unless you allow fear of who knows what to interfere. Mallory, life is short. Believe me. You have so much less time than you think. Do not look for your joy and happiness in perfection. Find it in the pursuit of joy and happiness. Do not discard in an emotional tantrum the opportunity to build your own barn, to marry and have children of your own, to be an outstanding international competitor and trainer, and to let me die knowing that you will have the life I always hoped for you."

"Mother, what will I do without you?" Mallory half-sobbed.

"I do not have the answer to that question. But you do, Mallory."

Mallory could see that Genevieve needed rest and no more conversation. "Thank you, Mom."

Cav called Spence and asked him to meet him that afternoon at the house. Spence became instantly inattentive to the men he was interviewing. He could not keep his mind on the candidates. He found himself drifting to nights on the Nile, to horses that make you feel wild and free, to ruins that triggered the imagination, to food, drink, and music that filled you with pure delight. But what he was feeling and remembering most was a woman that touched his soul like no other. Later that afternoon could not come fast enough for Spence as he waited.

When Spence arrived, he knocked and entered the house. Cav met him in the foyer and led him into his office shutting the doors behind them. Spence assumed they were here to receive or initiate a call with someone in Egypt. He wondered if he would get a glimpse of Sekhmet.

"Okay Spence. You need to be on a plane heading to Cairo on Monday. The Zabr's are expecting you and the collection and delivery will be duplicated from your last trip. You will of course be responsible for the transport."

"Monday is fine with me, but I am concerned about Mal. She was in a temper this morning when she left and has not been around most the day."

"Mallory is fine. She spent time with Genevieve this morning who was able to persuade her of the importance of this transaction being completed. This is for your future as much as anything."

"Put your traveling shoes on Spence. You know your way around over there now, so make sure nothing occurs that is out of the ordinary. We cannot afford another suspicious incident. This must go as smooth as Egyptian cotton."

Spence came home to a different Mallory. She was chatty as she made spaghetti and served him an appetizer of wine and cheese and fruit. He recoiled at the thought of ruining this mood by telling her he was leaving for Egypt on Monday. But as it turned out, he did not have to.

"So, I know you had a meeting with Dad today. I went by the house to drop some samples off for Mom to look at and saw your truck. When are you leaving?"

"Monday."

"Wow! I figured you would be on a plane tomorrow. Four days before you leave. That should help me get things organized so I can take over for a few days. I have decided to withdraw from Japan on my mother's counsel. That will take a lot of pressure off of me until next fall. Then Sky and I can come back with a vengeance!"

Surprised at her total acceptance of his departure in four days, Spence listened, wondering where this complacent and content Mallory was coming from.

"Besides then I can concentrate more time on the barn and wedding. And more importantly I'm not asking the inevitable question every evening do I train with Sky or go see my mom?" Mallory barely got "mom" out of her mouth without breaking down. "In the beginning I could justify dividing the time. But I looked at the calendar one day realized that I might only see my mom less than twenty times before I never see her again," Mallory sobbed.

Spence put his arms around her. His heart was splitting in two. He loved Mallory. He had loved her for almost forever. Her pain was his pain. It had always been that way and it would always be that way. Once her tears subsided, the evening turned into a romantic dinner by candlelight sitting at the kitchen island, a little too much wine and the best lovemaking that Spence could remember in a long, long time.

Chapter 39

That evening Cav sat beside Genevieve holding her hand. "I believe you worked your magic again today, Genevieve."

Genevieve was paler and more ashen than usual. Cav grieved as he sat looking at his beloved wife of more years than he could remember. She did not know he was there. The evening drugs had been administered earlier, so she slept peacefully in between coughing and wheezing. The doctor told him she was developing pneumonia and although they had done everything to prevent it, her lungs were filling up at a fast pace. All her organs were under duress, it appeared the lungs were the weakest and would pull the trigger. He silently blamed decades of the dust, hay, and hair she had lived in. But at this point who, what, when or how doesn't matter. All that mattered was he was losing her.

Winning Genevieve had been particularly difficult. He was in the throes of overcoming his affair with Stella Claire Harvey. The betrayal by Stella Claire had been shattering on many levels. None of which he was emotionally or mentally prepared to handle. He and Gil were in their early twenties when Stella Claire came into their lives like a wrecking ball. Unfortunately, neither of the King boys were particularly good looking. Both were relatively short, stocky, and not fair of face. Because of the constant conflict between the boys, their personalities were also seen as unattractive most of the time. Girls had never been a major factor in either's life until Stella Claire.

She came for a year. She attended a local university in Dallas, but her roots were in Kentucky. She was an amazing rider having grown up on the back of racehorses. But more than just a great rider she was beautiful beyond anyone that either Cav or Gil had ever imagined. She had long, luxurious sandy blond hair that framed a perfect face with big brown eyes and sultry lips. She looked amazing in riding breeches and tight tops which revealed an alluring figure.

When she spoke, it felt like honey had just been spilled and her laughter was Christmas bells ringing across the arena. Cav fell in love with Stella Claire immediately. Before any contact at all, he knew he loved Stella Claire.

The relationship started as many have. They were just barn friends. She seemed to be impressed that he was a King. He gave her a few tips on riding, but she did not need much improvement. In Cav's mind you could not improve what was perfect. It was close to Christmas that year before he had the comfort level to approach Stella Claire from a romantic demeanor. She was riding the inside arena cantering circles on a seventeen plus hand Thoroughbred. It was late and she and Cav were the only ones in the barn. She was laughing as she rode past Cav waving before bringing her steed down.

She trotted over to Cav and hopped off. Cav had never seen a female rider throw one leg over the other and hop off their horse. Most use the stirrup and climb down. But Stella Claire did not do anything like other girls. She did not walk, talk, or act like other girls. She was outrageously flirty and seemed to know what sex was all about. He felt she knew much more since he had only barely kissed a girl one time in his life. But until Stella Claire he had not been concerned about sexual drive. Now he was obsessed.

"Hi Cav!" she chirped.

"Hi, Stella," he responded always with a shy tone.

"What are you up to?" she asked.

"Just watching your ride. If you like, I'll meet you at the gate and help you untack. We can have some hot chocolate to warm up before going outside."

"Sure," flashing him a bright smile.

He opened the gate and Stella began to lead her horse through when she stopped. She looked at Cav, reached up, took his hat off and kissed him. And she didn't just kiss him. She gave him a lesson on the art of kissing. Arms were around each other. Breasts were pushed against him. Tongue was pushing and searching, and what he was feeling was unlike anything he had ever even thought possible.

"Now, Cav. Right now!" She was breathing in his ear. He could not believe he had this creature of beauty in his arms asking him for what he was not absolutely sure. But he was willing to find out. They parted but still touched and stopped again to share another kiss. But Cav knew how to kiss her now. He was beyond go. His male heat had taken over.

When reaching the tack room, they entered with him pushing miscellaneous contents out of the way as he watched her unabashedly strip down. Before he knew it, he had Stella's breasts, butt, and darkness before him. She was breathtaking and his pants were so tight he thought they would bust open. She reached for him. He heard the zipper.

Everything became a big blur of ecstasy and wonder. He knew he explored her body as she purred and moaned and even showed him how to touch, kiss and love. She seemed to know that this was his first experience and she wanted it to be remembered forever. She instinctively knew to pull away and make him change positions to prolong what became the best moment in Cav's life. He was in love. He was hopelessly, ridiculously in love with Stella Claire Harvey.

The next couple of months were the most intense of Cav's life. He opened his eyes thinking of Stella and he went to bed thinking of her. His objective everyday was to see her and if given the chance to be intimate. She was always willing and actually set up scenarios to make it happen. She loved being in strange places for encounters. He didn't care where they were. Peeling her thong panties off was his life now and pretty much all he lived for.

It was in April that Cav noticed some significant differences. Stella began to be around a lot less. Cav would look for her to show up at the barn but more often than not she was a no show. However, she assured him as he lay on top of her that he was the one and he was her man. Cav was certain they would be together forever.

His moods began to be based solely on when his last rendezvous with Stella occurred. He knew in a matter of days Stella would be going home. He could feel her pulling away. He was going nuts trying to figure out how to get a commitment out of her.

But then that fateful night. The night that he knew two things without a doubt. One, he hated his brother more than anything in the world. Two, Stella Claire Harvey looked like an angel but was a whore from the word go.

He caught them. Plain and simple. He had waited at the arena for her. But she again did not show up. He was walking out when he swore, he heard her laughter. He kept walking, turned out the lights and went into the common area to leave the arena. But he knew. He had heard her. And he was familiar with that laugh and what it meant.

He circled around and came in quietly through the backdoor and stealthily crept to the tack room, walked in, flipped on the light, and behold. She was laying over a saddle while Gil was mounting her from behind. They were both naked, sweaty with matted hair and apparently had been engaged for a while. Cav turned around and walked out to the aisle and lost his guts.

The turmoil and devastation were deep. If Cav and Gil were not arch enemies before, there was no doubt they despised each other after Stella. She returned to Kentucky not realizing or caring that in an already fractured family, she had put the final wedge between the King brothers. Grace and Porter were destroyed by the anger and hate that the boys spewed at each other and behind each other's back. Some say that it sent both Grace and Porter to their graves early.

Porter was astonished by all the strife and bitterness from over the years. Of all things, they go and fall in love with the same girl. A girl that obviously played both of them. Neither could see past their detest of each other to see that they did not do this to each other. Stella Claire did it to them. After constant public and private verbal assaults of each other, it finally became physical one evening. They beat each other up with years of pent-up rage behind each pommel. Cav awakened the next morning, packed his bags, and left.

He went to California and joined a barn that belonged to a friend of his father's. He hired on as a hand and did the mucking, feeding, grooming, and any other task that came up. He believed the only way to rid himself of the feelings of inadequacy and low self-esteem was to work until his muscles hurt and his body demanded sleep. Cav spent little time thinking of Stella or Gil. He had written them off. He was a broken man headed nowhere when he met Genevieve Maddox.

He did not pay any attention to the ladies at the barn. Stella had cured him of any misdirected passion. He never saw himself with another woman again between his trust issues and his injured ego. But he began to hear about a girl in the barn that was a rising star and considered a prodigy. He became curious. He hung in the barn one day just to see who she was and watch her ride. His first thought was she was a typical serious equestrian. Short hair, thin and lanky, and all business. He was, however, impressed when he watched her train and ride. Cav was not sure he saw prodigy, but he did see potential. He would always remember how wrong he was in the long run.

The friendship developed slowly. Genevieve was at the barn for the horses. She spent almost zero time socializing with anyone. If you did find her in conversation it was of equine content. He did not see Genevieve as a romantic interest. But he was interested in her equine knowledge and her natural abilities coupled with her work ethic. The whole package was so unlike any female he had ever encountered. He was intrigued with Genevieve and sought her out as a friend. But Genevieve did not make friends. She was the most private person other than himself he had ever met.

So, even the friendship came hard. It was a quick conversation here or there. A passing greeting. He noted the morning she actually smiled at him. Cav was not confident and knew that his overall score in attractiveness was low. But he was beginning to come into his own as a man. He was no longer a young man. He was beginning to realize that he wanted his own barn. He had his own ideas on how to manage and promote a world class barn. And as fate would have it, his dreams of the ultimate barn and Genevieve's dreams of becoming a respected prominent horseman brought them together. It was as though they only trusted each other not to laugh at their aspirations. He was mucking stalls, and she was riding borrowed horses. But together they could dream of the future and not feel ridiculed.

After five years of absence, Cav returned to the King Ranch with his wife Genevieve. Grace had passed a couple of years earlier. Cav and Gil attended the funeral and for their father's sake did not interact. But now Porter was in failing health. Gil was living and playing cowboy in Montana. So, Cav and Genevieve moved into the big house to care for Cav's father and began to make their dreams come true.

Cav wiped his eyes and nose with a handkerchief as he looked at Genevieve lying quietly. He could hear her labored breathing, or one would think they were looking at her corpse. She was always a tiny thing, but she exhibited strength. Remembering how they came to be who they were and where they came from brought a frog to his throat. He could not believe that it was over. For so long, they had been a team, an unbeatable team. Losing Genevieve would be impossible to overcome.

He said a prayer thanking God for the peace she seemed to be in at the moment and asking for his grace and comfort in the days ahead. He kissed Genevieve's hand and left the room and a lifetime of memories.

Spence was awakened about three in the morning by his phone lighting up. He leaned over and read the message from Mohammed in Egypt.

Take flight directly to Alexandria arriving at 10:00 PM

Cleopatra and Mark Antony

Cleopatra was young when Caesar died! But as Caesar's companion, she was experienced in Roman civilities and uncivilities. She rivaled Caesar in knowledge, political science and, more important, charm. She demanded respect and recognition, and she had a treasure that she felt sure was the key to ruling the future Roman Empire. She had Caesar's son! But what unfolded was as surprising to Cleopatra as to the world!

He was a handsome, educated, successful warrior! He had demonstrated his courage and finesse in battle repeatedly bringing wealth, property, and honor to Rome. His popularity was second only to Caesar. And like two stars colliding, the second love story of Cleopatra exploded before the landscape of Rome and Egypt. His name was Mark Antony.

He enticed Cleopatra to join in his Parthian and Armenian wars with funding and support. The partnership of Mark Antony and Cleopatra resulted in a torrid love affair that has been forever chronicled for posterity. In their quest to conquer their enemies and put Cleopatra's and Caesar's son on the throne, they too became stupid with love. They were both young, vital, and sexual. They found excitement and contentment in each other's arms. They discovered support, sustenance, and acceptance in each other's eyes.

While popularity in both Egypt and Rome failed, they arrogantly and stubbornly continued with their war and plans and love affair. Only when shameful defeat became evident and public humiliation became reality, did both Cleopatra and Mark Antony take their lives. A love borne out of tragedy, ambition and arrogance that ended as most Egyptian love stories do ... in loss.

Chapter 40

The flight to Alexandria was filled with emotions for Spence. He could not believe he was on his way back. The previous few days had been unbelievably busy. He had to call on Carson, who of course showed up to help. Watching Mallory walking in his footsteps so she would step into his ongoing issues was amazing. He did not know what had occurred, but he suspected Genevieve was behind Mallory's newfound confidence.

Mallory had been nothing but supportive and encouraging. She was not worried or fretting because her world was not perfect. She was stepping to the plate strong and undaunting. He had so much love and respect for Mallory. She had kissed him passionately on his departure with no tears or whining. It was hard to leave her with all the trials and tribulations pending.

But here he was. Going back to Egypt. Soon he would feel the Egyptian sun, walk among the ancient ruins and pyramids, feel the joy of the pounding hooves on the desert sand, and as guilty and remorseful as he was in his deepest soul, he would see Sekhmet. He could close his eyes and see her in Egyptian robes with jewels in her dark hair which framed those enchanting black eyes and inviting lips.

How can one kiss affect a person forever. How can one feel the longing, the loneliness, the isolation of one's soul become whole with one kiss. Never in his life had he ever thought such emotion was possible. Sekhmet completed him in a way that he craved and feared at the same time and tomorrow he would see her he hoped.

Mohammed, his friend from the last trip, met him at luggage. "My friend, welcome back to Egypt!"

"Mohammed, I wasn't sure you would be here to meet me! I'm so pleased to see you," Spencer replied.

"Assan will get your luggage. The car is waiting for you to take you to your lodging. Are you hungry or thirsty? We have provisions in the car if that is agreeable."

They walked out of the grey, concrete airport into the warmth of the Egyptian sun. Spencer raised his face and absorbed the rays and felt peace. He was back in the land of Pharaohs, pyramids, and Sekhmet. Texas seemed far, far away.

The ride thru Alexandria to his hotel was typical Egypt main street. Every kind of vehicle, camels, donkeys, horses, carts, etc., were crowded into the street until they reached the Corniche. The Corniche was a boulevard that curved inward from the Mediterranean Sea. It is seawall on one side and shops and eateries on the other much like an American boardwalk. But to see the sea that Cleopatra and Marc Antony sailed across the street from his hotel was incredible.

Mohammed and he visited, and Mohammed did share a tidbit that caught Spencer unaware. It seemed that Cav and the Zabr's were discussing Mohammed's grandson coming to America as a trainer at the King Equestrian Center. Before Mohammed could share details, they arrived at the hotel. It was located on the Alexandria corniche and faced the Mediterranean Sea. The hotel itself was historic with 15th century furnishings and original wrought iron elevators from the early 1900's. His room had a balcony that overlooked the bay and the busy street below that paralleled the water. Although early, his jet lag had kicked in, so he took a quick shower and fell into the comfort of the soft bed with Egyptian sheets. He slept like a baby his first night back in Egypt.

****

Mallory spent her first day in Spencer's absence concentrating on barn management. Spencer ran a tight ship so amazingly enough it had been business as usual with no critical crisis having to be resolved. Carson was invaluable knowing the ins and outs of certain customers and barn tribal knowledge. Mallory was able to concentrate on the training and trainers at the barn. That night as she sat on her parents' patio drinking a glass of wine, she felt that if the next few days would go this smoothly, this would be a walk in the park. She had come by for her nightly visit with her mom and ended up here thinking of growing up in this house.

Her earliest memories were not dolls and tea sets. She walked among horses as a toddler and was riding almost before she was walking. Would she have had it any other way? Would she have traded the blue ribbons from horse shows for trophies from dance contests? Would she give up the endless hours of training for a cheerleading camp? Would she have traded her famous equestrian mom for a mom like Spencer's whose sole purpose was comfort and happiness of her family? Would she give up the dream wedding of the year for a quick romantic beach elopement with Spence?

There was really never any choice. Her life was like a Danielle Steel novel. You knew what was going to happen before it happened. She had no choice. This was her life. She had to live it. She was blessed she knew that. Why did she hurt inside when she had so much? Mallory finished the bottle, continuing to wonder about the ins and outs of her perfect life. She found herself in her childhood bedroom and she lay on her bed and slept. She slept like a baby Spencer's first night in Egypt.

****

He awakened early surprised he had slept all night. His first action was to draw the curtains open to look out at the sea. He could almost see Cleopatra and her fleet coming through the bay to land in Alexandria and begin a legend that would live through the centuries. He showered again and dressed and went upstairs to the top floor to have breakfast on the veranda overlooking the sea.

When he walked out to the veranda after grabbing a cup of coffee, there she sat in a white sundress looking like an angel with the wind whipping her hair. She raised her hand to hold it out of her face and then caught his eye. For a second the world stopped. He stood like a statue looking at her. She sat still entranced with her hand holding her hair, so he had clear sight of her eyes. The moment ended with both breathless when she stood up as he walked toward her with both reaching to hug their greetings. Spencer was surprised that their emotions at seeing each other led to a hug in public. But he was feeling whole by simply being in the arms of Sekhmet.

"Sekhmet I am so happy to see you!"

"Yes, Spencer! Fate has been kind and brought us together once more," Sekhmet said. But Spencer could not help feeling there was a hidden meaning in her voice. The waiter brought his breakfast, and they sat down to eat.

"I have been up since early prayers and have eaten already. You must enjoy your nourishment because we have an industrious day in front of us and a flight tonight to Aswan," Sekhmet stated. The rest of the breakfast was spent in conversation that somehow came so easily between them.

Their first stop that morning was Alexander's Library. The building was new, modern, and colossal. It held thousands and thousands of books and was a museum of history in itself. They walked for two hours immersing themselves in Egyptian history. Sekhmet, as she had before, offered many insights into the exhibits, increasing his knowledge of ancient world history.

From the library they visited the Pillar of Pompeii. The Pillar was fascinating and as always standing close to ancient history humbled Spencer. When he turned and looked at the buildings that surrounded the site, he was struck with the culture make-up. Tall buildings maybe ten or fifteen stories each, standing side by side like a picket fence. They were all a brown stone and lacked any color except the laundry hanging from the hundreds of balconies that were visible. He was despondent that the pillar would be surrounded by an apartment style residential neighborhood. It seemed disrespectful to him.

The next excursion was to the Citadel on Quaitbay built in 1477. The fort was mainly stone and sandstone with several levels overlooking the bay, the views were outstanding. The corridors had small porticos that extended from the main walkway with portholes for shooting at the enemy in ancient times. Images of Sekhmet looking out the portholes with her silky hair blowing in the breeze against the blue of the sea would be forever burned into Spencer's memory.

Few people make it to the top of the structure. But they did and they began to play hide and seek popping in out of hidden crevices and hiding spots. Spencer felt like he was ten years old laughing and playing with Sekhmet in the corridors of this structure that had been a foothold on the Egyptian coast since the 15th century.

Lunch was at a fish market restaurant sitting on the water. Customers pick their fish and preparation method. Again, conversation came easily between them as did the good times. Spencer was absolutely enchanted. As different as they were, they were alike. They enjoyed exploring their diverse backgrounds and lives. But in almost all conversations they ended up in the same place.

As good as their lives were, they were trapped. Both were living lives based on the other's expectations and plans. Neither could really fault the hand dealt to them. That was expressed by both. But somehow the good life came with strings. And as the beautiful day wore on, it became apparent that part of the attraction to each other was due to the sense of cutting the strings.

"So, are you having a good time, Spencer?"

"Certainly! The food is beyond delicious!" Spencer leaned back in his chair and took in the view through the half walls that served as outside walls of the restaurant. Alexandria was in full view across the bay and the Citadel stood tall and stately a little further down the corniche that was the shoreline of the Mediterranean.

The sea was blue and peaceful. Gulls flew the perimeter hoping to be gifted with tidbits from the patrons. Spencer closed his eyes and breathed in the moment. He now knew why Mallory strived so hard for perfection because the moment right now was perfect. He understood the satisfaction of everything being in harmony and rhythm.

"What are you thinking Spencer or are you napping?"

Spencer sat up straight looked Sekhmet in the eyes and said, "I am not thinking Sekhmet. If I were thinking I would not be here entertaining the feelings that I am feeling." There he said it. They had been pussyfooting around the elephant in the room all day. There were feelings and he was certain they were not one-sided. But he also knew that Sekhmet's cultural conventions would look upon the feelings that Spencer referred to in a totally different light. But in any light, any fulfillment of the feelings was wrong and a betrayal to their integrity and loved ones.

"Spencer, I will not deny my attraction and like of you. But our time together is just that, a short episode in our lives. This is not our life … this is an escape from our life. This is you and I leaving who we are behind to be who we want to be for a brief passing moment."

The levity of her comment weighed on Spencer. For the first time that day he thought of Mallory with immediate consequences. He was here across the world staring into the eyes of this beautiful creature sitting across from him with lust in his heart. That alone was disloyalty at minimum, and he was seriously considering total betrayal.

Sekhmet was right. He needed to think this through, but the truth be known, he didn't want to. He didn't want to make the right and honorable decision. He wanted every second with Sekhmet and he wanted to feel her close and intimate. That was what he wanted.

The afternoon was spent at the Catacombs of Kom El Cosafa. They wandered through the sarcophagus graveyard admiring the hieroglyphics and inscriptions. And then took the spiral stone staircase down into a hole to enter the actual catacombs. It was overwhelming row after row of four to six coffin-like chambers where once dead bodies lay. In some places there were scenes carved out of the stone walls depicting Egyptian gods and the burial rituals. Again, walking in a cemetery of thousands of years was inspiring and amazing for Spencer.

They left Alexandria by air and flew to Aswan that evening. They enjoyed cocktails after takeoff and the conversation drifted to what Spencer had been dying to ask Sekhmet. "Aswan ... why Aswan and not Luxor?" Spencer inquired.

"Well, they are making preparations for you in Luxor for the collection. But we can be less discreet in Aswan than in Luxor. Besides, Aswan is beautiful, and I think you may enjoy the peace and beauty there."

"Sekhmet, there is something I want to ask you."

"Yes, Spencer."

"The previous trip, the specimen that was tampered with ..." Spencer began to stutter. He was for all intents and purposes accusing the princess of the Zabr family of unmatched treachery.

"Spencer," Sekhmet interrupted and continued, "Even if I were the culprit in this narrative, I would tell no one for fear of consequences. My family's wrath would be insurmountable." She smiled and he knew the answer. She had made up her mind long before him that she was willing to live with the aftermath of their decisions. He was not ahead of her in feelings. He was playing catch up.

They arrived at the villa in Aswan and Spencer was in awe. The architecture was Nubian with brightly colored mosaic tiled floors and six-foot walkways with twelve-foot ceilings. A beautiful patio overlooking the Nile River with high ceilings and wide-open arches was inviting with plush benches and chairs. The river flowed between the rocky banks with small waves and a glistening foam in the moonlight as the river pushed toward its destiny.

Sekhmet smiled, "It is even more beautiful in the daylight when the scenery on the shore is visible." She noticed that Spencer seemed taken with the surroundings. Spencer turned to her. Sekhmet sat on the short stone wall that surrounded the villa patio. The moon was behind her illuminating her smiles with the Nile River serving as backdrop. Her dark smoky eyes and dark hair framed the most beautiful face he had ever laid eyes on. She was breathtaking.

He could not help but feel desire. She was the zenith of legendary Egyptian beauty. She was perfect with gemstone onyx eyes, creamy olive skin, full lips that he so wanted to kiss. He could not believe he was here under the Egyptian moon, on the Nile River with this Egyptian goddess come to life and she was feeling him. He was in disbelief that she would turn her head his way for a minute. In his opinion he did not have swag or good looks, was from a horse ranch in Texas, and did not have a suave, smooth, polished bone in his body.

But here he was sitting in the bright moonlight with a vision that would fulfill any man's fantasy. He was not sure if he felt like the luckiest cowboy in the world or the most doomed cowboy in the whole world. "Yes ... I am looking forward to seeing all of this in the daylight," Spencer responded.

"Well ... how about I meet you for breakfast early in the morning here on the patio. We'll take it easy tomorrow. Maybe go to the market. You might be interested in some of the sites here in Aswan. We'll plan our day in the morning. It has been a long day for both of us. I think it is time to retire."

"Yes ... I agree. I am exhausted and could use a shower."

"I will see you in the morning, dear Spencer," Sekhmet looked deep into his eyes.

Chapter 41

He almost felt she was sending signals that he should stop the separation and stay together. But his gentlemanly manners and his fear of rejection led him to acknowledge agreement. As if by magic, an attendant appeared and motioned he would show Spencer to his room.

He followed the attendant through the huge open hallways to a room at the end of the foyer. Spencer was immediately impressed with his accommodation. He loved the Nubian architecture featuring white stucco walls, arched shuttered windows, arched doorways, and a red brick dome ceiling. The bed was a stone platform with a mattress. There was no furniture. The shower stall was in a corner of the room surrounded by a stone wall as was the toilet area. A stone dressing table with shelves and mirrors stood between. The contrast between the solid white room and the red brick that populated the ceiling and edged the doors and windows was unique and charming. It felt like a cave but bright and beautiful.

But the appeal and comfort of the suite did not lend itself to a good night for Spencer. He tossed. He turned. He found himself in the middle of the night looking out the window at the black thread of the Nile. The moon fully illuminated the banks exposing ragged rocks with the lights from a village on the opposite bank.

As serene and pleasing as it was, Spencer was not at peace. His mind was at warp speed replaying the day. One image after another of Sekhmet pervaded his consciousness. Her beauty, her Elizabeth Taylor voice, her laughter, her magical eyes, her curiosity about him and who he was, all of it played over and over as he felt his desire and love growing for Sekhmet, a forbidden fruit at best.

He almost jumped out of his skin when his phone rang! He was clicking on to FaceTime thinking that middle of the night here was evening in Texas. Mallory was calling him.

"Hello."

"Hi, I wondered if you would answer. You don't sound like you're sleeping," Mallory queried.

"Well, actually not. I have had a restless night." Spencer explained.

"Are you sick?"

"No, no. Sleep is just eluding me. Are you okay, Mal? You sound a bit blue." Spencer wanted to get the subject off of him. He felt like he had been caught with his hand in the cookie jar. He did not want to admit to himself or Mallory that he could not sleep because he was lusting for another woman. The absurdity of feeling that he had been caught with another woman when he was alone in his room was sobering. But he knew in the dark corners of his mind, he had been.

"Blue? Why would I be blue? My mother is dying, my father is beside himself, my fiancé is across the world, and I have a barn to run. Why would I be blue?" Mallory instantly felt bad that her second sentence to Spencer was dumping on him. She called because she was lonely. She was tired of being lonely. But the moment he answered the phone, he sounded like a stranger. Her Spence that she had known a lifetime, that was soon to be her husband, that had shared everything with her, seemed unfamiliar. What was it about Egypt that caused such apprehension and insecurity within her?

"Mal," Spencer started but Mallory finished.

"No, Spence. I'm sorry. I didn't call to rag you. Actually, right the opposite. I know it's late and you need sleep, but if we could just visit for a few minutes."

"Of course, Mal. Tell me what is going on with your mom and the barn."

And so, she did. They spent over an hour talking on FaceTime. Talking about everything that mattered to both of them. Genevieve, Cav, the barn, the horses, the clients, the gossip, all of it. They talked as though they were at the kitchen table not separated by an ocean. Spence found the conversation relaxing, comforting, and easy. Mallory was elated to feel a connection and to know that he was alone, sleepless in the night and she had been his answer. Seeing each other was consoling and heartening for both.

"I feel like you have been gone forever," Mallory lamented.

"I know, Mal. It's having been here, back home and then back again. This will be the last trip," Spence said with assurance that his internal dialogue rebutted. To never come back to Egypt was not a totally pleasing thought.

"Yes, please bring dad his dream back and then maybe you and I can live ours." Mallory felt instantly guilty that she would talk about living her dream when her mom was dying. Spence caught the vibe immediately. He had been Mallory's confidante for many years, and he could read her well, even on FaceTime on another continent.

"Mal ... don't! Don't you know that is what she wants? Whether she is alive or not, that is all Genevieve has ever wanted for you. You must not feel guilty or remorse that you have a life and dream to live. She would want nothing less."

The tears started. The tears that Mal had been holding back for so long. She had been trying to be strong and resilient, coping with everything in a stalwart demeanor. But inside she was crumbling. She was weak. She was tired. Spencer felt so helpless. He could not hold her. He could not pet her hair or caress her. All he could do was offer solace via FaceTime.

"Mal, Mal, I'm so sorry. I'll be home soon, and we'll get through this together, I promise."

Mallory began to compose herself. "I know. I know. I assure you I will be okay." Mallory gave a half-hearted chuckle. Then her brow furrowed big time. "What is that?" Mallory exclaimed with surprise on her face.

"Ohhhhh, that's prayers," Spencer answered.

"Prayers … Isn't it in the middle of the night?" Mallory questioned.

"Yeah … well they start about four … four thirty," Spencer responded yawning as he said it.

"Wow, that is one way to wake up. And you sound beat. I have kept you up all night, Spence. I'm sorry."

"Don't be silly. You found a restless, sleepless soul and entertained him to slumber, Miss Sandman," Spence was beginning to feel the long night.

"Well, Miss Sandman has spread her sand so say good night and get some sleep," Mallory began to bid goodbye.

"Good night, Mal. Hang in there. I'll be home soon."

"I will, Spence. You get some sleep."

"I love you, Mal."

"I love you, Spence."

Spencer laid his head down and closed his eyes welcoming the fatigue that overwhelmed his body. His thoughts quickly went over his conversation with Mallory. He truly was empathetic with all she was dealing with. One thing piqued his curiosity. They talked for a long time and Mallory did not mention the wedding. He was slightly intrigued, a little concerned and somewhat surprised that Mallory never mentioned their wedding. He wasn't sure what to make of that.

He awoke to men yelling at each other outside his window. He opened the shutters and found himself looking at about twenty or thirty sheep with three guys herding them to a destination. Another man was in a small wooden cart pulling a wagon brimming with hay and being pulled by a beast of burden, a donkey. The men were in long robes, barefooted and carrying long sticks as staffs. It looked like a scene straight out of the Bible. Spencer's first thought was,

"Only in Egypt." He was groggy and shocked that it was after ten and he needed a shower and a cup of coffee.

A little later, Spencer was relaxing on the patio being served a delicious brunch of fresh vegetables, fruit, cheese, pita bread, beans, and boiled eggs. So, his plate was full as he took in the lush abundant environment. Natural beauty and sounds of the Nile rippling along the way completed the morning ambiance. Spencer felt like he was on the set for a Hollywood movie. He mused that almost anywhere one goes in Egypt that was the sensation. You felt that you were on a set for an ancient biblical saga.

Spencer was looking at his phone enjoying his cuisine when he felt someone approach from behind. His heart skipped a beat. He had berated himself in the shower that morning after his conversation with Mallory the night before. He was engaged to another woman. He was here to conduct business. He had made a very good friend in Sekhmet, but he must draw the line on any romantic encounter. His feelings were confused because he was far from home, and he was in the company of an alluring woman. He needed to get control of himself and be the gentleman he was and get through this and home to Mallory. He ignored the little voice that kept echoing his good intentions with suspicion of exactly how he would do this.

Spencer looked up and it was not Sekhmet, but Mohammed. Spencer enjoyed Mohammed's friendship. He was the first person he had met in Egypt in what seemed so long ago and turned out to be a dear friend.

"Mohammed!"

"Spencer, I apologize for obviously startling you."

"No, not at all. I thought you were Sekhmet."

"Sorry to disappoint. But may I join you?"

"Sure, please."

Mohammed took a chair and smiled at Spencer from across the table. Spencer in those few seconds suddenly felt that Mohammed was bringing bad news. It crossed his mind immediately that Sekhmet was gone and would not be back. He suddenly regretted sleeping late and not seeing her early this morning. He knew she rose with prayers. The server interrupted his thoughts.

"Hibiscus tea, please," Mohammed requested.

"Yikes, that is one Egyptian delicacy you may keep in Egypt," Spencer scoffed.

"Really?"

"Yes, do not care for it at all. Now on the other hand mango ... can't find mango juice like this in Texas."

"I see," Mohammed seem to be comparing the two beverages in his mind.

An awkward silence ensued which was unusual between Spencer and Mohammed. Finally, Mohammed broke the ice. "Spencer, plans have changed, and I am the emissary to deliver the news."

"She's gone," Spencer half spoke have choked the words out. The realization that he might never see Sekhmet again wrenched through his whole body. He instantly became self-vexed that he felt this way after his resolutions this morning.

"No, my friend this does not concern Sekhmet." The relief was apparent through Spencer's whole body and expression. "No, Spencer ... this concerns a contract I have made with your beih, Cavanaugh King." Spencer squinted with curiosity. He could tell that Mohammed was emotional about whatever this sudden mystery involved. "I will introduce you shortly to my eldest grandson, Yousuf. Plans are now for him to accompany you on your trip home." Mohammed continued, "Your beih is aware that Yousuf is what we refer to as a champion horseman at a very young age. He has developed a reputation locally for winning the games and training the horses that win the games. Many bring their horses to the Zabr stable to be trained by Yousuf."

Spencer couldn't help but think to himself that Cav was as sly as they come. No wonder he felt no fear of Gil or Gil's filly. Spencer began to put two and two together. He remembered a previous conversation with Cav wherein Spencer asked who was going to train this Arabian prodigy. Cav replied, "a trainer of Arabians naturally." Spencer began to see that this was in the cards the whole time. Cav was negotiating not only for the horse but for the trainer. He was never concerned with Gil because he knew all along, he was ahead in the game. Cav would end up with the prize Arabian horse and the prize Arabian trainer.

Mohammed continued. "Yousuf lost his parents at an early age. I am his what you would call a guardian. Yousuf has always been with me." Spencer instantly understood. Yousuf was not just Mohammed's grandson. Yousuf was like a son he had raised. "However, I have decided that it is in Yousuf's best interest to go to America and start a new life."

Spencer became all ears. "Pasha King has kindly offered to house, educate, and give my grandson opportunities in America to pursue his passion. He and I have talked on this matter, and it is agreed that he should welcome this opportunity." Spencer could see true emotion in Mohammed's eyes and face. "Spencer, I share this with you because I know you will be in Yousuf's life. I come to you because I respect you. I ask that you watch over Yousuf. I know Pasha King is a man of age and I do not want Yousuf left on his own accord before his education is finished and he is in manhood."

Spencer was surprised at Mohammed's request. He met Mohammed just a few months ago, developed a surprising friendship and trust of each other, and now he was taking his grandson under his wing. "Of course, Mohammed. Your grandson will always have a place at my table."

Mohammed took a deep breath and closed his eyes. "It is done then."

"Mohammed, you love this boy, why are you sending him to America?"

"I am an old man. I will die soon before he is an established man. There is nothing here for him in Egypt. He will go into the military whereas in America he will be attending university. This is his best life path. I will die a man at peace knowing Yousuf is in a good place."

Spencer was sensitive to the fact that this man was giving up his grandson for a better life. But it was obvious the sacrifice was telling on Mohammed.

"You must meet Yousuf. Let me call him," Mohammed stood to leave the patio to fetch Yousuf.

Spencer fell into deep thought again about the ruse that Cav had pulled off. He was bringing THE horse and THE trainer back to Texas. Both were of Egyptian heritage and legacy. Cav was determined to have his Arabian empire over and above Gil. Spencer pondered exactly when Cav began hatching this coup to surmount Gil at his own game. And Spencer came to two conclusions as Mohammed and a young man walked up to him. He surmised first that Cav had probably been planning this since he met his friend, Saad at the show in England years ago. And secondly, never underestimate Cavanaugh King.

Mohammed entered with a young man and began introductions. Spencer was taken aback because he remembered seeing the boy at the different horse demonstrations he had attended. On a horse he seemed older and more confident. He remembered the boy in particular when he watched the games which is the equivalent of a Texas rodeo but Egyptian style.

The riding was hard and fast on Arabians decorated in bright colors and gemstones. He recalled watching a young rider that was truly a delight. The young rider not only was skilled and talented, but while other horses just went different gaits mainly fast, this young man's mount performed while gaiting and was definitely a favorite of the crowd.

Spencer found himself looking at the young lad, supposedly sixteen but looking more like he was twelve. He had a mop of dark hair, dark eyes, beautiful olive skin with a quiet, respectful demeanor. Spencer looked deeply in the youth's eyes and extended his hand.

Spencer did not realize when he first looked Yousuf in the eyes that he was looking into the eyes of a boy that would grow into manhood and be known as one of if not the greatest Arabian trainer in the world. Spencer did not comprehend he was looking into the eyes of a lifelong friend that would work and train side by side with Mallory until both were distinguished in the industry. That his friendship and support would stand in for Genevieve in Mallory's life. Spencer did not understand that he and Mallory would someday feel that Yousuf was their younger brother or even a son. He did not comprehend that Yousuf would someday marry a beautiful soul and have children who would call him grandfather. Spencer could not see what an honorable, spiritual, and respected man Yousuf would become. Nor could Spencer fathom that as he grew older it would be these eyes, eyes of a lifespan friend, that would offer him solace and comfort till the end.

The introduction of Yousuf was interrupted by the entrance of an animated Sekhmet. She was dressed in riding gear and obviously coming in from a ride.

"Hello, everyone! Spencer, you are awake. You are not ill, are you?"

"Good day, Sekhmet. Yes, I am awake and not ill and visiting with Mohammed and Yousuf."

Mohammed nodded a greeting to Sekhmet when she arrived. Yousuf knew Sekhmet because he had ridden with her many times in the desert. She had always been kind to him. So, he smiled at his greeting.

"I see. I just came off the desert. I am on my way to wash it off of me. I will be back in short time, and we can explore Aswan."

"I would enjoy seeing Aswan with you."

"Yes! I will return and we will go!"

Sekhmet nodded a goodbye to Mohammed and Yousuf and headed off to dress for the rest of the day.

Mohammed and Yousuf made their exit very shortly afterwards leaving Spencer alone on the patio. Spencer sat watching the Nile, the longest river in the world, heading along its own way. This Father of African Rivers had run its course since the beginning of time. Spencer felt a kinship with the river because he felt he was also drifting. He misjudged how just seeing Sekhmet would affect him.

It was not just mental or emotional, he physically reacted to her. His heart beat harder and faster, his whole body went on alert, his brain turned into mush and his tongue became thick and unmanageable. She was an electric shock, a bucket of ice over the head, a sudden tack in the foot. Her very presence was enchanting but riveting. He savored her company and no matter how wrong he knew his feelings were, they were his feelings. She was the light, and he was the moth. And everyone knows the fate of the moth.

Chapter 42

Mallory tackled the morning with more than her usual fervor. Her conversation with Spencer the night before had been very comforting. She needed that closeness, that support. She needed Spencer and she had never realized that before. She loved him, she liked him, she and he were and always had been partners, but she had never needed him. As she walked the barn and considered this new paradigm, she promised herself she would never take Spencer for granted again. Never.

The day was for the most part uneventful until early afternoon when she came out of the barn office and ran into Murdach. "Murdach! I'm surprised to see you," she exclaimed.

"Mallory, I thought I would come by and give you the news personally."

"The news?" Mallory questioned.

"Yes, I felt that you would want to know."

Mallory was confused. She could not guess what Murdach was talking about. She had just spoken to her Uncle Gil yesterday. So, she did not think the news had anything to do with barn business unless …

"Okay, what is up, Murdach?"

"I am giving my notice this afternoon to your uncle."

"Wow, that was fast!" Mallory wasn't sure how she felt about Murdach leaving her uncle so quickly. She felt he was disloyal to the whole family. First, her mother and now her uncle. She had immediate defensive feelings towards Murdach. Her next thought was he was looking to come back. She knew it would not be her decision but a combination of her father, Spencer and her. And her vote was an absolute no. He was disloyal.

"Mallory, if I may impose, I would like to discuss a couple of matters with you."

Mallory resisted the urge to say, "if you are looking to come back here as a trainer the answer is no," but she did not. "Okay, let's sit down." Mallory turned around and led Murdach back into the office. They both took seats. Mallory did not sit behind the desk. She did not think the conversation would last long. He would ask and she would say it would have to wait until Spence returned and she and her dad and her fiancé could discuss it. Thank you very much and goodbye. Oh, and I don't care what happened between you and my uncle … nothing would surprise me.

"Okay, Murdach, what is on your mind?"

"Mallory, I am giving my notice to your uncle and want to explain why."

"Murdach, you do not need to explain anything to me about why you might be leaving my uncle. That comes as no surprise to anyone."

"Mallory, I am not leaving because of issues with your uncle."

Mallory became a bit confused. "So, why are you leaving?"

"I have a more lucrative opportunity both career wise and financially."

"What? Where?" Mallory could not think what might be more lucrative than owning part of the King Ranch especially with that Arabian filly in the deal.

"I have been offered a partnership with an outfit in England. I can pursue my goals in the company of English greats. It is a career move I would have to make no matter where or who I was with. It is unmatched in the US quite frankly."

Mallory was not sure how to take the last statement, but she felt it was a bit of shade on both the King ranches. Later that night she sat on the swing porch with thoughts of the day. Murdach had delivered his news and left shortly after. She expected a call from her uncle all afternoon, but it did not occur. She laughed to herself about what Murdach would think if he knew what Spence was bringing back to the ranch. Let him go to Europe to seek his fortune, the fortune her mom had given him on a silver platter.

Thoughts of her mom brought her down instantly. She rose, went to the kitchen, and poured herself another glass of wine before returning. The sun was setting, and the night was beginning to creep in. Mallory drifted to thinking that soon that sun would start a new day in Egypt. Maybe Spence will be home in a couple of days. He arrived yesterday, collection today, and flight home tomorrow. She hoped and prayed he would be that quick, because when she thought of her mom, she knew that it would not be long. She stared into space wondering where she would be when the call to come to her mother's deathbed happened.

Chapter 43

Over the years when Spencer remembered this day, he remembered it as perfection. It began with Sekhmet's return looking ravishing in a colorful sundress, with a wide-brimmed hat and sandals. The excitement that both felt knowing that they were spending the day together was tangible. Albeit Spencer drifted between rapture and guilt when Mallory crossed his mind. But Sekhmet was intoxicating, and he could not quell what he was feeling.

They crossed the Low Dam to arrive at a dock on the Nile providing ports for small motorboats. They motored across the Nile to Philae Temple. Philae Temple was originally built on Philae Island in the sixth century. But due to the dams on the Nile the Island was overtaken by the Nile and Philae Temple was submerged almost entirely. The temple was relocated stone by stone to nearby Agilkia Island and is now a must see in Egypt.

The complex itself was one of the most memorable and beautiful of the ruins that he had toured. The entry of the temple was preceded by an expansive tiled pavilion that was edged on each side by massive, engraved columns. The face of the temple displayed well preserved engraved images across the twenty-foot walls. Spencer recognized the images as the images often shown in Egypt documentaries in America. Sekhmet explained the temple was in honor of the love of Isis and Osiris and their son, Horus.

They wandered the temple finding the nooks and corners with Sekhmet reading the hieroglyphics. The temple was unlike many tourist attractions in that it was open with areas to sit and appreciate the temple. It was a wide, open patio so not crowded and aesthetic with palm trees and flora.

Small open temples built by the Romans offered scenic places to sit and take in the beauty and history. Spencer was once more overwhelmed as he had been many times since arrival in Egypt by the history that stood before him. He was standing in the midst of the oldest civilization on the planet. That was considerably bigger than Texas was all he could conclude.

Images of Sekhmet as they wandered the ancient ruins would forever be burned into Spencer's brain. She was like the changing seasons. One moment she was reading a hieroglyphic serious and intent, other times she was relating the story of Isis with emotion and passion and the next moment they would find something that would send them into throes of merriment. Sekhmet was not only an exquisite beauty, but she also had a personality that was compassionate, humorous, intelligent, and intuitive.

They found themselves taking a break in one of the sitting places overlooking the Nile. "Is your water cold enough?" Spencer asked after purchasing a couple of bottles at the refreshment center.

"Yes, it is excellent!"

"This place is amazing, Sekhmet. Thank you for bringing me here. The hieroglyphics are some of the finest I have seen and the images on the front of the temple are awesome. In America we think those images are of aliens from space you know."

"What! Space people? You are being amusing, yes?" Sekhmet queried.

"No, actually the round circles on their heads look like space helmets."

Sekhmet laughed out loud! "You Americans are so dramatic! Ancients wore elaborate crowns and headpieces. The drawings were simplified either by the artist or time. But they are not space helmets," Sekhmet proclaimed.

They sat for a few minutes taking in the sights and watching people. The complex was very quiet as though visitors recognized history and the human effort to respect and preserve antiquity. The atmosphere was similar to being in a cathedral but most of the site was outside.

"I hope that you will not let Yousuf believe such nonsense," Sekhmet commented.

"Well … if I recognize whatever as nonsense," Spencer responded.

"Aliens, space helmets on an ancient ruin! Surely, you are an intelligent person and would know that is nonsense."

Spencer just raised his eyebrows and took a drink. He had a passing thought that you only know what is fed to you and the American media was not always trustworthy in his opinion. Sekhmet was absolutely right. Sometimes people do not use their common sense because they believe in the false reality that is held widespread.

Spencer went on to express his feelings about Yousuf. "I felt for Mohammed this morning. I know he loves that boy very much and will be heartbroken when he leaves."

"Yes, but he must do this."

"Why? Why can't Yousuf thrive here in Egypt? He has connections, he is a recognized expert already, surely the Zabr family can offer him everything Cav can," Spencer argued.

"Spencer, do you see that tree?" Spencer looked across the courtyard and eyed the tree Sekhmet was pointing out. "The Zabr family is like the trunk. Old, strong, built by centuries of generations, branching out over and over again but always connected to the trunk. The closer a branch to the trunk the stronger it is. The newer branches are not as strong and massive. But the newer branches are still connected to the trunk for strength and nourishment through the trunk roots."

Spencer continued to listen to her analogy. "So, it is with Zabr family. Our family has a very old and strong core. But there are many families connected to us. Several tribes and hundreds of families. All connected to the trunk and expecting to be considered in turn for any advantage that might be available such as education, health care or vocation."

Sekhmet let this sink in, but she could tell Spencer still did not get the picture. "In brief Spencer, no matter who or what Yousuf Zawahiri is, he is not a Zabr. He would always be a stable boy in Egypt." Sekhmet's statement had a major impact on Spencer as he processed the difference of Yousuf's life compared to what he would experience in America. "You must remember, my dear Spencer, our culture is about family."

They soon left the Philae Temple and Spencer felt his life had been changed by the ruin. Sekhmet pointed out how American life is still influenced by ancient Egypt. Philae is sometimes called the Temple of Love while historic Philadelphia is known as the city of brotherly love. She also pointed out that while in Cairo he visited a part of the city called Memphis. He left knowing and thinking about matters he never imagined he would.

On the motorboat back to the dock, Sekhmet promised him a real treat for a late lunch. They went by car to their lunch location. After a scenic ride, they pulled into a driveway of what appeared to be a huge hotel of red sandstone and white trim around doors and windows. Getting out of the car, Spencer noted above the door was a sign that said Old Cataract. They walked into a foyer that was Old Cairo at its best.

The entry to the hotel boasted shuttered windows draped beautifully and dramatically. Grand chandeliers of golden brass hung from the 14-foot ceilings. Zebra covered chairs along with brown leather sofas offered seating. The room was semi separated by a massive circle arch with a checkerboard white and brown sandstone pattern.

"Do you know where you are at?" giggled Sekhmet. She asked as the attendant was escorting them to a round balcony that overlooked the Nile with a gazebo roof and a view that was 180 degrees. Spencer almost lost his breath as he took it all in. The Nile was a blue thread below between green palm tree lined banks. Palm trees and quaint bridges crossed the lengthy hotel pool that followed the bend of the Nile. Sailboats were abundant in the scenery that most likely came from the village on the opposite bank. The city boasted a fair size marina with numerous sailboats and small motorboats. Spencer thought it looked like a puzzle.

"Spencer come and sit. It will not go away. I ask again. Do you know where you are at?"

"One of the most magnificent places I could ever hope to be," Spencer responded as he took a seat at the table set for two.

"This hotel is most famous in Egypt. Celebrities and political figures from all over the world have stayed here. But it is most known as the hotel that your American author, Agatha Christie resided when she wrote the murder book."

"Sure, <u>Death on the Nile</u> … very well known in America." They settled down for a scrumptious Egyptian lunch beneath the canopy watching the activity on the Nile.

"You have shown me such a beautiful and magical Egypt, Sekhmet. I can never thank you enough."

"You have found Egypt pleasant?" Sekhmet quizzed.

"Yes, it is almost like a drug. You become lethargic in its beauty and tranquility, but at the same time you are excited and thrilled to ride magnificent steeds across the desert. When all the while immersing yourself in the music, the food, and the people all with the backdrop of ancient history. It is a mighty stout potion." Spencer did not add that being in the company of the most alluring woman in the world added to the exhilaration and intoxication of Egypt. But he had to admit that the day had been without tension. He and Sekhmet had been more like good friends than romantic interest. Spencer's conscience was somewhat at peace. Perhaps he would escape Egypt unscathed.

They left the Cataract and returned to the Nubian village that was near their hotel. They walked the dirt alleys where one craftsman, farmer, artisan after another displayed their goods. All manner of goods including fabrics, grains, herbs and spices, brassware, clothes, rugs, bird cages, and more. They found a little tea and coffee bar at the end of one street.

They took their shoes off and entered the tented establishment. They sat on mats on the floor. The far side from the entrance was totally open to reveal another Nile pallet. A small Egyptian band played in a corner. They sat close to the outer wall so they could absorb the setting of the Nile and the palm treed bank.

Sekhmet ordered for them, and Spencer was surprised when the waiter sat a shi-sha water pipe in front of them. They had tea from a China tea set which Sekhmet served. They shared the apple flavored shi-sha tobacco. Spencer was not one for smoking, but he found himself enjoying the whole scene. Again, he felt like he was on a movie set.

He noted the band and asked Sekhmet about the instruments. The main instrument which served as a guitar was the lute. It was backed up by a harp, a goblet drum and an Egyptian flute called a ney. The music was lively and uplifting as is most Egyptian music. After a short while, the lute player noticed Spencer's attention to the band and the music.

He came to their table and gave Spencer a quick lesson on the lute which Spencer, being a guitar picker caught onto quickly. Spencer took the lute and sat thinking of what he might play. He was seeking something simple and easy. He began to strum and sing ...

"Puff, the magic dragon lived by the sea
And frolicked in the autumn mist in a land called Honah Lee
Little Jackie Paper loved that rascal Puff
And brought him strings, and sealing wax and other fancy stuff
Oh, Puff the magic dragon lived by the sea
And frolicked in the autumn mist in a land called Honah Lee

Puff, the magic dragon lived by the sea
And frolicked in the autumn mist in a land called Honah Lee"

Sekhmet was obviously delighted with the tune. And the few people in the bar clapped their appreciation. Spencer handed the lute back to its owner. The band picked up on the tune and began to play a very soft, sensual version of the song.

Spencer gave Sekhmet his hand. She looked at him quizzically but rose to follow him to a small space and began the first and only two-step in her life. In all Spencer's daydreams and fantasies of Sekhmet, never did he realize how he would feel when he put his arms around her. He had to laugh to himself as thought of the fairy tale where the baby bear items were not too big and not too small but just right. That is exactly how Sekhmet felt in his embrace, just right. He was dancing a dance of love to Puff the Magic Dragon. Only in Egypt is everything distorted to be romantic, intriguing, and captivating even a children's rhyme.

They finished the dance as two different people than when they started. The desire and passion had won both over. There was no need to verify or confirm what each other was feeling. They were on that cloud where there was no doubt of feelings and desire. It was not a matter of one giving in to the other, they were both succumbing to each other. It was as though they made a mutual silent pack that they would put all reasons to not be together aside.

They left the shi-sha bar and walked hand in hand back to the hotel.

Chapter 44

If Spencer lived to be two hundred years old, his memory of this night with Sekhmet would never fade. It was not just a night of physical indulgence of unimaginable ardor, but a connection of souls, a bond of intimacy and joining of hearts.

They walked together through the mosaic patio past the full moon shining on the Nile to the arched entry to Sekhmet's room. He found his room charming and unique, but Sekhmet's room was another level. It also was all white stucco with red brick trim over the arched doorways and dome ceiling. But her window was actually two wide glass doors that attached to a private patio and sunken tub. Palm trees and flowered shrubbery gave total privacy and created a lush and aromatic atmosphere.

It was not awkward nor cumbersome. Their kisses were long and passionate and exploring feelings neither had ever envisioned. Sekhmet was an unbelievable seductress. She stood before him and did a silent strip. She was not exotic or erotic. She was an illusion of sexuality turning slowly in the shuddered moonlight letting his eyes devour every curve and nuance of her body. She smiled her invitation and walked into the pool.

Under the glow of the Egypt moon he undressed and joined her. They intertwined in the pool naked body on naked body. Spencer was out of his mind with lust. Sekhmet was perfect in every way. He devoured her creamy brown breasts that were perfect natural mounds for his pleasure. Her body was tight and lean with long legs that led to heaven. Sekhmet took the time to sensually apply oils on her body putting some in his hands and letting him massage her while she did the same.

Being with Sekhmet attacked all his senses. The oils enhanced the sensual touch and pervaded the aura in carnal scent of bodies in heat. Sekhmet's body was beautiful to feast his eyes upon with perfect curves, tight and muscular but yet soft and feminine. Her breathing and gasps only increased his frenzied indulgence of everything she offered.

When the union occurred, Spencer was in another universe. The love exchanged before the actual joining had him in a sexual corridor of ecstasy and fantasy. He did not have to close his eyes to imagine the perfect place, the perfect woman, the perfect love making. He was living it.

And even as the night progressed and the intimacy continued until the moon began to fade into the rising sun, Spencer wondered where this would all lead. How could he ever leave her? How could he stay? Who was he anymore? Where is Texas now? Where was home? Fury absorbed his brain as he bounced between total rapture and total uncertainty as to what would happen in the light of day. He did not want the night to end.

In the morning light as Sekhmet slept in his arms, he counted the hours until he would have to say goodbye. Twenty-four hours …twenty-four short hours. One day and one night and then he would have to make choices. The second set of prayers started and awakened Sekhmet. As the prayers echoed from wall to wall, Sekhmet crawled on top of him. He again climbed the ladder of pleasure and excitement with Sekhmet and for a while forgot the matters that plagued him.

They lay in each other's arms till mid-morning. Saying very little to each other. Just relishing holding and cuddling each other. Both knew the other was wrestling with the reality that this would soon end. Both were wondering how they would cope with not only the permanent loss of each other but the guilt of betraying family, religion, and fiancé. Holding each other gave them comfort, but both felt the burdens they would shoulder when they left this bed.

"We cannot lie here all day, Spencer. We must bathe and eat. I thought we might ride this afternoon. You must experience the Sahara one more time," Sekhmet's voice trailed off. Both had the same ending to the sentence "for the last time."

"Sekhmet, I don't how I will say goodbye to you … to all of this."

"We shall deal with tomorrow … tomorrow. Today we sail the Nile and ride the Sahara. We will eat, drink and be joyful tonight in our …" Sekhmet stopped there. She could not bring herself to say "love."

Spencer knew that both were shy to speak about the feelings that were so overpowering because both knew that there was no future for the feelings. It seemed wrong to acknowledge them and wrong not too. As Sekhmet rose to dress, he thought to himself that as much as he was looking forward to spending more time with Sekhmet, this would not be an easy day.

Chapter 45

They dressed and had breakfast on the patio. Spencer could feel the heaviness of knowing he would never have the time again to sit and bathe in the peacefulness and splendor of the Nile. He would forever be in awe of the longest river in the world with history that was ancient and notable in the chronicle of mankind.

"You are pensive, Spencer," Sekhmet commented.

"No, not pensive … just trying to absorb it all," Spencer smiled as the prayers began to boom across the tranquility. "And I shall miss the prayers perhaps most of all."

"Most of all?" Sekhmet exclaimed, raising eyebrows in amusement.

"Well … speaking of Egypt not of the treasured friendship I have found with you I assure you. I'm not sure missing you describes the agony I feel, Sekhmet."

"We have been favored to have had what little time we have shared. This will be a dream that I will dream often in my future. To not have this time with you would have been a travesty in my life. But I will always have you in my memory, my dreams."

"Dreams," Spencer echoed the sentiment sadly as he realized that after tomorrow Sekhmet would only exist in his dreams.

Spencer was always amazed that when you think you have seen everything to see in Egypt, there is another surprise around the corner. He had seen the Sphinx, pyramids, Luxor Temple, Karnak Temple, the beautiful Dendera Temple, mummies, ancient churches, hieroglyphics, tombs in Valley of the Kings including Tut, but nothing prepared him for the scene that stretched before him when they boarded their boat. He knew it would not be like the taxi boats that dotted the river connecting the banks in Luxor.

However, the driver dropped them off in a vista that belonged in biblical times.

He first noticed that there was no dock with other boats. The only boat was a wooden galley sailboat with a wooden plank propped on the ground to board the deck. On the shore skeletons of enormous ships being built were sitting waiting for the next nail or board. They looked like different stages of Noah's ark being built. Spencer had never seen anything like it. It was like he stepped back in time to the 1500's.

The pasture that made up the shoreline was green and lush. An Egyptian farmer was crossing the pasture with a loaded cart pulled by a donkey. Another donkey was pulling a manual plow. In the water a small rustic craft was bringing straw to be loaded on the cart. Spencer could not believe he was witnessing agriculture from the 3rd century transpiring before his eyes. As he watched the manual antiquated methods to cultivate and move their crops, he thought of all the equipment at home. The tractors, excavators, four-wheelers, irrigators, bulldozers, cultivators, the list went on. And here he was witnessing farming as it had not been done in centuries in America.

They climbed the plank to the deck and although the boat seemed old, the deck was beautiful wood with plush pillow furniture to stretch out on and relax. They had barely found their place before beverages were served. The boat was pulled into the middle of the Nile by a motorboat. The sails were raised, and they settled in for a few hours of total relaxation.

The recollections of the few hours that ensued are a myriad of beauty, tranquility, and ease in conversation, connection, and enjoyment of another human being. Sekhmet took his breath away more than once. With the Nile banks as her background, she endeared him with her beauty and animation. Snapshots of her laughing with her head thrown back and her hair blowing in the breeze, looking aloof, and absorbed as she also contemplated the next day were filed away in his memory. The mood vacillated between extreme merriment and quiet preoccupation.

A delicious mid-afternoon lunch was served which resulted in a conversation about what would happen the day after tomorrow. "I will return to Luxor to offer counsel to my father and brother. I suspect Mohammed Ahmd will choose a bride for the future which I will train to be a female in the family. Although many say that I have no respect for my place in the family," Sekhmet laughed at herself for being a mentor for appropriate behavior for any family member. "What about you, Spencer? What will your return entail?" Sekhmet queried.

Spencer took a deep breath. Talking about home seemed surreal sitting on this galley boat with a modern-day Egyptian goddess on the Nile, river of mystery. He had forced thoughts of home from his consciousness, telling himself he would deal with home when he had to. But Sekhmet was gazing at him anticipating an honest answer. "It's hard to think about being home sitting in this environment. It is like home doesn't exist. Home feels like another realm. To tell you the truth I don't know what to expect when I return. Mal and Cav, I expect will be pretty somber considering the situation with Genevieve."

Spencer went instantly dark as he chastised himself silently for being here in paradise renouncing his years of prior promises and vows, he would soon take. Vows that in actuality had been in place for years. He had selfishly quenched his desire and lust without any guilt in the moment. But as he looked in the eyes that had led him down the path of uncontrollable want and hunger and even now left him needing and craving more of her, he knew his reckoning was coming. "I am sure both Mallory and Cal are exhausted trying to cover the barn and coping with Genevieve's pending death. I do not expect my homecoming to be a jubilant event. More like a relief to have another pair of shoulders to carry the burden of sadness and death."

Again, Spencer retreated to a dark place as he thought to himself that he had not been there to support Mallory. He had been back and forth to Egypt when she needed him most. When he was home, he was living in Egypt in his thought and heart. Guilt penetrated his very soul.

Sekhmet was dismayed at seeing the internal struggles Spencer was experiencing. She too was carrying remorse for the betrayal to her family when she substituted the collection to bring Spencer back to her. There was no one in her life that would condone or understand that action. She put the Zabr legacy and reputation at risk for a rendezvous. Totally unforgiveable. But just as Spencer could not help himself, she could not help herself. She also bore shame for sleeping without marriage and blessings. She knew that together they had both been blasphemous.

"Spencer, we cannot undo what is done. Our choices have been made. What matters after this is our choices going forward. By continuing to choose to keep the onus to ourselves then other lives will not bear consequences for our actions. To do otherwise would result in chaos and irreparable damage in their lives for naught. It would not change the circumstance that we cannot be together. But that means we must be strong to keep our time a secret unto ourselves until we are no more."

Spencer heard her say not to confess misbehavior to Mallory or anyone else. To simply walk away and keep the memories, the feelings, the pain to oneself. In other words, pretend that none of this happened. Spencer had only kept one secret from Mallory in all their relationship and that was at the request of her father and dying mother. Spencer seriously questioned his ability to remain stoic for the rest of his life. But he also knew that knowledge of what had occurred in Egypt, especially the depth of his feelings for Sekhmet, would destroy Mallory.

Sekhmet rose saying, "We are close to docking. Wait ... I have something for you." She disappeared below deck leaving Spencer to take in for one last time Egypt from the Nile. While he waited, Spencer amused himself looking at a small village on the bank. Spencer noted that the villages that dotted the banks of the Nile all looked very similar. The buildings were hard to distinguish because the walls were all the same sandstone color. The exceptions were the brightly colored houses indicating the occupants had been to Mecca and the lofty prayer towers that soared high above the other buildings. The boat pulled over to an embankment where a couple of goats were grazing, and an older man was fishing with his son or grandson.

Sekhmet ascended the galley stairs holding a small red velvet bag. Spencer immediately became embarrassed that she would have a gift for him when he had none for her. She stopped to talk to the sailors briefly.

"The winds have shifted. We will have to be pulled by motorboat back to our destination. The crew is going to have lunch, but hey will put the plank down and we can walk a bit on the bank. But first, Spencer, this is for you." Sekhmet handed Spencer a small bag. "Sekhmet, I am so humiliated that you would gift me when I have nothing to give back."

"Shhhhhh ... open it." The bag was a drawstring bag from which Spencer pulled a solid gold bracelet with a unique Egyptian link and a clasp that when closed was two of the letter "S" connected. The bracelet was not only one of a kind obviously but was expensive and exquisite. Egyptian men and women wore elaborate bracelets, necklaces, rings routinely. Spencer was not prone to do so, but the bracelet was manly and looked perfect on his wrist. "This is magnificent, Sekhmet. I don't know what to say."

"Spencer, my hope is that you will seek comfort for what is lost and courage to live the future. When you look at the bracelet remember no one is lost who is not forgotten. Remember me ...

remember us … but without consequences to those we love." Spencer looked deep into her eyes and saw her wisdom. He was desperate to kiss her and hold her. She was fully modestly clothed, but Spencer knew what was beneath the fabric shield. He knew her milk and honey body that yearned and demanded to please and be pleased. But eyes were upon him, and he couldn't even touch her. He could only wait for tonight for the protection of darkness to fulfill the lust that filled his loins like nothing he had ever felt before. In the meantime, he knew she was right and so help him, he would figure it out. He would have to leave her. There was no option. But he would not destroy Mallory. He was resolute in that.

"Come, they have the plank down," Sekhmet exclaimed heading to the wooden, slatted beam to the ground. He followed, admiring the bracelet, and watching his step going down the plank that led to a grassy field. They walked a few yards and suddenly Sekhmet kicked her sandals off and waded into the Nile. She held her dress up exposing her beautiful shapely legs and Spencer experienced a flashback of them wrapped around him. He stopped and took a moment to look at her. He took her in much as he had last night when they were making love. He wanted to absorb the image of how beyond gorgeous this exotic maiden was that shared his bed and his feelings so deeply. Her smile and eyes reflected pure bliss as she twirled in the water laughing and jeering him to join her.

He walked into the water and if a medal could be given for self-restraint, he would be wearing it. He wanted to wrap her up in his arms, peel those clothes off of her, and love her here in the Nile, under the sun. His desire was tangible and panoptic. And he might not have been able to stop himself, but the water was ice cold and brought him to his senses very quickly.

"You tricked me, you made me think it was warm," Spencer bellowed. It was only up to his knees, but the water was ice cold.

"Who ever heard of a warm river?" Sekhmet scoffed.

"Well believe me we have rivers in Texas that are not straight out of the Arctic."

Sekhmet giggled and continued to turn in the water. Spencer again admired how lovely she was with her bare legs peeking out, her black hair swinging in the sunshine, her eyes like jewels catching his as she circled by. She knew what she was doing to him, and she was enjoying it. She was dancing the dance of seduction. He felt he was in a dream as the gold bracelet glistened in the light while a vision of beauty and sexuality pirouetted directly to his libido. His senses were in a state of confusion as the cold water collided with the hot that was running in his blood.

He couldn't stop himself. He came closer. They were not touching but they could feel each other. For one brief second, he thought they were going to kiss. But the sailors were yelling from the boat. It was time to go back. Spencer knew what he had seen in Sekhmet's eyes, and he knew they were destined to fulfill the promise that evening.

Going back to the boat Sekhmet let him know they were about thirty minutes from their destination. They both needed to dress to ride. Horses would be waiting for them when they docked. They would ride the desert one more time before sunset.

When they reached the boat, Sekhmet went down to the bedroom to dress first. Spencer sat on the deck again feeling melancholy. The time was going fast. He was on an express train to a big heartache. He could not imagine how he would say goodbye to Sekhmet and leave her. Spencer knew he was leaving a different man than he was when he first stepped onto Egypt soil. He hoped that only he would ever know that.

"You can come down now," Sekhmet peeked out from the stairwell, "I am done I just need to grab my scarf." Spencer went down the stairwell and, in a small hallway to the bedroom and bath, Sekhmet and he found themselves alone. The very much coveted alone with no eyes or ears. Neither had a second thought as they passionately wrapped themselves in each other sharing the kiss and promise they could not share earlier. Spencer was almost dizzy with his yearning that now was an ache he wanted her so much. But eventually they pulled away. Both knowing that suspicions would surface if Sekhmet did not. She went up the stairwell to the deck, Spencer put his hand on her thigh and caressed her slightly. She looked down, blew him a kiss, and disappeared above.

Chapter 46

He dressed and by the time he reached the deck they were docking. Sekhmet was correct. Two exceptional Arabians were waiting for them on shore. Both were magnificently adorned in Egyptian tack and stood proud and ready for what would be Spencer's last desert ride.

They walked a few streets through the village and then came to massive gates that opened onto the Sahara Desert. Once on the desert, they rode out. It crossed Spencer's mind that Sekhmet was trying to run away from the inevitable. Although they seemed isolated in the desert, Sekhmet let him know that eyes were still everywhere, and they must continue to practice decorum.

They galloped between the dunes while wild dogs eavesdropped from afar. The sun was beginning to start its decline and Spencer felt wild and free. He was racing an Arabian stallion across the desert with prayers in the background. He knew it was his last time and as they rode together, he acknowledged to himself the last ride could not have been more perfect. Sekhmet was as beautiful on the back of a horse as she was giving a hieroglyphics lesson in a pyramid, sitting across the table a jeweled and adorned Egyptian queen, or wading in the Nile, or lying in bed looking up at him as they both experienced ecstasy beyond rapture.

They stopped on top of a dune as the sun began its dip behind earth. The ride was coming to an end and Sekhmet was giving Spencer one last opportunity to enjoy the beauty of the desert. The Nile was visible in the distance with the lush green foliage contrasting against the desert brown and the blue of the river. The sky was beginning to turn with shades of yellow, purple, and pink. It looked like a panoramic painting. Spencer knew that among the many things that he would never forget in Egypt this sunset was one of them.

"Spencer, do you see that rider coming towards us," Sekhmet broke his trance as he also eyed the rider.

"Yes, it does look like he is coming our direction ... fast," Spencer said in agreement.

At that moment the rider waved a greeting to them. "He is coming to us," Sekhmet commented as they continued to watch. Because he was obviously coming to them, they began to ride and met him a couple of dunes over. When they reached him, Sekhmet immediately started a discussion with the rider that Spencer could not understand. He waited as they continued to converse. At first, he felt Sekhmet's tone had been somewhat confused as though she needed more information. And whatever the information was Spencer could see it was not pleasant and was upsetting to her. By the time she had obviously dismissed the rider, Spencer knew things were not right. He noted the rider only went away he did not ride away. He was waiting.

Sekhmet turned to him, "Spencer, Genevieve King has died," she took a deep breath as she let her words land on Spencer.

"What?" Spencer was dumb founded.

"She has died that is about all I know to tell you. You will have to obtain details elsewhere. But Spencer they have made arrangements for you to leave Aswan tonight, witness collection tomorrow morning in Luxor, and then you and Yousuf will fly to Cairo and leave on a nonstop flight to New York at 3:00 PM."

Spencer was looking at her in total shock. Although they had known for months that Genevieve was dying, he was shocked. He couldn't imagine her being gone. He couldn't imagine Mallory there without him. In one sentence, all of it came crashing down on him. The reality of his life versus this fantasy had wrapped him up like a Christmas package. But in that same breath, something else came crashing down on him.

"He's waiting on me," Spencer motioned to the rider.

"Yes, they have a car waiting for you to take you to the hotel to fetch your belongings and then the journey to Luxor. You should arrive about midnight."

"I should arrive about midnight," Spencer questioned emphasizing the "I".

"Yes, Spencer only you. I can't come with you."

"Later, you will come later?" Spencer questioned again.

"No, Spencer. I can't come with you or to you. You will be in company that would be opposed to our friendship. You are here for business, and they expect nothing less. You must go now."

"Sekhmet, we can't say goodbye like this! Come with me now!"

"Spencer, I cannot. We must say our farewells now. But I have something for you."

"What," Spencer asked showing not only his anguish but surprise.

"I had not planned to hurriedly give you this," Sekhmet said as she handed a small package to Spencer, "but here. When you are in privacy dispose of the draw you receive tomorrow and replace with this."

"Sekhmet, what is this?"

"Spencer, take it and follow my instructions but you must never reveal to anyone this exchange."

Spencer could come to only one conclusion regarding what he held in his hand and where it came from. He realized that she was handing him the Zabr heritage. The magnificent animal that she had introduced him to his last trip was in the bottle he was holding. "Sekhmet, I really don't know what to say … this is huge."

"It is a wedding gift for your bride, Spencer."

"But Sekhmet …"

"No buts ... she deserves the best ... just be sure she never knows that she has the best. With Yousuf as a trainer, she will exceed all expectations. Choose the filly carefully. You are beginning a legacy ... a legacy unsurpassed ... the King's Arabian empire in Texas."

"Sekhmet, you're the most amazing woman ... no ...human being I have ever known and will ever know. Your kindness is humbling. I know what you are giving me. I am forever beholden to you!"

"Oh, come Spencer. You are a world away ... no one will ever make the connection. But you will have the opportunity to introduce the very best of the best to another continent. Let the posterity carry the royal genes across the globe. Only you and I will know. Our final covenant, Spencer."

Spencer slipped the priceless package into his pocket. There were no words to express enough gratitude for what Sekhmet had given him. Both could be executed no doubt for such treason. The lineage from ancient ancestors to future generations of the Zabr Arabian stable was in his pocket. But Spencer felt like a trapped animal. He had no choice of his own to change, postpone or stop what was happening. This was the last time he would see Sekhmet or hear her voice or her laughter. He would never kiss her, touch her, or feel her again. Not tonight, not one more time, not ever. "Sekhmet, I don't know what to say. I don't want this to be the end not like this."

"My Spencer, no end would be acceptable. Our stars crossed but they are now on the path of their destiny. We cannot change the stars. I wish only the best for you, my dear Spencer, but we will always live on two continents under one sun. I will always hold you in my heart and forever in my thoughts."

"Sekhmet what you have meant to me is ineffable. I leave a part of me here with you. I love you Sekhmet. I love you more than you can ever know." Spencer could not believe he was professing love.

But he felt it and he felt he needed her to know that there had been real feeling behind the time shared.

"I know Spencer and I love you. Now you must go. Go with love. Inshallah."

She blew a kiss with her lips and those were the last words that Spencer ever heard from Sekhmet. Both knew that further contact would result in the consequences that both had sworn they would not inflict on people they loved and who trusted them. She watched Spencer ride to the other rider. That was her last sight of him before she rode. Spencer turned for one last look, and he memorized for future recall the splendor of the silhouette standing on top of the dune. She sat proud and beautiful with her hair blowing in the desert breeze on a steed that arched his neck and paraded his tail. They were striking dark images against the setting sun. And then like the wind they were gone.

Chapter 47

The return trip was nothing short of horrendous. Spencer was in shock as they drove across the desert traveling further and further away from Sekhmet. He wanted to cry, he wanted to scream. He felt trapped in the plane going to Cairo, he couldn't believe he was leaving her. Over the years when he looked back on this long sad journey, he could not help but wonder. Did Genevieve somehow across the ocean know how weak he was? Did she die to keep him from getting up tomorrow and blowing his, Sekhmet's and Mallory's world apart because he wasn't sure he could have left her tomorrow. He just wasn't sure. But he wondered with Genevieve's impeccable timing she was so well known for, did she know? Did she save him from himself?

His stress and anguish at leaving Egypt was apparent to his young companion, Yousuf. Yousuf was with Spence for the collection and at his side until they reached Cairo. Spencer went to the toilet leaving Yousuf in the waiting room and there he followed Sekhmet's instructions. He considered keeping both specimens, but out of respect and the risks Sekhmet had taken, he followed her instructions exactly. He walked out only with the zenith of the Zabr Arabians.

That fact should have elated Spencer. But elation is hard with a broken heart. And not only was his heart broken, but he could see that Yousuf was beginning to also realize that he was leaving home for what he did not know. Both were nursing woe as they said bye to Egypt. Spencer thought he was going to be physically sick. It was over. He was going home.

Arriving at JFK in New York was a shock to Yousuf. He noticed immediately the change of pace between New Yorkers and Egyptians. He was amazed at how new and clean everything seemed. But he was in awe of the rain. New York was having a deadly storm off the ocean and Yousuf had never seen rain like this in his life. He did not know what to think of this soggy, strange land.

Texas was not much better. Although not pouring rain as in New York, it was cloudy and threatening bad weather. In the Uber taking them to the ranch, Yousuf asked.

"Is there not sun in America?"

Spencer felt like someone had punched him in the stomach. He could hear Sekhmet's silky voice, "We are under one sun on two continents."

"We have a magnificent sun, Yousuf. But we have four seasons. You are here in the winter and rainy season. The sun will come … the sun will come."

Spencer said as much to himself as he said to Yousuf.

Chapter 48

Yousuf's introduction to the ranch was sobering at best. The ranch was in mourning. No matter who you talked to or where you went there was grief, sadness, and condolences. Flowers were everywhere as a reminder that an occasion was in progress, but they were not happy flowers. Spence found himself pondering how flowers knew it was not a happy occasion, but they definitely spoke death and funeral.

Mallory and Cav were both devastated. It took Spencer exactly two seconds to forget his internal struggle and begin to support and console both. Genevieve had tried to prepare them for her demise. But no matter, one is never prepared for the finality of the end of a loved one's life.

It took the ranch months to recover from losing Genevieve. She was everywhere but yet nowhere. Mallory decided to postpone the wedding. And then later at her request they had a small ceremony with family and a few friends and spent two weeks in Maui. She couldn't go forward with a big wedding without Genevieve.

It was several weeks after Genevieve's funeral that Mallory came to the barn. Her timing was perfect because Yousuf was working Sky. Mallory developed an instant admiration and respect for Yousuf as she watched her horse perform under his saddle to perfection. This was the seed that turned into a lifetime of partnering and friendship. Although Yousuf could not replace Genevieve's mentoring, he fulfilled the role of peer. Together they could solve any horse issue. And together they exceeded all expectations and dreams that each had. The pairing was God send for Mallory. There was never competition or jealousy. Yousuf was the little brother that Mallory never had. And Mallory along with Spencer replaced the family that Yousuf left behind in Egypt.

Genevieve's dreams and predictions held true for Mallory and the King Ranch as it became known again.

As is often the case, when one spouse dies, the other follows close behind. Cav lived long enough beyond Genevieve to see their dream of the ranch becoming a dominant player in the Arabian circles come to fruition. The colt that the specimen threw was impeccable and the posterity that followed was unbeatable at any discipline they were a part of. As fate would have it, Gil also developed cancer and after a short illness succumbed. Gil left everything to Mallory. So, the two ranches originally split between the two dueling brothers were combined back to the one ranch as it was to begin with. Spencer found himself dealing with a ranch twice the size and million plus dollar horses. Cav achieved the goal of handing an empire to Mallory and Spencer. And Mallory and Spencer were faultless custodians of the legacy of the King Ranch.

Chapter 49

And here he sat a lifetime later with a letter from Sekhmet in front of him. He could smell her, feel her, hear her, and see her as he unrolled the scroll. He had lived a good life full of all the good things and he knew he had been blessed. But always in the deepest darkest corner of his mind and heart she lay silent. Now she speaks.

My Dearest Spencer,

I know we have an agreement to not contact the other, I ask forgiveness for breaking our covenant. At this juncture in our lives, I hoped it would not be an intrusion. As I write I feel a bit foolish not knowing if you have held close in your heart our time together as I have. However, I believe in the sincerity of our sentiments those many years ago.

I had the opportunity to visit Yousuf while he was here. He has become a remarkable gentleman! His skill and knowledge are legendary in Egypt. The respect he has brought to his family is notable. He has risen to the highest of stature in the world of Arabians. I regret that Mohammed died before he could see the future of his young Yousuf. But I believe inside he knew. He did not need to live in pain and suffering to see it come to pass. I congratulate you on his absence on the outstanding guidance and opportunities you have engineered for Yousuf. I also thank you in Mohammed's absence. When Yousuf told me he had three children that call you Grandpa, I knew you were the same Spencer that I once was fortunate to know briefly.

Many years ago, a special delivery was received here at the compound. It was about three months after you left. There was no return address or card, only a package addressed to me. The box contained a gift of a beautiful gold and diamond music box. When I opened the music box, a beautiful black horse in Egyptian tack spun to the music. Other's eyes were wide because no one recognized Puff. But I assure you that all my nieces and nephews for two generations are now very familiar with Puff and Honah Lee.

I have never had the occasion to thank you for the music box. I have it here in front of me as I write. It is a most prized possession. It has brought light in the dark, hope in the bleakness, comfort in the difficult, but above all it is reminiscent of a time of love in my life. Shukran, Spencer, shukran. I have waited eons to express this.

I think perhaps you might be wondering why after over three decades I am writing this letter. I have always known that someday I would, but I had to wait for the right time. And the right time is now Spencer because time is short. I believe Yousuf came at this time so I could have this delivered discreetly. The gods have always smiled on our friendship and opened avenues for us.

But I have been diagnosed with a terminal illness and may very well not see the next year. I realize this is abrupt and news of impact. But I do not want you to grieve needlessly. Our grieving occurred years ago. Life will be no different. We have always been in different places on two continents under the same sun.

As always Spencer and to my death, I carry you in my heart and memory of you in my soul. I find joy in passing knowing that sometime our stars will cross again in another life.

Inshallah my friend.

Sekhmet

The letter lay on the desk as Spencer hung his head in his hands. The ink smeared and stains appeared as tears fell on the paper.

Chapter 50

Across the world on another continent Priyanka stood at the window overlooking the compound sumptuous gardens. Sekhmet sat on a bench below with children at her feet telling them a story. They were wide eyed and intent on every word as she mesmerized them. Mohammed Ahmd's son, Sekhmet's nephew, came into the room and joined her at the window.

"Do you think she is okay?" Priyanka asked her husband.

"I think perhaps. She is a lady of great strength and faith."

"Yes, she most certainly is that. But I wonder about how she feels right now about her choices in life. Never marrying, no children," Priyanka mused out loud.

"She dedicated her life to service to the family and to my father. I know he has always depended on her counsel."

"I wonder why? Why did she not make a life for herself," Priyanka was so sad that Sekhmet had never married and had a family.

"Well, she was married as a young woman and from what I gather although it is never spoken of, abused in all manner. She never sought the attention of another man after that. She made a life with her horses and other pets. She was a wonderful aunt when I was growing up. Full of fun, stories, teaching me and my cousins how to ride. Always on the right hand of father helping with family matters. I believe her life was full just not in the same way as most women."

Priyanka seemed to accept that assessment. But again, she went on. "She is so beautiful ... even now at this age and ill. But all her life she was exceptionally handsome. Surely, she had opportunities to make different choices."

"Yes! I believe father had to turn them away at times. But Aunt Sekhmet never had any interest. She has lived exactly as she has chosen. We must accept this. But she will be missed unbelievably by all. She is loved Priyanka. She is loved."

In the garden, Sekhmet finished the story. The children wanting to move about and stretch their legs jumped up. "Let us hear … Aunt Sekhmet … let us see … please," the children begged.

Sekhmet raised the lid on a beautiful, jeweled box and a shiny Egyptian adorned black horse began to spin as the tune began to play to the delight of the children.

Puff the magic dragon lived by the sea.
And frolicked in the autumn mist in a land called Honah Lee
Puff the magic dragon lived by the sea.
And frolicked in the autumn mist in a land called Honah Lee

THE END

Acknowledgements

Lynda Scott, Editor— No words to thank you enough for the hours upon hours of editing my mess.

Ride Egypt, the organization that planned and facilitated excursions to Egypt including the magnificent horses.

Saber Khodary, friend and handler in Egypt. Without his friendship and sharing of his home and country, this book would not have happened.

BOOKS BY THE AUTHOR

CAPROCK

SILENCE ON THE HILL

Printed in the USA
CPSIA information can be obtained
at www.ICGtesting.com
LVHW041205160724
785412LV00001B/92